ANCESTRAL VOICES

By the same author

ON BORROWED GROUND

'Once in a while there comes a book which is quite extraordinary in its ability to recreate times past, to bring us an evocation of a whole way of life now gone and to encourage us to remember with affection mingled with a little awe what was, as distinct from what might have been. This is such a book ... Amid a welter of modern mediocrity, this is one of those rare gems.' — *The Cork Examiner*

REPRISAL

'... a human and humane account excellently told' — Kevin Myers, *The Irish Times*

'... a finely written historical novel that is at ease with time and place' — *Sunday Press*

THE KYBE

'... a well-researched, well-constructed and well-told tale' — *The Irish Times*

'... an attractive and well-told story with fresh dialogue and a strong Irish sense of place' — *Irish Press*

ANCESTRAL VOICES

Hugh FitzGerald Ryan

WOLFHOUND PRESS

VANDAMERE PRESS

First published 1995 by
WOLFHOUND PRESS Ltd
68 Mountjoy Square
Dublin 1
Ireland

© Hugh FitzGerald Ryan 1995

British Library Cataloguing-in-Publication Data
A catalogue record for this book is available from the British Library

ISBN 0 86327 438 2 paperback
ISBN 0 86327 457 9 hardback

Published in the USA 1995 by
VANDAMERE PRESS
A division of AB Associates
PO Box 5243
Arlington, Virginia 22205

ISBN 0 918339 32 4

Wolfhound Press receives financial assistance from the Arts Council / An Chomhairle
Ealaíon, Dublin, Ireland

Cover typography: Joe Gervin
Cover illustration: Katharine White
Typesetting: Wolfhound Press
Printed in the Republic of Ireland by Betaprint, Dublin

To Margaret, whose contribution to this story is incalculable
and to my mother of course,
for the story of a thousand years of Wexford.

Foreword

Echoes of the American Revolution reverberate through the events of 1798 in Ireland when a government bent on provocation goaded the populace into revolt.

The Republican ideals of the United Irishmen, inherited from Revolutionary France and from the signatories of the American Declaration of Independence so alarmed the Protestant ascendancy government in Dublin that many saw their only safety in a union of the kingdom of Ireland with England.

Anyone who spoke of conciliation or moderation was dismissed and a free hand was given to the militias and yeomanry to provoke and intimidate the largely Catholic peasantry. Paradoxically in Ulster, where the Republican movement had taken root among the Protestant middle class, the Catholic militias of Cavan and North Meath were employed to inflame sectarian hatred.

The spectre of a French invasion lent a greater urgency to this work but the burning of a small chapel at Boolavogue in County Wexford was the final spark that set the country ablaze. That summer saw peasant insurgents, armed mainly with pikes, bring seasoned veteran troops to a standstill. But inexorably the force of numbers took its toll and by the end of the year the Commander in Chief, Lord Cornwallis, could confidently declare that the country had been pacified.

At night, they say, a listener may still hear the sound of ghostly regiments marching and the echo of battles long ago.

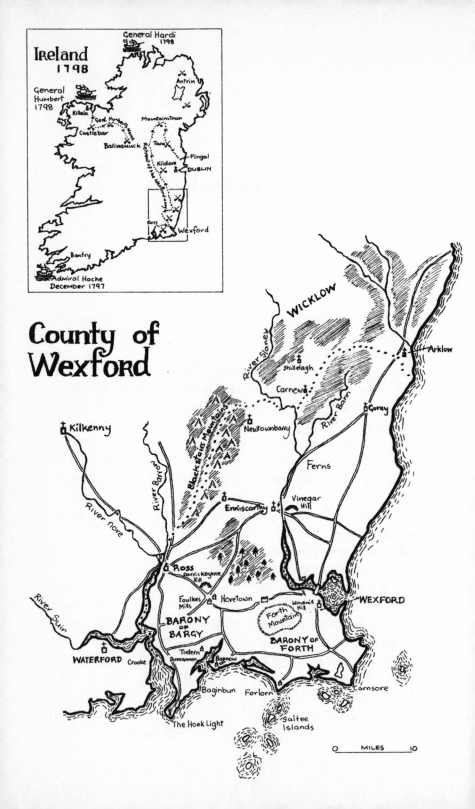

Ireland
1798

General Hardi
1798

General
Humbert
1798

Killala
Gen. Hum.
Castlebar
Ballinamuck
Mountainstown
Tara
Kildare
Fingal
DUBLIN
Antrim

Ross
Wexford

Bantry
Admiral Hoche
December 1797

County of Wexford

WICKLOW

River Slaney
Shillelagh
Carnew
Arklow

River Bann

Kilkenny

Black Stairs Mountains

Newtownbarry

Gorey

Ferns

River Barro

Enniscorthy

Vinegar Hill

River Nore

Ross
Carrickbyrne Hill

Foulkes Mills
Horetown

Windmill Hill

WEXFORD

River Suir

BARONY
OF
BARGY

Forth Mountain

BARONY of FORTH

WATERFORD
Crooke

Tintern
Duncannon

Bannow

Baginbun
Forlorn

Carnsore

The Hook Light

Saltee Islands

0   MILES   10

CHAPTER ONE

When Dempsey saw Tomgarrif with its solid old farmhouse and stone outbuildings, he loved it at once. He took in at a glance the high gabled roof and the shell of the ruined Norman keep that abutted one end of the building. Leafy sycamores sheltered the farmstead and a dark slanting cedar tree stood before it like a sentinel.

'Well here we are,' said Elaine glancing at him sideways, aware that he was impressed.

'Wow!' he exclaimed, slowing the car to a halt at the gateway. 'This place is as old as the hills.' The expression suited, as the farm nestled in a declivity looking as if the buildings had grown naturally from the ground.

'You could say that,' she agreed.

He felt a slight touch of apprehension at meeting her family but if they had ever suspected that he was some Dublin jackeen with his eye on a rich farmer's daughter they gave no such impression. Mr and Mrs Synnott received him warmly and Elaine's two younger sisters, who had spotted the car from an upper window amid great excitement, shook hands shyly and giggled at each other sharing some huge joke. Elaine had brought home a young man from away up there in Dublin, quite a normal looking young man, he assumed, with the requisite number of heads, arms and legs. The girls stared at him with barely concealed hilarity and then scampered away to compare their first impressions.

Dinner was served in the long dining room although the family usually took their meals in the stone-flagged kitchen with the workmen. Dempsey knew that he was under a kind of scrutiny and wondered how he was doing.

Elaine's parents probed him politely about his family background and about his prospects but he realised that it was more from a genuine interest than from suspicion of his motives. As he relaxed, his practised eye took in his surroundings. Inevitably he noted that there were some very nice pieces of furniture and silver that had probably been in the family for generations.

Over the fireplace hung a long black powder flintlock with the stock picked out in silver. The stock he noted had been broken and rather inexpertly put together again. He felt that he would like to get his hands on it and do a proper job.

'So your father was in the army then.'

'Aye. Practically all his life. He left it the day after the Congo funeral. Do you remember that?'

'Indeed I do. The Balubas. Oh, a terrible business.' Mrs Synnott lamented the poor Irish boys massacred in a jungle ambush.

'They're still arguin' about that ambush,' put in her husband. 'Some say they should've stood their ground sooner.'

That was Dempsey's father's phrase. 'Stand your ground. Keep your gloves up.'

'Fight their corner, like,' agreed Dempsey. 'Balubas is the Da's worst term of abuse.'

They laughed. It was all a long time ago.

'So he's retired now?'

'From the army yes, but he got a job with the Corporation after that. He's getting on a bit but he likes to have something to do.'

'I dare say,' agreed Mr Synnott addressing himself to his food.

'He's a night-watchman,' said Dempsey and the word reverberated momentarily in the void that lies between the strong farmer and a beat-up ex-soldier sitting by his brazier. Dempsey caught a flicker of amusement in Elaine's eyes as she watched her parents.

Mr Synnott chewed thoughtfully and swallowed.

'So how did you get into the antiques business then, Jack? That's a comical business to be in.'

'Matter of chance really. Studied History, Fine Art, that sort of thing. Just lucky I guess.'

'Oh, very brainy Jack is,' cut in Elaine and he could see that she was teasing him, exhibiting him as a prodigy. 'Jack won a scholarship to university, didn't you Jack?'

He mumbled. 'Always interested in history and stuff. No big deal.'

'Well I'm very proud of him, anyway,' said Elaine and patted the back of his hand with a distinctly proprietorial air. The scholarship explained a lot without further probing.

'I dare say there's a few bits and pieces in this place that would take your fancy,' said Mr Synnott indicating the furniture, with a wave of the hand.

That's what everyone imagines, thought Dempsey. People warm themselves with the notion that the grandfather's old tankard or spindly legged table would be worth a fortune if only they could bring themselves to part with it.

'Not that I'd let any of it go, of course. It's all been in the family since God knows when.'

'Don't worry,' smiled Dempsey, but without rebuke, 'I'm on a weekend off.'

Dentists probably have people coming up to them in pubs with a finger in the corner of the mouth, gargling some incomprehensible information about a back molar. Things could be worse, he reflected.

'These of course are our own strawberries,' said Mrs Synnott proudly. 'Picked by these two young ladies for the occasion.'

The girls blushed, pleased to be acknowledged. It was an important day after all.

Mr Synnott pushed back his chair and stood up from the table.

'We'll take a turn around the fields,' he declared, 'Jack and meself.'

There was no arguing. The day was fine and it was dry underfoot. Mr Synnott carried a shotgun in the crook of his arm.

They went down by a stream and crossed it by an old mill dam. The water was black and deep. Dempsey looked at the gun. Perhaps this was how the Synnotts disposed of unwanted suitors.

'And the Mammy isn't well, you tell me.'

'That's right,' said Dempsey and it was as if a cloud had passed over the sun.

'Ah, that's too bad, too bad altogether.'

They went on up a steep headland until they came to a gate set into stone gate pillars. Mr Synnott sat down on the top of the stile. They looked down over the farm.

'You can just about see the sea from here,' he said pointing towards a thin line of light on the horizon. 'Down there is where the Normans landed.'

'Baginbun?'

'Aye. We came here with the Normans.'

'You've been here awhile then.'

Mr Synnott ran a finger around the neck of his collarless shirt. He slapped the stone pillar beside him.

'This is one of the original boundary stones. I could step out the margins of Tomgarrif the way they were set out in the original grant. A lot of history in these here stones.'

He took a pipe from his pocket and filled it from a tobacco tin. A wraith of blue smoke surrounded him and was borne upward on the light afternoon air. He was the picture of contentment.

'Do you shoot, Jack?'

'No.' Dempsey shook his head. 'I grew up in the Curragh. Had enough of it, I guess.'

'A gun is a beautiful thing.' He stroked the stock of his shotgun. It gleamed from long handling like old treen. 'A thing of beauty,' he mused.

Dempsey waited. He wondered about protocol. Should he begin with 'Sir, I have the honour to ask for your daughter's hand in marriage?' Or should it be 'the honour of your daughter's hand in marriage?' Tricky.

'I'll tell you a story.' Mr Synnott interrupted his line of thought. 'I was standing here one day years ago. A day just like this; the sun splittin' the trees as they say and all of a sudden I saw this young fella', a lad about your own age in fact. He's just standin' there where you are, lookin' down at the house. A tinker, says I to meself, with a gun under his oxter. Well I can tell you I was very wary even if I had me own oul' shotgun with me.' He patted the wooden stock as if patting a faithful old dog.

 ' "What do you want here?" says I. Well he looked around at me and smiled. "I just wanted to hear the echoes," says he and raised his gun up like this.'

Mr Synnott snapped the shotgun shut and pointed it skywards. He fired. Dempsey flinched in sudden alarm. The report came back to them from trees and hillsides and crackled away into the distance. Startled pigeons fluttered overhead and rooks rose from their perches in the high woods. Dempsey watched them rising and falling in a crazy dance and heard their raucous cries with a kind of childish pleasure at their discomfiture.

'That's exactly what I did,' said Mr Synnott, 'and when I turned around there was nobody there, just the gun, broken and rusty on the ground.'

Dempsey felt a prickling on the back of his neck. He looked around.

'Is that the same gun over the fireplace?'

'It is that,' nodded the older man. 'I cleaned it up as best I could. I never saw the young lad again but I think I know who he was.'

'You do?'

'Aye. There were two brothers went away from here and fought in the Rising of 'Ninety Eight. Only one came back alive and even at that he was hardly in it at all.'

'And you think you saw the other one?'

'That I do. I like to fire a shot up here for him now an' again. It's a kind of a salute, d'you see.'

There was a long silence. Dempsey leaned on the gate.

'The Rising was all around here I suppose.'

'Oh, aye.' Mr Synnott roused himself from his reverie. He tapped his pipe out on the stone and pointed with the stem.

'Do you see those woods away beyond? Now that's Horetown.

Beyond that again is Foulkesmills where Sir John Moore put his artillery.'

'The famous Sir John Moore? "We buried him darkly at dead of night"?'

'That's the man and a very decent man by all accounts.'

'That's a funny thing to hear from a Wexfordman — a good word about a Redcoat.'

'Well it's a fact. Anyway the battle was fought all across those woods. That was after Ross of course.'

He spoke as if it was common knowledge, as if he was discussing recent events with a neighbour. The rights and wrongs of it were alive to him still.

'This place is steeped in history. That hill over there is Carrick-byrne where the camp was.'

Dempsey could just about descry the rim of a jagged hill peering above the skyline. It was difficult to imagine the shouts and the din of war sounding across such a pastoral scene.

'And the brothers?' he prompted.

'The younger one was killed at Foulkesmills. They never found his body. Thrown into some Croppy grave I suppose. The other one came home eventually. He would've been my great, great, probably great-grandfather.' He told off the generations on his fingers as he spoke. 'That'd be about right. Aye.'

Dempsey's gaze travelled to the ivy covered ruin of the keep. The Synnotts, he reflected, knew where they stood. When they broke the soil with ploughshares they knew that it contained the sweat and the very bones of their own people. The tower house gave testimony that they had spilled their blood too in defending this land from wild mountain men from the north. He felt presumptuous, an intruder.

Mr Synnott rose and stretched. He slipped the pipe back into his pocket.

'So you're going to marry our daughter then?'

Dempsey was caught off guard. His prepared speech deserted him.

'That's the plan,' he blurted hoping it did not sound too much like a *fait accompli*. There is still a protocol somewhere in these matters.

'You'll be good to her then, I dare say. She's a fine lass.' The matter was settled.

They walked on through a field of young barley and across grazing land where placid cows raised their heads and regarded them with consuming interest. When they returned to the house Mr Synnott took out a bottle of Hewitts' whiskey.

'We'll just have the one in view of the day that's in it. Come into the kitchen here Jack, where a body can relax.'

Elaine looked up from the newspaper which she had spread on the white deal table and raised one enquiring eyebrow. Dempsey grinned broadly and pantomimed the wiping of sweat from his brow.

Mr Synnott put his head round the door into the hallway and bellowed: 'Come in here Mother and have a drink with us. It seems this young fella-me-lad is about to marry your daughter.'

'Do you think I haven't got a pair of eyes in me head,' said Mrs Synnott bustling in with a basket of eggs. 'Any excuse for a jar,' but she smiled and accepted a glass.

Dempsey raised his glass. He felt a speech was in order but he was too happy to speak. Elaine took his hand in hers.

'So there,' she said defiantly. 'I knew you'd like him.'

'We'll have our tea in here,' declared Mrs Synnott. It was the final seal of approval.

~

The unfamiliar sounds of a strange house woke Dempsey early in the morning. He listened intently. A heifer coughed in the misty paddock. A pail clanked somewhere in the yard and voices, made unintelligible by distance, greeted each other, muttered outcrops of sound, vowels without consonants. Water ran through pipes and was cut off suddenly with a rattle of protest.

Tom was up early, he thought. It was a private joke. When he first heard Elaine mention her home place he thought Tomgarrif was a person. 'You must come and see Tomgarrif.' In fact it was Elaine who

usually got the wrong end of the stick, scrambling a familiar phrase
— one man's meat is another man's gander; out of the frying pan
and into the soup — very often a big improvement on the original.

For Dempsey Tomgarrif would always be there, a sturdy man of
Dorset who came across with Strongbow, a man who spoke in Old
Talk, old Chaucer English they claimed and played Tom Fool with
the mummers. To Dempsey, he was the presiding genius of the place.

He stood at the window. Low morning sunlight was lancing
through mist. Trees stood out like islands in an ocean of white, like
leafy green nunataks. Crows were already abroad, rising and falling,
anxious to be off about their business.

There were no voices raised in argument. He almost missed the
familiar sound of his father grumbling into wakefulness. Even in his
benign moods, Dempsey's father could not put aside his drill ser-
geant's manner and when he was angry it was as well to stay out of
his way. Had Dinny Dempsey grown up in a rural setting like
Tomgarrif, would he have been a quiet easygoing man? His son
wondered about it. Dinny was a child of the barracks square. What
passed for a family album showed other Dempseys in British army
uniforms, pill-box hats, bum-freezer jackets, two generations of
them, all fighting men. If there was no fight going on, Dinny
Dempsey could start one, himself and his old mate, the Mad Gunner
McEnaspie who joined the Free State Army on the same day.

Dempsey began to shave. He looked a bit like his father he had
to admit, except for the nose. He turned his head sideways. A touch
of Marlon Brando about the nose. That was the legacy of a battle lost
in a boxing ring in Drogheda. The Da was furious with him about
that.

'What did I tell ye? Keep your guard up.' Drogheda was a grey
town with a brown river sweeping into the darkness. The minibus
stood in a pool of water and the rain pelted down.

'Come on, Dinny,' the Mad Gunner said. 'You can't win them all.'

He recalled looking like the Phantom of the Opera for a few weeks
but definitely the nose was an improvement on what had been there
before. Dinny relented after a while and spoke to him earnestly
about keeping up his guard.

Dempsey towelled his face vigorously and made his way quietly down the stairs. He looked at Elaine's room and pictured her sleeping with her hair perhaps spread on the pillow like a halo. Soon he would have no need to wonder. He let himself out into the yard and strolled around to the front of the house. The sun had scattered the last of the mist.

He swore under his breath when he noticed the flat tyre on his Volkswagen. The car was a constant drain on his finances. It always seemed to wait until he relaxed and then it sprang some new ailment on him. Yet when it worked it gave great satisfaction. On balance it probably earned its keep.

He got out the jack and began to change the wheel. He struggled with the wheelbrace. They always tighten them too much. He cursed again. A shadow fell across him where he crouched.

'Here,' said Mr Synnott, 'try this.'

He had a length of gun-barrel piping in his hand.

'Put this over the T bar for leverage. It's a great man altogether. The theorem of Pythagoras or one of those old fellas.'

It worked. The nut squawked and surrendered.

'Begod, you're right. Archimedes or whoever was no fool.'

'You have to be able to improvise in this job,' said Mr Synnott. 'No, no, keep it. It's bound to come in handy.'

Dempsey hefted the length of pipe. Tool-making animals, he thought, though another theory says weapon-making. Either way it was a handy thing to have around.

'I will then. Don't want to be stuck somewhere on the road. It's a funny thing,' he added, 'but I hate a flat tyre. It always depresses me, like breaking a shoelace when you were a kid, or the buckle coming off a sandal. It's not being able to keep up with the others I suppose.'

Mr Synnott laughed. 'Well you're a gas man, Jack. You wouldn't want to have my job where there's somethin' bust every second day. I spend half me time fixin' machinery.'

He straightened up. 'It's a wonder now herself didn't get you out early.'

'It is early,' protested Dempsey glancing at his watch. It was eight o'clock.

Mr Synnott snorted. 'Herself has been out these two hours.' He pointed towards one of the far fields where Dempsey made out a figure on horseback going at a brisk canter.

'You have to be up early to keep up with Elaine. I take it you haven't had any breakfast. I'm just on me way in.'

Dempsey threw the jack into an old leather holdall and slipped the length of pipe onto the shelf under the dashboard. He rubbed his hands together as they went indoors. There was a smell of bacon frying. This is the life, he thought as he listened for the clatter of hooves in the yard.

~

Marrying Elaine was so obviously the right thing to do that it came as a surprise that anyone should regard them as too young. He told his father about their plans late one night as Dinny dozed in front of the television.

'I have a bit of news for you.'

'Huh?'

'A bit of good news. Elaine and I are going to get married.'

'Good Jasus! When?' Dinny sat bolt upright.

'In about a year. Early next summer.'

Dinny subsided, visibly relieved. 'Aw, that's all right then.'

Delicacy prevented him from saying what had first come into his head and Dempsey laughed. 'You needn't worry. Give us a bit of credit.'

'Right, right,' he mumbled and conceded, 'that'll be a big day out, I suppose.'

'We hadn't thought that far ahead. I suppose we'd have to have a bit of a do.'

Dinny grunted then sat silently for a few moments with his hands joined over his shirt front.

'Big step, big step,' he muttered.

'Aye. I suppose it is.'

'You'd want to be sure.' Dinny exhaled slowly.

'Oh we're sure all right.'

'You'll have to go and tell your Mammy.'

He hardly ever referred to her. 'Not that she'll understand a thing about it.' He spoke almost impatiently.

'No, I suppose not.' Dempsey felt guilty that in contemplating his own happiness he had overlooked the fact that his mother would know nothing about it; that she had opted out of the mainstream of their lives.

Dinny shifted in his chair and grunted. 'Poor Ginnie. She deserved better.'

He fumbled for a handkerchief and blew his nose loudly. Dempsey sat still, taken aback by the remark. This was a facet of his father that he had never suspected.

Dinny stood up slowly and sniffed.

'Aye, well I'm glad for the both of ye. She seems a fine girl. Mind you don't let her down.'

That's a good one coming from you, thought Dempsey but let it pass. He was thinking about his mother. He would not want her at the wedding to be stared at and commented on. For her sake he would not want that. He wondered though, whether in his inner-most thoughts, he was really thinking of his own sake. Life is a series of opportunities for doing the right thing or for letting other people down. We live with the consequences. Who would escape whipping?

~

His employer, Paddy Sedgwick reacted with predictable irony to the news.

'Jasus, another good man down.'

Being happily married with a brood of five sons he felt entitled to denigrate the institution of matrimony. He had, he claimed, put up his hours. He invited them to dinner and Elaine confessed that she found the Sedgwicks absolutely charming. She had been a bit wary of meeting someone whose name appeared in gold lettering on a

prestigious Dublin premises. She expected pomposity and condescension at the very least and was surprised to meet Paddy in his
shirt sleeves, sweeping the front driveway as they arrived.

Two young boys were kicking a ball around the lawn.

'Kids,' he said by way of greeting. 'They always come right to the
point. Do you know what they said?'

They shook their heads.

' "Who's coming?" You'd think I never tidied the place in my
whole life.' His cigarette wobbled up and down as he spoke. 'Come
inside,' he continued, 'and meet Maureen. By the way, Jack, I picked
up a couple of volumes that I know would interest you.'

The dining room opened onto the lawn at the back of the house
and once or twice Paddy had to leave the table to mediate in some
dispute or other between the boys.

'And tell me,' said Maureen, leaning her elbows on the table.
'How did you two meet?'

Elaine smiled. 'As I recall it you admired my new hat.'

'That's right. All the nurses had to wear hats for their final exams.
We used to sit on the steps in college and whistle at them. Very
sophisticated.'

'Well I was late that day. In fact I had to go and buy the stupid
hat and then I got soaked in the rain. I asked this scruffy looking
student where the Medical School was and he insisted on coming
with me. I thought I'd never get rid of him. He kept going on about
my hat.'

'Right and didn't I wait to see how you got on too? At considerable expense be it said.'

'I needed that coffee too I can tell you. You see I took a tranquil-
liser to calm me down and it nearly put me to sleep. My examiner
said I should get a boot in the backside.'

'Not very gentlemanly of him,' remarked Maureen.

'Maybe not but it woke me up enough to pass the exam.'

'Leave that bloody bike alone,' shouted a young voice outside and
again Paddy left the table. There was a sound of a door slamming
and raised voices and Paddy returned.

'Thanks be to Christ the rugby is starting soon,' he said in exasperation. 'They are little bastards during the summer. During the rugby season they get on fine. It's all that testosterone. There should be a bottle for it in the chemist's.' He subsided. 'You used to box, Jack, didn't you?'

'That's right. I wasn't much good at it though. The Da always said it would make a man of me. He was pretty nifty himself I can tell you.' He told them about his father's fear of book-learning and how his mother had encouraged him to read. It was yet another point of disagreement between his parents. Dinny had no time for her people the Comerfords and in truth they had no time for him. He would beat the Comerford influence out of his son if he had to take his belt to him to do it.

'Jasus,' groaned Paddy, 'if a kid isn't aggressive, for Christ's sake don't try to make him aggressive. Do you know what one of those little gets did once? He shoved his brother down the stairs on his rocking horse. Right out through the glass he went. Some argument about whose turn it was, that's all.'

'Good lord,' said Elaine, 'was the child hurt?'

'No. Funny thing, there wasn't a scratch on him. They were disappointed that the glass didn't break in the shape of his horse, like in the cartoons.' He shook his head.

'Why did you give up boxing then?' asked Maureen returning to Dempsey's story.

'It sort of gave me up in a way. I was in the gym one day watching two lads sparring. One of them was a doctor. Pretty useful too he was. Anyway I saw this thing running along the ropes. I thought it was a mouse but it wasn't. The retina of this eye,' he pointed to his right eye, 'had become detached. That's what your man the doctor said anyway and he whipped me round to the Eye and Ear Hospital to have it checked. He was right too. Told me to give it up or I could go blind. The Da was disappointed in me. It didn't matter that I passed my exams. I think he took it as evidence that university had ruined me altogether.'

'You never told me about that,' said Elaine in some alarm. 'When did that happen?'

'There was no need to worry. It hasn't got any worse. Just a kind

of a bubble that distorts things a bit — puts a kink in a straight line.
It was the day after we went up the mountains to the Hellfire Club.'

'Ho ho,' said Paddy 'and what were you up to up on the Hellfire?'

'Not a lot,' said Dempsey. 'Would you believe your woman here
was in a hiking club? I just went along.'

'You were a grumpy so and so too if I remember,' Elaine put in.
'In fact I told you to feck off and get the bus back into town. I think
you were just afraid of being murdered 'cause you wouldn't go back
down.'

'Is that what you thought? Well I can tell you now I wasn't being
grumpy just for pig-iron. If you must know my bladder was full and
the trees were too small to give decent cover. I could hardly think of
anything else. I didn't want to disillusion you at such an early stage
of our relationship.'

They laughed at his explanation.

'And to think that we hiked all the way over to Bohernabreena.
Oh Jack, you must have been in agony,' she laughed.

'I nearly died I don't mind telling you.'

'But what's all this about being murdered?' asked Maureen.

'Oh we had a guide, a bloody knowall. Kept going on about rocks
and trees. Told us all about the famous Hellfire murder case. All the
gory details.' Dempsey still harboured resentment of the guide.

'Oh yes, that business,' said Paddy stroking his chin. 'One of your
better Dublin murders if I recall. Two blokes battered to death by a
man and a woman. I forget the outcome of it all. It was years ago.'

'Some well-known artist, according to our guide.'

'That's right. A fellow called Clifford, if I remember rightly. Very
big in the forties. He was excommunicated by the bishop I think. I've
come across some of his work now and again — did a bit of stained
glass as well.'

'A strange story,' nodded Dempsey and the talk turned to other
matters. They talked about the wedding and finding somewhere to
live and Paddy, mellowing as the evening advanced, extolled the
joys of the married state and assured them that the best was yet to
come. In fact he agreed to be best man although he called it aiding
and abetting.

CHAPTER TWO

The following morning Dempsey found two books on the glass topped counter at the back of the showroom, *The Diaries of Sir John Moore*. There was a note from Paddy who had 'nipped out for a few minutes'. Dempsey smiled wryly and regarded the chaos on his desk. It was a high desk which he always imagined for some reason, might have belonged to Mr Pickwick. There was a high stool to go with it. All it lacked was an ink pot and quill pen. Paddy was threatening to get the whole business computerised. He said it with distaste.

There was a list of items to be included in a forthcoming sale. There was a supplementary list of items which had arrived too late for inclusion in the catalogue. There was a third list of items previously overlooked and items that had been described over the phone but had not yet arrived. Asterisks indicated the customers who were likely to be awkward. Paddy had an ascending scale of asterisks, a kind of private Richter scale.

Dempsey turned the books over and flipped through the pages. They looked like something to be saved for a few days in bed with the flu. A line caught his eye: Sir John's opinion that the people in his district in Cork were cutting timber for firewood, not for the shafts of pikes. It seemed a bit rough that a fellow might be hanged for trying to keep himself and his family from freezing to death.

He read on. Moore seemed to feel that the country was being

driven into rebellion by its own rulers. 'One good man could save Ireland.' He recommended conciliation but the gentry wanted war. Dempsey pushed the lists to one side, hiked himself up onto the stool and turned another page. Moore described the progress of the army from Cork to Wexford. Stan and Ollie would not have been out of place amid such incompetence and poltroonery. Dempsey laughed aloud. He looked up at the sound of a cough.

There was an old lady standing at the counter. She had one of those fox fur stoles with the paws hanging down her lapels and a very crafty looking fox peering from below her right ear.

'I beg your pardon,' said Dempsey sliding quickly from his stool. 'I didn't hear you come in. As a matter of fact,' he added quickly, 'I was reading a rather interesting book.'

'Oh, I'm sorry for disturbing you,' she said with a tremor in her voice. 'I can come back later if you like.'

'Not at all, not at all. What can I do for you?'

'Well,' she began. 'Frances told me to ask for Mr Dempsey. Would you be Mr Dempsey by any chance?'

It figured. This old lady was another of the secretary's acquaintances. They were like clones, either from the bridge club or some parish organisation. She always advised them to consult that nice young Mr Dempsey about the disposal of their treasures.

'Yes indeed,' he said heartily and braced himself for a disquisition on some piece of family silver which must be worth a great deal of money, you see, because it belonged to an old relation who brought it back from India. No, there was no hallmark, but it was always believed to be solid silver. Very, very old. It was always hard to shatter their illusions.

'And what can I do for you? Would you like me to go upstairs and tell Frances you're here?'

'No, no that won't be necessary. I just have some things I'd like to sell,' her voice trembled again.

'I'll get you a chair,' he offered and she nodded gratefully.

'I came in on the bus, you know.'

He nodded and she took a brown paper envelope from her handbag.

'They go very quickly,' she went on, 'and they don't give you enough time to find a seat before whoosh! they're off again.'

'I know. You have to be very careful.'

'These belonged to my husband, you see,' she said placing a pair of spectacles, a fountain pen and an old pocket watch on the counter.

'Do you think someone might buy them?' She looked at him anxiously.

'Ah,' said Dempsey at a loss.

He picked up the watch. 'Rolled gold' said the inscription on the back but most of the gold had long since rolled off.

'Difficult to say.'

He leaned his elbows on the counter and spread his hands.

'Are you quite sure you want to sell them? I mean...?' He was not sure what he meant. She pulled a glove through her hand with the quick jerking motion of a little bird and all at once she reminded him of his mother.

'He was a very good man you see.'

It was important to her that he should understand.

'We were together for forty-eight years. It would have been forty-nine this August coming.'

'I see,' nodded Dempsey looking down at the items on the glass, the sum total of a man's life. 'I'm very sorry.'

'We never had any children, you see. There were just the two of us. If we had children I could give these to them but there's nobody.'

'Are you quite sure? There wouldn't be a great demand nowadays, I mean. I don't think...'

He trailed off watching the glove sliding through her bony fingers.

'It's just that I can't bear to look at them in the house. It's almost as if he had just popped out for a paper. You do understand, don't you? I'd prefer that somebody would get some use out of them.'

'I understand,' he said gently. 'I'll look after things for you.'

'I would be most grateful if you would do that,' she said getting slowly to her feet. She touched the items one by one and then drew on her gloves.

'Frances told me everything would be all right.'

Dempsey mumbled something indistinct and glanced at the name on the envelope.

'Don't worry about it,' he assured her. 'We'll do all we can.'

He showed her to the door and held it open.

'I could call a taxi, if you like,' he offered, 'that is if you don't want to risk the bus.'

'No, no, the bus will be fine. We mustn't give in to them too easily.'

He wondered who 'they' might be, the massed bands of Kamikaze Dublin drivers, perhaps. The fox watched him with basilisk eyes and then the old lady was gone, tottering along the flagstoned pavement as if a gust of wind might waft her into the river.

A man should leave more than that behind him, he mused and opened the drawer of his desk. A bit of jiggery pokery would raise a few pounds for her. He could include them in a job lot. He wondered if she also needed the money. Maybe the old man had set his life down on paper with that pen. Perhaps he too had written a diary. Maybe she had read it after his death and found a strange and secret man whom she had never known. Who knows? Sir John had felt it necessary to tell his story to posterity. Dempsey wanted to get back to it but duty called. Carefully he slipped the items into the envelope and place them in the drawer. He slid onto his stool and began to decipher and check the lists. He heard the phone ring upstairs and the sound of Frances answering it. All was well. If there was a problem, Frances would have the solution. He decided to skip lunch and treat himself to a good read instead, even wander over to Stephen's Green for three quarters of an hour and take advantage of the fine weather.

~

To a background prattle of insistent and fearless waterfowl Dempsey read Moore's account of the battle around Foulkesmills and Horetown. I know those fields, he thought with a sudden excitement. I can see where Moore placed his guns. So that's how it happened. It was as Elaine's father had described it with the pikemen holding the line against all the odds. Now here was a story worth writing down, a story to stir the blood, and through it all gleamed the fundamental decency of Moore himself trying wherever possible to alleviate the suffering of the people he had been sent to pacify.

The phones rang incessantly throughout the afternoon and he found his temper beginning to fray. Dealers and other prospective buyers came and prowled around the showroom. Elaine rang to say that she had to do night duty for a friend.

'Balls,' he muttered, disappointed.

'I'm sorry,' she said, 'but I couldn't get out of it.'

'That's okay,' he conceded. 'Maybe we'll have forty-eight years to make up for it.'

'What was that?'

'Never mind. I'll explain some other time.'

'Right,' she said and there was a tinge of puzzlement in her voice. 'Love you.'

She put down the phone. He felt the evening stretching before him like a void.

'Balls,' he muttered again with more vehemence.

'I beg your pardon.'

The speaker was a tall, thin man of about sixty, in a well-worn tweed jacket with leather elbow patches. His closely trimmed moustache, the merest dusting of colour on his upper lip, and his air of languid authority proclaimed his background.

'I'm sorry,' said Dempsey putting down the phone, 'a bit of bother.'

The man drummed his fingertips on the glass.

'May we come to the point. An item sent in. Not in your catalogue.'

'I see,' said Dempsey. 'Perhaps it arrived late. It must be on the supplementary list, Mr eh ..?'

He looked up interrogatively.

'Don't you realise who I am, young man? I'm Colonel Humphreys of Ringwall House.'

'Humphreys, Humphreys,' muttered Dempsey running his finger down the sheets of paper. Hump off, Humphreys, he thought.

'Doesn't appear to be on this list.'

That left only the disaster list.

'There is some more documentation.'

'This is outrageous, young man. Where is your employer?'

'Mr Sedgwick is not available, I'm afraid. He was called away urgently.'

'I was under the impression that I was dealing with a reputable firm, not one staffed by incompetents.'

'Sir, if your property is here there will be a record of it. Can you describe it?'

'Not damnwell good enough. This is a valuable piece of silver, Georgian wine cooler; worth a considerable amount of money.'

Dempsey furtively consulted the final list and found the name Humphreys with asterisks clustered about it like spiders. Where's me pike? he thought. There had been a conversation over the phone but it seemed the good colonel had decided in the long run to entrust the sale to a different firm.

'We don't appear to have it, Sir. It seems that you decided to patronise one of our competitors.'

He leaned slightly on the word patronise, giving it, he thought, a nice sarcastic edge.

'Preposterous! Are you telling me I don't know where I send my own property?'

'That's how it appears, Sir. You did apparently discuss the matter with Mr Sedgwick but in the final analysis...'

The man looked as if he might explode with anger. He clenched his fists. Dempsey braced himself. If he tries anything I'll flatten him, he decided.

A look of doubt flickered across the man's face. It seemed to slide like a cataract across his eyes. He frowned.

'Good heavens!' he murmered. 'Good heavens,' and slowly his anger changed to confusion.

'Ah Colonel Humphreys! Have you decided to come back to us after all?'

It was Paddy arriving just in time to resolve the situation.

'I trust our Mr Dempsey has been looking after you properly.'

'Bit of a misunderstanding, I'm afraid,' said Dempsey.

The man looked somehow older and almost pitiable. Paddy conducted him to the door and shook hands with him, inviting him to call any time.

He rolled his eyes upwards as he returned.

'Poor old chap. Gets a bit confused at times. Still, these are the people who pay the rent.'

'He's a new one on me.'

'Comes in very occasionally. Forgets what he's bid on. Raises all sorts of ructions.'

'So I gathered from the asterisks.'

'Still it wouldn't be a good idea to belt him one. I think I arrived just in time.'

Dempsey smiled and shook his head.

'No, it wasn't him as such. Just his manner. Eight hundred years of arrogance bred in the bone.'

Paddy laughed. 'What's all this about? Up the rebels?'

Dempsey looked a bit sheepish.

'He just got up my nose, that's all. Don't see why we should have to put up with it.'

'We? Who are we?' Paddy put his head to one side and regarded him quizzically.

Dempsey felt at a bit of a loss. He admitted that there was an old prejudice there that he had never really thought through, a vague inherited resentment of the gentry, the big house, a world virtually vanished and yet still a powerful shaper of attitudes. Not so long ago a government minister had rejoiced at the destruction of Georgian houses because they represented everything he detested in Ireland's history. Dempsey put this point to Paddy.

'If you really think that Jack, you're definitely in the wrong business.'

He gestured about.

'And where would I be for a living? Think about it. There's always more than one side to any story.'

Dempsey felt rebuked and immature. That rather sad old man could hardly be held responsible for eight centuries of foreign

domination. Putting his head on a pike would have been a bit rough.
He shrugged.

'I'll have to think about all this,' he conceded and went back to
work.

~

When Dempsey came back from visiting his mother he found that
he could not settle. He had a nagging feeling that he should have
been able to arrange something better. Darkly he wondered if that
was what the future held for Elaine and himself. He took up the book
again and read of ancient battles and a long straggling pursuit
through Wicklow and his interest began to quicken. It would make
a great film or even a novel. The idea seized him. He looked at his
watch. It was two o'clock in the morning. He went quickly and made
a flask of tea and drove around to where Dinny sat by his brazier in
contemplative solitude.

'Thought you might like a fresh drop,' he said as his father
inserted the blade of a shovel under a railing to make a seat for him.

'Don't sit too near them fumes,' Dinny warned him. 'Many's the
good man was found coiled up in the mornin' from fumes.'

Dempsey drew back. The night was mild and he felt no need of
sleep.

'Are you never worried out here all night by yourself?' he began.

'Worried? No, no. I can take care of meself. Anyway I like to sit
here and have a good think.'

'Aye.' They sat for a while watching the blue flames flicker in the
heart of the fire.

'You went to see your mammy then?'

'I did,' nodded Dempsey. 'I'm afraid she didn't really understand
what I was saying. Alzheimer's, they say it is.'

'I could do nothing for her in the end,' said Dinny after a while
and subsided again into a brooding silence.

A high ululating cry came to them from afar echoing through the
silent streets, a cry full of loneliness and the hurt and despair of exile.

'That's the gibbon above in the zoo,' said Dinny. 'I hear him every night.'

Dempsey knew the gibbon well. He lived on an island in the lake, a master of his element. In summer he levitated from tree to tree and in winter he crouched in his shelter looking with hurt and bewildered eyes at his captors, pining for his beloved rainforest.

'Wouldn't you hate to be locked up?' Dinny was in a talkative mood. 'I couldn't take it at all.' His train of thought was interrupted by the sound of a group of youths conversing long-distance as they parted company for the night.

'Balubas,' snorted Dinny. 'Why can't they just go home quiet like anybody else? Y'know they'd swipe me lamps, given half a chance.' He stood up and looked down the street. 'Though the toffs are worse — dress dances an' all that. I dunno what it is that they have to destroy somethin'.'

There was a dim light in the east. The cry of the gibbon came again, a cry from the pit of ages, a protest against those who had chosen to walk erect with sticks and stones in their hands and set themselves in dominion over all creatures.

'Probably raining in Borneo,' said Dempsey and Dinny looked at him oddly.

'Oh yes. I see what you mean.'

Dempsey rose and stretched. He could go home through the treeways like Tarzan but it might be easier to drive.

'I'll see you in the morning then,' he said.

'Aye and thanks for the tea.'

The treeways, sycamore, courtesy of the Corporation. He had worked one summer in London with a little fellow from Cork. Five foot two at the very most and always starting trouble. He used to goad the West Indian workers with a running gag: 'They're cuttin' down all the trees on this street, boys. Ye fuckers are goin' to have to walk to work any more.'

All very well until one day a chap picked him up by the front of his overalls, a big fellow about the size of Sonny Liston, and said in mellifluous Jamaican: 'Now listen, Sean Ban if ya doan stop with dese remarks I'm goin' to beat seven kinds o' shit outa' you.' He said it politely, even considerately and Sean Ban gave it a rest for a day or two but like Tarzan he had an instinct for the jugular even at the risk of his own life. Dempsey wondered what had become of him. There had been another time when the foreman said: 'Put these two Paddies to work at the conveyor belt,' and Sean Ban went for him. Racism, he learned, is a two edged sword. They didn't stay long in that job. 'Have to teach them respect,' said Sean as they trudged out into the street. Sticks and stones may break your bones but names in the long run do a better job. It was too late to go to bed so he read for a while, then shaved and went out.

When Elaine saw him outside the gate she smiled and he felt a great surge of joy.

'What in the name of God are you doing out at this hour?'

'Waiting for you,' he said casually. 'I missed you.'

'How long have you been up?'

'All night, like yourself. I've been walking and thinking about things.'

'And?'

'I think things are going to be great. Don't you?'

'Are you sure you don't mean walking and drinking?'

She tucked her hand into the crook of his elbow and they walked slowly, avoiding the cracks in the pavement. It became a game, trying to make the other step on a crack.

'And what conclusions have you reached?' she asked after a while.

'Just that we shouldn't waste any time. We should get married straight away, have a raft of kids and by the way I'm going to write a book.'

She laughed

'A prolific author.'

'Okay, okay but I know it's in me. All your old man's yarns and so on. Wait till you see.'

'You will consult me I hope, about the other part of the plan.'

'The children?'

'Yes.'

'You'll be the first to know.'

'Not today though,' she said yawning. 'I've no energy for any of that carry on right now.'

'Not even a bit of research?'

'Not a chance,' she repeated. 'I have to work tonight.'

'We really must get together sometime,' he said as she kissed him lightly and skipped up the steps to her door. He turned to go and the early morning sunlight flooded round him gilding the pavements and the railings of the elegant old houses.

~

By comparison with Elaine's people, Dinny seemed ill-at-ease in his good suit and collar and tie. Dempsey had wondered at times whether his father would travel down to the wedding and at times he half hoped that he would not. Dinny was not a man for polite small talk and chit-chat. His speech at the wedding breakfast was awkward and mercifully brief. He looked as if he wanted to escape. Sweat stood out on his forehead but he went so far as to wish them health and happiness and sat down, looking embarrassed at the ripple of applause and murmurs of agreement. It was accepted that Jack's father was a man of few words.

Yet Dinny had the capacity to produce the occasional surprise. When Elaine claimed a dance with him he waltzed with unexpected grace. She smiled at him and shared a joke. Dempsey saw his father relaxing. Maybe the few drinks had had a beneficial effect. He was obviously pleased with himself.

Elaine led him back to where Dempsey was standing. She held him by the hand. Dinny looked positively smug.

'You never told me your father was such a good dancer.'

'Well, there you are now,' said Dempsey, 'a man of many parts.'

'It's a while now since I put a foot under me on a dance floor,' said his father, slightly out of breath, 'but the oul' legs aren't finished yet.'

Paddy Sedgwick took him by the elbow and steered him towards the bar.

'You always described him as a bit of an ogre,' Elaine said with a kind of challenge in her voice. 'I think he's very nice.'

'Nice? Maybe I don't know the man at all.'

'Well I think he is. He's had a sad old time of it. That's what I think anyway.'

'I'm glad you get on with him. He thinks you're not so bad yourself, y'know. He even went so far as to say so once.'

'Indeed? And what do you think?'

'Oh, I'm inclined to agree. Ask me again in five years' time.'

Dinny returned and diffidently interrupted.

'I'm goin' to slip away quietly now. I want to get the late train back to Dublin.'

'But you could stay over in Tomgarrif,' said Elaine, laying a hand on his forearm. 'There's plenty of room.'

'Ah no,' said Dinny. 'Your father said as much but I told him I have to get back.' He fumbled with his almost empty glass. 'I better get back tonight.'

Elaine looked at Jack. 'Well then you'll have to drive your Dad to the station. It'll only take a few minutes.'

Dinny protested.

'Nonsense,' she retorted. 'Anyway it'll give him a chance to check on his car.'

'Aye,' said Dempsey, 'to make sure those eejits haven't covered it in toothpaste and whatever.'

'Well then,' said Dinny relenting, 'if it's not too much trouble.'

He took Elaine's hand awkwardly in his own. 'Look after each other,' he said, 'because if ye don't, as sure as God, nobody else will.'

'And you take care too,' she replied and kissed him lightly on the cheek.

They were the only people waiting for the train. A sharp breeze blew along the platform scattering sweet papers and whirling them onto the track. A signal wire groaned.

'Where did you learn to dance like that?' asked Dempsey kicking at an empty matchbox. It skittered along the platform and disappeared over the edge.

'Aw, you never lose it,' said Dinny dismissively. He smiled at some secret memory. 'The mammy would have enjoyed the day, if she was in the whole of her health.'

'Aye. She would have, at that.'

'Aye.' Dinny walked a couple of steps and turned. 'You get on back outa' that. There's no need to wait.'

'It's no trouble.'

'No, go on, for God's sake. I can look after meself.'

'I wouldn't like to leave you on your own.'

'Go on, go on, man. It's your weddin' night for Christ's sake.'

'Well, if you think so, then I'll go along. And listen, I'm glad you came.'

'Aye. So am I. Enjoyed the day, whatever.' He ducked and feinted with his left and caught Dempsey playfully on the jaw with his right.

'Always fell for that one.'

Dempsey laughed. 'You never lost it.'

The train rumbled in and screeched protestingly to a halt.

'An' by the way ...' Dinny reached into his inside pocket. 'Somethin' here for the both of ye.'

He put a creased envelope into Dempsey's hand and swung open the carriage door. 'Go on now and don't be hangin' about here.' He climbed up and shut the door abruptly, anxious to be gone. He glanced back briefly and raised his hand. Dempsey raised the hand that held the envelope and shook it, at a loss for words.

The train lurched forward with couplings straining and began to move away into the darkness. Dempsey stood watching the lights dwindling in the distance. He shivered at the thought of his father travelling alone through the night with the great black void of the sea on one hand and ghostly shapes of trees and mountains flitting past on the other.

You could have stayed, he thought, with a little human warmth about you, if only for one night. Awkward bastard, making people feel guilty. He slit the envelope with a finger. There was a fifty-pound note inside. No message, just a smooth new banknote folded carefully in two. The sucker punch again, he reflected, just when I was nearly glad to see him go.

There was no reason for him to feel guilty. This was the happiest day of his life and the future with Elaine would be even better. There

were things to do and standing brooding on a windy railway platform was not going to get him anywhere. Time to put aside childish
things and get on with his life.

~

Elaine's father refused to learn Irish. It proved no disadvantage in
the raising of cattle and barley and a few horses. There was no extra
percentage gain for using the Gaelic tongue. No cattle jobber
haggled with him in Irish. No mart offered him a few extra pounds
for transacting his business 'through the medium'. But his refusal
sprang from a far deeper reason, an ancient grudge that coursed in
his very blood. 'It was Gaelic speakers that hanged the men on the
bridge at Ross.'

Something like that is never forgotten, especially not in Wexford.
All other wars and risings become flimsy sideshows when a
Wexfordman begins on his theme.

Mr Synnott would rise from the dinner table to demonstrate the
use of the pike; the hook to cut the bridle and reins and the point to
finish off the dismounted yeoman. Yeoman service was no
compliment in his vocabulary.

'The fighting men cut staves from our own ash trees.' He showed
Dempsey with pride, the hedgerows that had equipped an army. He
would stop suddenly on a country lane.

'This was where the fighting men brought the army to a halt. My
ancestor shot two soldiers in the cattle pound at Foulkesmills.'

Elaine rolled her eyes upwards and laughed. 'Don't start him on
the fighting men,' she said, 'or he'll be at it 'til midnight.' She had
heard it all before but Dempsey was fascinated.

'All right then,' she said with a glint of mischief. 'Just ask him
about Scullabogue.'

That was the only time he had ever seen his father-in-law angry.
It was a personal affront. 'It wasn't the fighting men who burned
Scullabogue.' The finger was pointed elsewhere. Dempsey was
taken aback by his vehemence but Elaine merely laughed. 'He'll

never hear a word against the men of 'Ninety Eight.'

~

On the first night he and Elaine spent as man and wife under the Synnott roof, they made love carefully but still the old iron-framed bed betrayed every movement. It twanged and jangled and they spluttered with laughter.

In the morning the sun streamed through the tall window and Dempsey woke again to the sounds of country life. He looked out of the window, noticing the mist still lurking under trees. He looked at his wife and wondered what he had done to be so fortunate. There must be some catch, he thought. She stirred in her sleep and a strand of auburn hair slipped from her bare tanned shoulder. The sun had brought up little freckles on her arm. She opened her eyes, smiled at him and stretched like a kitten.

'Come back to bed,' she said softly and he felt again an over-whelming need for her. He was young and he had plans and the tintinnabulation of the bed was not important.

At breakfast she was demure. Her father concentrated on his food and the day's work ahead of him. Her two younger sisters exchanged smirks and watched Dempsey with interest. As yet they had not made up their minds about him. He felt uneasy under their scrutiny. No topic of conversation presented itself to his mind. He glanced at his watch.

'Oh, that's funny,' he said. 'I forgot to wind my watch last night,' — and everybody laughed.

CHAPTER THREE

Dempsey saw his son come into the world, unusual in those times. He stood there feeling stupid with a silly hat and a robe tied at the back and held Elaine's hand. They gave him something else to hold aloft, a bottle or a bag, he could not be sure, to give him the semblance of usefulness. Elaine watched him with concern but there was no need. He was master of the situation.

The little chap slipped easily into the world, wet as he was and streaked with blood. He glared around with sightless eyes and clenched his tiny fists. I'll have to warn him about holding his thumb inside like that, thought Dempsey incongruously. Presumably somebody slapped him. Dempsey could not be sure, but he heard the little voice, rasping and aggrieved. There was more business but the room had become hot and had begun to move.

'Don't worry, Mr Dempsey,' said the ward sister, a formidable woman, 'we've never lost a father yet.' Then he was outside on a chair in the corridor, grinning foolishly at people who did not appreciate the momentousness of the occasion.

When they brought Elaine back to her room they had tea and biscuits together and laughed delightedly at their own cleverness. He looked at her in wonder and awe. He drove home singing and beating time with the accelerator. Not until he saw frost glistening in the headlights and felt the wheels give a premonitory flutter did he come back to himself, Jack Dempsey, champion of the world.

~

Dempsey's mother faded unobtrusively out of this world not long after that. His father stood morose and pugnacious looking at the graveside. There were few mourners to mark her passing. Old McEnaspie the Mad Gunner was there and a tall stooped man who did not come forward to commiserate.

'Did you see him?' said Dinny afterwards. 'What the hell did he want comin' here? Damn all time he had for her when she was alive.'

'Who?'

'The tall fella' with the big car. That was your Comerford uncle, oul' bastard. He had no business comin' here today.'

'Comerford? Her brother. Well that's a bit of a turn up all right.'

'Ah well. Water under the bridge. She's better off where she is. A bitter oul' bastard, he is.'

Dempsey wondered if there was another side to the story. He knew nothing much about the Comerford side of himself except the few stories his mother had told him about her childhood. The Comerfords, he knew, were a force to be reckoned with in their part of the country but they might as well have been from Montenegro for all they meant to him.

He had other matters to occupy his attention. His son was taking his first few tentative steps — a natural athlete. He was experiment- ing with words — a prodigy of intelligence. They were happy and had begun to put money aside for a house. There was no time to mull over old grievances and feuds of long ago. He enjoyed his work and had an instinct for a bargain. He had developed into something of an expert in the field of antiques and was highly valued by Sedg- wicks.

There were summer weeks in Tomgarrif where the little boy sat in front of his mother as she trotted her quiet horse around the meadow and there were long lazy days at Bannow raking for cockles or bathing in the sun-warmed pools of the undulating beach. And all the time there was Mr Synnott and his stories of the Rising.

'It'd make a powerful book. You should write it all down when you get time.'

'Time is the thing, isn't it? Going around those old country houses you're very concious of time. There's an atmosphere about them that just gets you — not just the damp and dry rot but like your story about the man on the hill, I often feel there are ghosts watching me when I'm cataloguing the contents.'

'Does it bother you?'

'No, funny enough. I'd like to talk to them but it would be presumptuous I suppose. After all I'm usually clearing out all their precious belongings. It's not something they would have looked forward to is it?'

Mr Synott chuckled. 'It might make your colleagues a bit worried if they saw you.'

'Aye, I look out the window and I can imagine a mob of peasants camped on the lawn like it was at Horetown, butchering the farm stock to feed an army.'

'Who could blame them though?'

'Well I don't know. It's all relative, isn't it? I was driving one morning past a flea-market, just a stone's throw from O'Connell Street and it struck me that I was rich compared to those people. It was just the look on their faces. The stuff was rubbish, I mean, the cast-offs of poverty and yet they were desperate to get at it. That says something, doesn't it.'

'A stone's throw you could be right.'

'The thing is, I felt guilty because I have a shirt on me back so I just kept going. If I stopped to offer advice I'd have got a dig in the snot for me trouble.'

'Write it down Jack, now that you have the bit of free time.'

'I will. It's taken a while to come to a head, like a good boil.'

~

'In the beginning was the Word.' That was a good start for any book and worth using again. Plagiarism is a matter of good taste. Everything began from the Word. He sat back and admired the sentence.

It had taken him a while to type it but it looked good, professional.

That was how the whole thing had started. Word came of fighting at Dunlavin. Kildare was in uproar. Word came of the massacre at Carnew, in the ball alley. Words fascinated Dempsey, Yeola, the Old Talk of South Wexford, the dialect carried over from Dorset and lodged in that small palisaded corner. Nobody spoke it anymore but it survived in an inflection or a turn of phrase. The deep burr of South Wexford suggested Somerset and Farmer Giles.

He pursued the dialect through the Quakers, going to their headquarters to see the original manuscripts. The people had been very kind and obliging, letting him stay after the library closed. The old gentleman addressed him as Friend and insisted on helping him with the card-index. His old hands shook uncontrollably and diffidently Dempsey tried to help, knowing what he wanted. The cards leaped in the air and fluttered to the ground like a wild-west poker game. Dempsey gathered them and began to sort them but the old gentleman intervened and started to replace them in the drawer. His coordination was gone. He aimed for alphabetical order but his hands created a random pattern. Leave it for Christ's sake. It is against the rules to clobber a Quaker.

'You're a fuckin' disaster area, Dempsey.' Someone had said that to him once. Everything he put his hand to seemed to go awry. Nails bent under his hammer. Switches came off in his hand. The Quaker families of South Wexford scarpered in all directions at his approach.

But the book would be right. The words were there in his head.

'In the beginning was the Word. Where did I hear that before?'

'There's a bit more to it than that,' he laughed. 'These things take time.'

It was her idea to take the cottage near the beach for a few weeks in the summer. He could get down to serious writing at last. She could relax with the child while he spun out his yarn. He had an enormous keyboard chart on the wall to which he had added coloured arrows, a different colour for each finger. Touch typing, he said. It helped the ideas to flow. You could patent an idea like that, the coloured arrows. Make a fortune.

'So what comes next?'

'Wait 'til you see.' He got up and stretched.

'That's broken the ice anyway. That was the hard bit, actually starting.'

'So what comes next?'

'Don't rush me. Don't rush me.' He sounded piqued. 'I have to shake it all down in my head. Let's take the lad for a bit of a walk on the beach and I'll tell you what I have in mind.'

They walked over the dunes of the sunken town of Bannow, a Norman town built in the wrong place and reclaimed by the sands, a lost city. Summer visitors sat in folding chairs, broiling in the sun. Dempsey spoke of them almost disparagingly as if they had no right to be there. This was their private place now and he resented intruders. John scampered ahead of them running over the dunes, always seeking the most difficult route. At six everything is an adventure. Everything is new and your Dad can fight anyone in the world. Dempsey chased him up through the marram grass and brought him down with a tackle. Elaine watched them rolling down the steep scarp in a flailing bundle of arms and legs. The sky was without a sign of cloud. They were young and healthy with all their life together to look forward to.

'You know, I've been thinkin',' Dempsey said trotting back to her with the child jouncing up and down on his shoulders.

'What was that?'

'Well, it's just, what would you say to me giving the writing a real try, maybe taking a year off? It makes a lot of sense really.' His voice tailed off.

She laughed. 'Stick with the day job,' she said. 'You're not really serious, are you?'

Dempsey grinned, self-deprecatingly. 'Just a thought. I know we couldn't afford it. A nice thought all the same.'

She looked at him sideways. 'There's lots of things we'd like to do I suppose, but they don't put bread on the table.'

~

Another time they stood on the rocky outcrop of Baginbun. The wind whipped around them and she held tightly to John's hand — an easterly wind out of Wales.

'This is where it all started,' he remarked. 'We're only one day's sailing from Wales. Even the tides are the same. Just imagine it.' He pointed to the ditch that ran across the neck of the headland and the gap where the invading Normans had charged with their cattle, putting the Norsemen of Waterford to flight.

'They didn't mess about, did they?' She was always infected by his enthusiasm.

'You can say that again. Look, here's where Raymond le Gros threw his prisoners over the cliff. Seventy-seven of them.' There was a shoulder of cliff jutting out over crumbling black boulders. He inched his way outwards with the wind plucking at his clothing. The very place tempted thoughts of self-destruction and bone-crushing impact. Far below the day-trippers lurked behind their windbreaks, their territories marked out, safe in their micro-climates. One peep around the end of the shield reminded them that a seaside holiday is a delicately balanced thing, part idyll, part disaster, where children snivel and relationships creak under the strain.

'Come back for God's sake. Don't go near the edge.'

'Seventy-seven men, one at a time. Jesus Christ.'

'Get away from the edge.' The boy made a movement to follow his father but she gripped him even tighter. Dempsey inched his way back, no longer blasé. They continued their walk over tough, wiry blue grass, rounding the head to look out at the low line of Forlorn Point. The wind, a half gale, battered at them.

'The very word is like a bell. I'm tellin' you, you could write volumes about this place.'

'Aye,' she agreed drily. 'I'm waiting.'

They climbed down to the small sandy beach where the Norman ships had made their first landfall. It shelved steeply so vessels of shallow draught could come right to the water's edge.

'*Landfall*. That's the name for the book. That's it. *Landfall*.' He was enthusiastic. 'I could make it bigger, take in the whole sweep, the selling of Ireland to the Normans. A blockbuster.'

'Why not do the one you had in mind? The 'Ninety Eight. As me grandmother always said about picking blackberries: 'Pick one bush clean before you go on to the next.'

'Your Granny. That's the one that never went up to Wexford town 'til she was nearly eighty?'

'The very one.' Elaine mimicked the old woman's tremulous voice, handed down by tradition — 'I'd never go over the pink mountain. They're all barbarians up there.'

Up there they disembowelled their neighbours with pikes and hung men in hanks on Wexford bridge.

'That's what I like about Wexford. It's the street corner of History. I guess I'm just a corner boy at heart. There was an oul' fella down in Tipperary where all the Ryans come from, Ryan Stand Idle they called him. An ex-boxer so they say. A bit punchy. Just stood at the street corner all day long watching the world go by. I think he had it made.'

She laughed. 'Are you sure it was only your retina that came adrift in the ring?'

'I coulda' had class,' he laughed, 'I coulda' been a contender.'

'No,' she said, 'you've too much imagination. You'd probably sympathise with your opponent's point of view.'

'The Da would have seen that as a weakness. He wanted me to be another Jack Dempsey or maybe a Marciano. He loved Marciano. He used to get up in the middle of the night to listen to his fights. There he'd be, slapping the radio, fists clenched, daft really. He always got me out of bed to listen. It was static mostly but he said it was history.'

The mention of his father made him pause. Sometimes he felt that he had some obligation towards his father but Dinny was all right. Tough as nails. 'Yeah Rocky sure was a great champeen but here's the next heavyweight champeen of the woild.' He grabbed the little boy's fist and flourished it aloft. 'John Dempsey, the winnah.'

It was almost a perfect day, except for the wind, that same wind that had filled the sails of the invaders and, in the winter after Cromwell, blew magpies across to Ireland, making their landfall on the storied point of Carnsore, the headland of the priests.

~

Then the word came of the fight on Oxmantown Road. Oxman, Ostman, the old word for the Norsemen. The Ostmen of Waterford had hurtled to their deaths on the black rocks. Oxman, oxen, dying like cattle. There was an abattoir near the cattle markets. No, there was no connection. Dempsey shook his head.

'What was that again, Guard?'

The policeman coughed and hitched up his belt. 'Well I'm afraid it's bad news. It was the only way you could be contacted. Your wife's people told us where you might be found.' He coughed and removed his cap to step under the low cottage doorway.

'Good afternoon, Ma'am,' he added as Elaine came in from the back of the cottage.

'It's the Da,' said Dempsey. 'He's dead.'

'Oh no,' she said putting her fingers to her lips.

'I'm afraid so, Ma'am,' said the policeman. 'We got word at the barrack.'

He had been found at home by his old friend McEnaspie who missed him after first Mass in Aughrim Street. There had been a row the night before with a gang of youths who had smashed some of the lanterns. Dinny, according to witnesses, had waded in and sent a couple of them flying. Dempsey could well imagine it. Balubas, every last one of them. But he had taken a bit of a hiding.

It was mindless, a flash of pointless violence. It could make some sense if they had tried to rob him but they had set out to goad and humiliate an old man. Dempsey clenched his fists at the thought. He probably would never know who they were. They ran away laughing and Dinny had died the next morning as he tried to make a cup of tea.

Dinny was an old son of a bitch but he was Dempsey's son of a bitch. He would have to go up to Dublin. He felt a surge of guilt as if in some way he was to blame.

'I'll have to go up,' he said.

Elaine said that she would leave John with her parents.

The policeman nodded approvingly. 'That would be best.' He felt a fatherly concern for these two young people.

Dempsey missed the right hand bend at Newtownmount-kennedy in the darkness and ploughed through the triangular bed of rose bushes that had been set there out of civic pride. Guiltily he reversed back through the flowers and sped off in the direction of the city.

'Catches me every time,' he muttered. Nobody would have been abroad at that hour. The witching hour of pub closing was long past. He had talked more about his father on that trip than in all the previous years that Elaine had known him.

'You know one thing that always bothered him?'

'What was that?'

'The camp in the Curragh where they interned the lads during Hitler's war. He knew they were tunnelling. They were at it all the time. He would report it and the CO would say, 'Never mind. Let them get on with it. Just let me know when they're five yards from the perimeter fence.' The Da knew exactly where they were all the time. His pal the Mad Gunner wanted to set up machine guns where they were going to come out. Did I ever tell you about that?'

'No, what happened then?'

'The CO would send in a steamroller and have it drive around the compound collapsing all the tunnels. Then they'd start all over again and the steamroller would come in again. It kept them occupied, the CO said.'

'And your Da was bothered. Did he want to stop them?'

'No. What bothered him was the clay. He could never find the clay. He searched high and low. For years he'd wonder about the clay. You'd see him sitting with a faraway look in his eyes and you'd know he was still trying to figure it out. He turned them out of their huts at all hours of the day and night but could he find that clay?'

'Did anyone ever find it?'

'Oh aye, but by the time the Da found out about it, it was common knowledge. It annoyed him more that people knew for years before he did.'

'And where was it?' She yawned, not from boredom but from the effort of staying awake. It is no harm to keep the driver from dozing off too. She noticed how he swore at undimmed headlamps.

'I heard of a fellow once who deliberately crashed head-on because someone didn't dim their lights.' An apocryphal tale but a strong moral.

'But what about the clay?' Dimmed headlights had led to the argument with the rose bushes though.

'Ah, he went down there a few years ago with the Mad Gunner. Just for a day. All the old compounds were abandoned. The huts were all vandalised. The clay was in the walls, inside the lining. They had made bags out of everything they could lay hands on, curtains, old shirts, anything. Little pooches, he called them. Every hut was lined with clay. He even laughed about it. "The cute huers," he'd say, "ye couldn't be up to them." '

Dempsey was silent for a long time except to swear under his breath at oncoming lights.

'He wasn't a bad old josser really. It's just that he was cut out for the army, not family life. He hadn't a lot of imagination. If you didn't understand something he'd start to shout. My mother used to go grey. I often think she had expected more out of life. He even admitted it himself once.' He was silent again for a while.

'I suppose he must've been quite a dashing figure at some time.'

'They weren't what you'd call well matched, were they — judging from what you tell me.'

'I couldn't really say.'

She had never really known Dinny and the mother was only a slim, delicate-looking figure in a couple of old photographs.

The city was almost deserted, a pleasure to drive in. Even the night people had slunk away to their lairs. Dustbins overflowed and lights glistened on the wet streets.

'Old McEnaspie,' he said, taking up the thread, 'was the only real friend the Da had. Hardy men by all accounts. They used to say that they could clear a pub of soldiers just for the hell of it.'

He chuckled at some memory.

'What's the joke?' yawned Elaine. She looked forward to the flat and a couple of hours' sleep.

'The Mad Gunner. I was just thinking about a time long ago when we caught him as they say, *in flagrante.*'

'Where was that?' Elaine's voice rose in surprise.

'Oh years ago when we were kids down the Curragh. We were out one evening just messing about, a few lads and myself — experimenting with Woodbines probably. Well we came across your man on top of a young one in a hollow in the furze bushes. She was probably out from Newbridge, doin' a bit of business with the soldiers.'

'So what happened then?'

'Well it was very interesting to tell the truth. She had a fag in her hand and took a drag on it now and again while the Gunner banged away. Then one of the lads rolled an oul' sheep's head down the slope just as she looked up and saw all these faces looking down at her. She let a scream out of her and we ran. It was a pity really. That was about all the sex education I ever got.'

'You've made up for it since,' said Elaine drily.

'A good tutor, I guess. But anyway the Mad Gunner came after us in a rage, pulling up his trousers. I don't think I've ever been so scared. He caught me with a whack behind the ear and shook the daylights out of me. He even told the Da and he took his belt to me but I could see even then that he was amused. I always wondered if your man went back to get his money's worth. Sheep, shit and soldiers. That was the Curragh for you.'

But Elaine had nodded off.

~

The funny thing was they gave him a flag on the coffin and fired shots over his grave as if he had died in battle. The Mad Gunner insisted on buying them a drink. He wore his good navy suit and brown shoes. His neck was too small for his shirt collar. His Adam's apple slid up and down between two tendons, like a lift in a lift shaft. He was deeply moved by the whole business and blew his nose frequently.

'By Jaysus, if I could lay me hands on them gougers.' A salvo of machine-gun fire would have been too good for them. 'Time was...' He left the sentence hanging in air.

'Always very proud of yourself,' he ventured after a while. 'Had a great regard for the education.'

Dempsey was surprised. He wondered if the Mad Gunner ever remembered the episode with the sheep's head. It was difficult to reconcile the memory of that day with the sad old man who slouched in the corner of the lounge. Was every person's life no more than a handful of anecdotes to be handed around after his or her death, until they became worn like old coins and eventually were not to be taken at their face value?

Already the story of the Mad Gunner and Dinny's shroud had gone into circulation. The neighbour's wife had sent him down to the woman in Ellesmere Avenue, behind the abattoir, for a habit.

'Is he enrolled in the Brown Scapular?' she asked.

'No,' says the Mad Gunner, 'he was wrapped in a fuckin' oul' white sheet when I seen him last.'

Dempsey had a few things to sort out so Elaine went down home on the train and phoned ahead for her father to pick her up at the station. Dempsey felt a strange fear descend on him as she left, almost a foreboding. Dinny knew all about clay now, he mused and shivered. He dreamt of tunnels and cave-ins and awoke sweating. A large spider made his precarious way across the ceiling — an attercop, a grim, black word. He reached out but Elaine was not there and he felt as he had felt as a child when he heard raised and angry voices in the night.

He began deliberately in his mind to write his story, forcing himself to concentrate. It was bright summertime and the people, elated by their initial successes were advancing to breach the walls of Ross.

~

'The army is a quare oul' business,' said the Mad Gunner. 'Could take years to make a decision about some things and then they could take a man out and shoot him in a minute.' He lifted his whiskey and gazed at it contemplatively. Dempsey waited. It was a civil thing to return the courtesy. Obviously the sheep's head had been forgotten or expiated by association with his father.

'Aye. Now there was a time I was on duty up at headquarters. We had this hut with one of them paraffin heaters. Great yokes they were.' He rubbed his hands appreciatively.

'I know them well. Still the oul' bottle gas is a great man. No smell, like y'know.'

'Aye, I suppose. Well anyway the wick burned out and there we were freezin' our balls off.'

'Why didn't you stick in a new one?'

He snorted. 'Are you jokin' me? They had to put it out for tender.'

'Go 'way.'

'That's right.' He leaned forward, his eyes bulging at the enormity of it all. His Adam's apple travelled up and down on its cables. 'Three weeks it took. I could have put one in for one and a tanner but that's not the way it's done. Half a dozen civil servants sittin' on their arses in there and us freezin' to death outside.'

'The Da never questioned the army way though.'

'The army is greater than the people that run it. That's what he always said. No regard for officers but great regard for discipline. Bit of a contradiction.'

'Well it just goes to show, doesn't it.' Dempsey was not entirely sure what it went to show but it filled a silence.

'But the point I'm tryin' to make is this.' The Mad Gunner introduced a few drops of water into his glass with the care and precision of an alchemist. 'The point I'm makin' is this. Durin' the Civil War they could take men out at the drop of a hat and shoot them.'

'I suppose, I don't know. Maybe it was necessary.'

'It was orders, don't y'see.' His hand trembled and the glass rattled on the table. 'Orders. We shot seventy-seven lads all told.'

'Seventy-seven?' Dempsey assumed that the 'we' was a generic term, the Free State army.

'We were only lads ourselves at the time, your Da and me but there isn't a day goes by I don't see some of those men.'

'You mean the Da and ...?'

'Aye, there's blood on our hands. Couldn't be avoided, I suppose. Blood for blood, wasn't that the way?'

Dempsey put down his drink. It had gone sour. There was a song of 'Ninety Eight:

'But blood for blood without remorse
I've taken at Oul and Tullow ...'

It was always the way. He shivered. Seventy-seven again. It was as if some invisible prompter was following him around.

'I never thought of it like that. The Da never said anything.'

'Ah, he wouldn't of. In the line of duty do you see. Everyone had to take their turn.'

Dempsey reflected that he had never really known his father. Surely there was a point where you could say no.

'Look, Mr McEnaspie, I'll have to be off and thanks for all your trouble. You were a good friend to him.'

'Through thick and thin, isn't that the way of it,' said the old soldier, holding out his sinewy hand.

There was still strength in it, thought Dempsey, remembering the stinging crack on the head. There was an obscene logic to it all though. The objective is to inflict so much suffering on the enemy that he sues for peace. He pictured the bodies jerking like marionettes in a gloomy prison yard, the punctilious formalities, the chaplain kneeling to give the last rites and his father marching off to clean his rifle. Could anything make sense after that? What could be important after that?

~

Dinny left him the house and some money that had originally belonged to his mother. Her people, the Comerfords, wanted her to have some independence but she never ventured to assert it. The money was still there. It might have made a difference, a little luxury or even a bit of fun but she seemed to have lost interest. In the end, it had provided only a bleak security.

A persistent idea kept knocking at the back of Dempsey's mind. It was ridiculous, like selling everything and putting the money on a horse, a racing certainty. It could never work. It was as crazy as selling all that you own to give to the poor. What does that ever achieve except to add one more to the endless multitude of the poor? He went to talk to Paddy Sedgwick.

'Paddy, I want to take a break. I want to write. No, I need to take a break, more like it.'

Paddy took a long drag on his cigarette and exhaled slowly. Smoke seeped like grey ectoplasm from his nostrils.

'Go on.'

'I have a story inside me. I just know it. I need time to put it all together.'

'Ah. Are you sure you're not just upset what with your father dying and all?'

'That could be part of it but I need time to think.'

He told Paddy about his father and the seventy-seven executions. 'I want to get down to the why of it and more to the point, the how of it. I mean, at what point do you give your consent?'

'I don't know. There must be a point where you just say to hell with it.' Paddy drummed his fingers on the desk. 'It'd be a bit awkward, Jack, to tell you the truth. It'd mean I'd be pinned down here a lot. How long had you in mind?'

'I was thinking maybe six months to a year. What would you say to that?'

Paddy shook his head. 'No chance Jack. I'd have to get someone else. Think now before you burn your bridges. What does Elaine think?'

'She'd be all for it. I know. I haven't gone into the details with her yet.'

'You mean you haven't mentioned it yet?'

He looked at Dempsey shrewdly. In the silence that fell between them a bluebottle buzzed furiously and dashed itself against the window. It rebounded stunned, and lay on its back, waving its legs feebly. Of all the things that human ingenuity has devised, thought Dempsey, glass must be the most confusing to other creatures. He thought of tropical fish nosing against an invisible barrier. It was just the same for himself: duty, obligations, responsibility.

'She'll understand.'

Paddy raised his eyebrows. 'You're asking too much I'm afraid, Jack. You know you're a valuable man to me. Are you sure this isn't just a brainstorm, a hormonal imbalance? You know that's what Maureen says about this whole antiques business. She was a biologist at one time, you know. She says it's some sort of twisted nesting instinct, this magpie carry on, salvaging bits and pieces of the past.' He chuckled drily.

'That's just what I want to do, don't you see?'

Paddy took an envelope and scooped up the bluebottle, which had resumed its persistent buzzing.

'Get out you dirty divil,' he said, opening the window and batting the envelope on the ledge.

'Well, if that's your attitude,' said Dempsey pretending to rise. Paddy smiled.

'Nah,' he said and stood looking out of the window. The only sound was the whine from an electric sander in the workshop below. Or maybe it was the bluebottle coming back with reinforcements. Dempsey looked at the envelope which Paddy held behind his back. Probably covered with germs, botulism, salmonella, microscopic bombs to destroy unwary humans. He pictured the insect sniggering and weaving its way across the river, homing in on the Knacker Keeffe's yard, agreeable particles of putrescence wafting up its nostrils. Lockjaw, that's the one. War to the teeth.

'I think you're mad, Jack. That's all I want to say. I could maybe manage a couple of months. Maybe up to Christmas, though that's a busy enough time. I seriously suggest that you talk it over with your good wife, though that's none of my business of course.' He paused. 'I don't want to lose you. Don't want to have to break in someone new, know what I mean. You could sort of act as our agent if you intend to stay down Wexford way. Those old country houses are full of stuff. You could keep an eye out for me. There'd be a bit of commission in it.'

It was as easy as that. No rancour or recrimination and if all came to all, no irrevocable decision had been made. All that remained was to break the good news to Elaine.

~

That was their first major row.

'You might have discussed it. What in the name of God are we going to live on? Answer me that.'

But still he could see no difficulty.

'Look it's all very simple. I let the house in Dublin. Get a few bob in from that. We can let the flat go for the moment and actually save money by staying here.'

'You're mad,' she said staring at him. 'You're absolutely round the bend.'

Let, he thought, now that's an interesting word. Let go. Leave go. Let or hindrance. A mill dam down in that part of the country is a laet. Pure Anglo-Saxon that. A word that means two opposite ideas.

'That's an interesting word, though,' he said aloud. 'Let. It can mean two opposite things.'

'Jesus Christ,' she screamed. 'Will you shut up?'

She snatched the child by the hand. 'I'm going home for a while 'til you come to your senses.'

'No need to shout. You've upset John.'

'*I've* upset him. Do you ever listen to yourself?' She threw open the door. 'Give me the car keys.'

'Right,' he shouted. 'Suit yourself. Just once in a while you could try being reasonable.'

The door slammed and he heard the engine coughing into life.

'Suit your bloody self,' he shouted. 'I don't give a damn if you never come back.' He aimed a kick at a half-open drawer and had the satisfaction of hearing the cutlery leaping like loose change and the agreeable splintering of wood. 'At least I'll get a bloody bit of peace around this kip.' He felt better and them immediately worse.

Still, she had been totally unreasonable. Women never appreciate the larger scheme of things. God dammit, the drawer refused to shut. One of its runners was shattered and when he pushed it in it sagged down into the cupboard below. 'Fuck it,' he swore and thought of kicking it again but he was calm now and reasonable. He had made his point. She could take it or leave it; like it or lump it; stew in her own juice.

He went and stood at the door. The sea was a metallic grey and the small waves drummed incessantly on the sand. A skein of shags flew in line astern, heading for the Saltees. That was the place to be, away from everyone, answerable to no one, free as a bird. On the other hand, the book could wait. There would be plenty of time in the years to come. Maybe she had crashed the car. At that very moment they could be lying under the wreckage. The policeman would be swinging his leg over the saddle to come and tell him the bad news. He felt panic rising in his throat. He began to run down the narrow road, skidding on the wind-blown sand and then with a great surge of relief he heard the car returning.

She rolled down the window. He could see that she had been crying.

'Forget it,' he said reaching through the window. 'It was a stupid idea anyway.'

'No, no. If it's what you really want to do.' She took his hand in hers. 'If it's what you really want, we can give it a try.' She held his hand tighter. 'Through thick and thin. Isn't that the way?'

He was too overcome to say anything. John regarded them solemnly.

'You shouldn't be fighting,' he reproached them.

She smiled. 'Everyone fights a little bit now and again, even when they love each other. But I'll want to see those bloody pages filling up. That's the deal.'

'Wait till you see,' he said going around to the passenger side. 'I will astonish you.'

'I must be out of my mind,' she sighed and turned the ignition key.

CHAPTER FOUR

From the window he could see the sea creeping over the sand. The small ripples edged apologetically inwards and broke on a low sandbar. Diffidently they crept around the end of the bar and invaded the calm waters of a little runnel. Although there was little or no wind, small tufts of foam were generated by the breaking of the ripples. These tufts drifted into the runnel like a flotilla of sailing ships. Gradually as the tide rose over the bar, the incoming waves encountered others pushing obliquely up along the runnel and passed through them in orderly fashion as bandsmen wheel and march back through their comrades, all the while making music and keeping to their wonted rhythm. Rhomboid patterns appeared on the surface as the waves crossed. He watched them for a long time. Inexorable was the word. Supposing they kept on coming. *In sequent toil all forwards do contend.*

The runnel was deceptive. He had waded through it and headed out to sea for a swim. When he came back he splashed knee deep across the sandbar only to find that the closer he got to the shore the deeper the water became. The land is the danger, the lighthouse men said. At night he watched the lights of ships far out to sea veering off to avoid the palisade of rocks that stretches seawards from the Forlorn. He speculated on how history might have read if the Norman invaders had fetched up in foul weather on those dragon-toothed rocks instead of making their landfall at Bannow. It was no coincidence that the same Raymond who slaughtered his seventy-seven hostages had built the first ever lighthouse on the Hook.

Ideas flitted through his head. Across the bay lay Tintern, a daughter house of the more famous abbey on the Wye. It was in that same year of seventeen-ninety-eight that Wordsworth and Coleridge had goofed off in Wales, that long, scorching summer that saw some agrarian unrest in south eastern Ireland. Little did Wordsworth know as he lay under the dark sycamore that not so very far away men were fashioning weapons.

He wrote a passage on the attack on Ross. He saw the cavalry charging up the steep cobbled street and the gunsmen taking aim. A shattering volley brought men and horses to the ground. He described the charge of the rebels and the fierce hand-to-hand fighting in the streets and the incredulous joy as the regular troops were routed and fled in apparent disarray. He described Harvey, the reluctant general standing on the heights with his spy glass, agonising over every decision until men turned away from him, averting their eyes and leaving him to his arid contemplation of tactics and strategy.

Then came the *ville gagnée*, the orgasmic release from fear and tension, the drinking. Ross was a Norman town, built by William who gave the land for Tintern. William understood *ville gagnée*, but he would have posted sentries.

General Johnson's cavalry descended upon the unwary rebels like a sudden cloudburst. There was no shelter and no quarter given to men exhausted and bleeding or just too drunk to stay on their feet. The rebels had reached their high water mark and had begun to ebb. They looked at their new general and saw defeat already in his eyes. And he too, although a priest of the Church, was a drinking man.

Dempsey shuffled his pages. Idea followed idea, like the waves on the beach, apprehended for a moment and then lost. The waves had left a wet rim along the sand. The tide was dropping. If he walked briskly to the pub he would refresh his mind. Guiltily he reflected how usually after a few pints, everything fell into place in his head and he set out again with renewed confidence. But he was keeping his part of the bargain. Pages were filling up. In moments of optimism he believed that he was getting there. Michelangelo got up early every morning to look at an unprepossessing block of stone that had been badly hacked by some journeyman. Ostensibly he was doing nothing but in his head he could see the features of David emerging from the marble. Jobs like that should not be rushed.

The runnel was emptying out with the ebb of the tide. The flotilla of foam tufts which must have been trapped up at the shallow end began to drift down-channel towards the open sea. He watched them turning, colliding, coalescing and breaking apart and bobbing up and down as they encountered the small rip-tide at the mouth of the channel. Bravely they set out to sea but soon they were battered by the waves and reduced to a drifting scummy stain. Everything in a state of flux. A brisk walk and a contemplative pint would clear the synapses, allowing the creative spark to leap the gap, like God and Adam, like a spark plug, like the first artificer striking stone on flint and seeing in a flash the future of the world.

That's good, he thought. I should write that down. He hummed as he stood and stretched:

'A rebel hand set the heather burning

And called the neighbours from far and near.'

He saw distinct possibilities ahead and jingled the change in his pocket.

~

Mr Synnott was inclined to be tolerant. He could understand Dempsey's compulsion to write, even if he was some sort of a jackeen from up there in Dublin. Still he was Elaine's man so he was all right.

'So how's the work going?' He was prepared to call it work because of the subject matter. Others might scribble away at romantic trash, all that Hollywood stuff.

'Did I ever tell you about me great-grandfather coming back from the Rising? Or was he me great-great? Old Clem Synnott.' This was what Dempsey needed, the living folk tradition, the vivid detail. Mr

Synnott pulled down the veil of his beekeeper hat and rooted in his pocket for a pair of gloves.

'You stand over there,' he shouted. 'Even though they know you they can get a bit angry.'

Dempsey watched him in his white coat and the strange mask. There was something familiar about him, like one of those scientists in the films who are called in to save the world from some terrible threat, giant ants, man-eating plants. The scientist always has a beautiful daughter assisting him as he fumigates the nest of the creatures from outer space.

'Aye, it was the year after. It was the bees that knew him first. They all came out to welcome him.'

'Are you serious?'

'That's what me grandfather told me. He wasn't alive of course at the time. The serving girl came in and said there was a beggar man at the gate and the bees were all out. They had a bit of a roof on the house by that time.'

He foostered around making puffs of smoke with his little machine like a priest incensing the altar for High Mass.

'His wife now, she was a Walsh from Effernogue. Her brother was married to a sister of Father John. No wait a minute ...' He puffed away and the smoke drifted around him in a thin blue haze, blue against the hedges and turning brown against the sky. Mr Synnott went on.

'Anyway they all went down to see this man. I think she must've known he was part of the family and there he was, the raggediest poor beggarman you could imagine and he afraid to come in his own gate.'

'I suppose he didn't know what he might find.'

'It was a neighbour that brought him home, a yeoman by the name of Sproule, that led him halfway across the county with a rope around his neck. That was the only way he could keep him safe.'

'A yeoman? That was strange.'

'They knew each other y'see. Old Clem saw him down injured in the battle at Horetown and could've killed him but he didn't. He left him with the Quaker ladies for safety. That was why Sproule claimed him. Said he was taking him home to hang him at his own front door. The Yeos let him pass because they thought it was a good joke.'

Nothing much had changed. The sycamore had a fine branch for hanging a man. The house had a slate roof instead of the original high, sloping thatch. Dempsey felt grateful to Jacob Sproule for his act of compassion. It was a story for a fine summer morning, an old man telling his tale in an orchard among somnolent bees. At any moment Jacob Sproule might canter past on his way to collect the rent from his cottiers. The Synnotts of Tomgarrif, strong farmers, freeholders, doffed their hats to no one.

'He was never the same after that. That long winter made him an old man. He had no time for talk of freedom or Mr Emmett's Rising. He had seen things, he said, that no man should have to look upon.'

~

Elaine taught him to ride a horse that summer. She was a natural horsewoman. It looked easy enough but the view from aloft was very different from what he had expected. He realised, first of all, that he had entrusted himself to a creature many times his own weight, a creature that quite obviously had a mind of its own. Furthermore there were no brakes. The steering geometry was a very makeshift affair that depended entirely on the goodwill of the animal. When it chose to drop its head to munch the wayside grass there was nothing in front of the rider but a long sloping ridge-backed neck that put him in mind of a ski run. He knew that the animal was laughing at him. It is a simple matter of matching the rise and fall of the rider to the horse's gait. Dempsey felt the base of his spine being hammered upwards with every step. Soon he imagined his vertebrae would start popping out through the top of his skull like loose cotton spools. There was nothing to hang on to in front.

'Just relax,' Elaine encouraged. 'You'll get the hang of it.' She rode in front, setting the pace. She certainly had an excellent seat he noted.

Her breasts jiggled appealingly under a light silk shirt when she turned to see how he was doing. His thighs were aching. She had said it was like holding a huge egg between his legs. Some trick.

'Okay,' she called, 'we'll try a trot.' She rose slightly on her stirrups and Dempsey followed suit. He was glad they were still on grass. At least the ground would break his fall. It is always the sport of country bumpkins to see the city man come a cropper.

She moved up a gear and Dempsey's mount broke into a canter behind her. He watched her every move, beginning to feel quite proud of his horsemanship. The horse snorted derisively, amused by the whole business. Dempsey felt the power under him and the animal's urge to accelerate.

Elaine noted the panic in his expression and changed down to second and back into first. Dempsey was a bit aggrieved.

'I was doing fine,' he protested. 'There was no need to slow down.' He would have liked to kick the animal into a gallop just to show her. Hadn't he grown up on the Curragh, for God's sake?

'I'd rather not gallop them on the road,' she said tactfully. 'We can walk them a couple of miles, nice and easy and come back through the woods. There's a place I'd like to show you. You'll be interested in it.'

'Where's that?' he asked, secretly relieved to be back at walking pace.

'A little place by a stream where our people hid out during 'Ninety Eight.'

It was impossible to get away from it. Every square inch of the land had its own story. The hooves clopped pleasantly on the road metal. They rode side by side along narrow country lanes. Their bodies swayed rhythmically together. Dog roses were tangled among the whitethorn hedges. Honeysuckle embraced the blackberry briars. There was a smell of wood smoke.

'This is a very sexy business. Did you ever notice that?'

She looked at him and smiled.

'Have you ever tried it *al fresco*?' he asked easing himself in the saddle.

'What kind of a question is that for a man to ask his wife?

Presumably you know the answer to that yourself.' She looked straight ahead with a smile twitching at her lips.

'Just testing. You know what nurses are like.' The horse snorted and danced to one side.

'Keep the reins short. Take a twist of his mane in your hand. Let him know you're the boss.'

'Keep your mind on the job, you mean.'

'In a sense,' she answered drily.

It seemed to Dempsey as if the horse exploded under him. He heard iron shoes clattering on stone and felt as if he was sitting on top of a hairy brown volcano. The acceleration threw him back in the saddle. The reins lengthened as the animal bolted. He considered abandoning ship but immediately Elaine was alongside again and had a grip on the rein. It was almost as if her hand was in the animal's mouth. He saw with great clarity, as if he was about to die, flecks of spittle on the cuff of her shirt and suddenly all was calm again. The horse's head came round and one enormous eye rolled back at him. Elaine tugged on the bit.

'Don't let him get it between his teeth,' she advised. 'He knows when you're afraid of him.'

'I'm not afraid of him,' said Dempsey stoutly. 'I'm afraid of falling off him. He can run off to hell out of it as long as I don't break my neck.' Vengefully he took a good twist of mane in his fist, anchoring the reins firmly. 'Right, you bastard. Don't try that again.'

'I don't know what that was all about,' she said puzzled. 'Something must have frightened him. It's happened along here before.'

'Maybe he saw a ghost,' said Dempsey lightly.

'Maybe he did,' she replied and was silent for a long time.

She led him along by a stream that trickled beside the hedgerows. At one point it vanished into a great thicket of whitethorn and bramble.

'It's through there,' she said, pointing to the tunnel into which the stream disappeared.

'What is?'

'The place I was telling you about.'

'Ah. But how do you get into it?'

'That's the whole point. You'd never know it was there unless you wade along the stream.' She swung down from the saddle and twisted the reins around a branch. 'Come on. I'll show you.' She splashed into the water in her boots and ducked into the tunnel. Dempsey followed, feeling the shock of cold water in his runners. The water rose almost to his knees. Only a few yards into the thicket the stream turned sharply, leaving a sandbar of coarse gravelly sand on the inside of the bend. The water purled and rippled along the edge of the bar. On the outer bend it ran brown and swift, cutting a deeper channel.

'Well, here it is,' said Elaine sitting down on the sand and tugging at her boots. 'What do you think of it? My great, great whatever she was, hid in here for weeks with her children. Just as well or I wouldn't be here.'

Dempsey whistled and looked about him at the impenetrable hedge.

'Very neat. No one could spot you here.'

'That's what I was thinking,' she said and began to unbutton her shirt. 'At least the family aren't around, especially those bloody sisters of mine.' Patches of sunlight and shadow moved on her warm skin as she lay back on the sand. 'Come on,' she said urgently. 'It was your idea.'

'So it was,' he replied and knelt over her.

'What's in it for me?'

'Sand, if you're not careful,' she laughed, reaching up to him and closing her eyes against the light.

Dempsey forgot about battles long ago and the niggling doubts about writing it all down and his finances and great-great-great-grandmothers and yeomen. He felt her warmth and vitality and her need for him and gravel on her skin and sun in his eyes and one foot in the water and then they were lying together, panting and shielding their eyes against the light. He closed his eyes, feeling lassitude seep over him. Gently she began to dust the sand from his body.

'Okay?' she asked.

He mumbled, enjoying the warmth and touch of her hand.

'It was a good idea.'

'I have to admit you're good for something,' she said lightly and sat up. He began in desultory fashion to brush the sand from her back, running his fingers down her spine.

'Whatever happened to the hat?'

'What hat?'

'The one you wore the day I first saw you.'

'Oh that. I stuffed it in a drawer somewhere. Never wore it again. Why do you ask?'

'No reason. I was just remembering. Maybe I don't say much but I wanted you from the minute I saw you in the new hat.'

He knew she was smiling but he could not see her face. 'We'd better get dressed,' she said. 'The horses will be wondering.'

For the first time he became aware of the sound of tearing grass and the occasional jingle of harness.

'I had forgotten about the horses. It would be nice to stay here for a while, wouldn't it?'

'I think you'd get a bit fed up after a few weeks.'

'I suppose so. But then I presume the former tenants didn't have live entertainment.'

'You wouldn't keep that up for long. Not on oatmeal and goat's milk.'

'Yaah. Is that all they had?'

'Aye. They used to milk the goat onto the oatmeal. They couldn't light a fire or anything of course.'

'No, I suppose not.' But he was not really listening. He watched her putting on her clothes.

'By the way,' she said almost as an afterthought, 'I've been offered a job in the riding centre.'

'Oh.' He felt a sudden stab of alarm.

She squatted beside him and threw him his shirt. 'Here, put that on. You look bloody silly.'

A job would take her away, he thought. She would be involved with other people. This was never part of the deal.

'This is a bit of a complication,' he frowned. 'I mean, I'll have to look after John.'

'Don't be silly. He'll be at school. You'll have the place to yourself all day. No one to bother you.'

It made a certain sense but still he resented her not being there. He knew that there would be other things to do, jobs to distract him. The niggling voice suggested that he would make jobs, even welcome them rather than face the real task. There was for instance the cutlery drawer.

The people at the riding centre would be suave and cosmopolitan. She would find them more interesting. She would find excuses for working late.

'What do they want you to do?' he grumbled.

'Oh, everything from beginners to advanced equitation. Beginners like yourself I suppose.'

'Advanced equitation. Well that should be no bother to you anyway.'

'Pig,' she said and punched him lightly. 'Don't look so grumpy. It'll work out very well, you'll see. Anyway, the few bob will always come in handy.'

For a moment the old atavistic fear struck him that people would regard him as less of a man, sending his wife out to work while he sat around the house all day. But he knew that it was different. At the very least he could hope for a fool's pardon. Writers, poets, that class of thing. They could not be expected to go out to work like normal people. He read their attitude in their amused tolerance or the curious glance that the rare passersby threw at the cottage and the diffident wave when they saw his face framed in the window. Only Mr Synnott appreciated the importance of the writing. Strange in the father-in-law who had such a respect for work and visible prosperity.

A few bob would of course be welcome until the money from the house in Dublin started to come in regularly. The first tenant had left after a month but there would be no problem in getting another.

'I suppose it could work out,' he said grudgingly.

'Of course it will. It makes sense.'

He was glad to walk the horse for a while. He walked stiffly like a cowboy.

'By the way,' he began, 'back there. Did you feel tendrils of fire coursing through your body?'

'What are you on about?'

'You know. Tendrils of fire. Nipples taut with desire. Tumescent maleness. All that thrusting stuff that goes on in books?'

She scratched her nose. 'I know the stuff. Why do you ask?'

'Oh, you know. Research. That's called fieldwork in the trade.'

'I see. Distinguished in many fields. Is that what that means?'

'If I knock around with you I suppose I might be.'

'Well,' she smiled, 'I'll be happy to assist you in your researches at any time if you think your manroot will stand up to it.'

'My what?' he guffawed in surprise.

'There's one for your collection,' she said laughing. 'Use that in chapter one and you'll have the readers gasping for more. Now I think we should remount and look a bit dignified coming home.'

Dempsey tried to climb aboard but fell back spluttering with laughter. 'I'm afraid I'll damage my manroot,' he explained and tried again, clambering with great difficulty into the saddle. 'That's the best I've heard today.'

'Well,' she said drily, 'if you want to be a best-selling author you have to learn the lingo.'

'You're not wrong there,' he said recklessly kicking the horse into a trot. Tendrils of pain shot through him. What was it Waugh said about a blow upon a bruise? Plagiarism again but that is the name of the game.

CHAPTER FIVE

As the summer waned and the evenings darkened, Dempsey began to write in earnest. He wrote of a man leaving his home to join the United Army. He wrote of the oath that Clem Synnott swore and the high-minded principles that bound him to protect all innocent people, irrespective of their creed. He wrote too the story of Clem's younger brother, a craftsman who had left home after a row to find employment on the building of the new bridge at Wexford.

Seventy-five piers of oak and two abutments, seventy-seven spans in all, carried the bridge across to Ferrybank. He concluded that as the contractor was an American, the piers were of American live oak, a tree that grows practically in the seawater. The bridge was to be a dominant theme in his story, a symbol of hope, a reaching out across the sectarian divide. At times he suspected the metaphor creaked under the strain. He knew that eventually the bridge would become the scene of terrible carnage, reciprocal slaughter and some astonishing acts of individual courage and compassion. Father Kavanagh, the leading historian of the period, never crossed that metaphorical bridge, always rationalising acts of savagery by the insurgent side on the grounds that the other side was a lot worse. His argument led to a never ending chain of self-justification. In ancient times no bridge was built without a human sacrifice — but that could wait.

Clem met his younger brother briefly during the battle at Horetown.

He saw him vaulting over the hurdle fence of the public pound. He saw him aim and bring a cavalryman down with his first shot. The boy turned and grinned at his older brother as he rammed home another charge. Then he aimed quickly and another cavalryman toppled backwards under the impact, a Hessian, a Hompescher, some poor bugger sold into military service by his Landgrave, a peasant who had probably killed American colonists and Red Indians with equal objectivity. The boy waved and leaped the fence again and Clem never saw him after that. There had been no time to speak or to reach out his hand but he knew that all was well between them.

Dempsey pondered on this engagement at great length. Father Kavanagh claimed that half of General Moore's force had been either killed or wounded. Moore mentioned ten dead and forty-five wounded, but both agreed on the extraordinary resistance put up by the peasant army. The tide however was ebbing. Moore, expressing his sorrow for the deserted country and the pillars of smoke rising from abandoned homesteads, kept up his remorseless drive towards Wexford. The rebel priest and newly elected general, Father Roche, saw the shadow of the gibbet reaching out across the land and he turned to his whiskey bottle. Meanwhile, a courageous woman hiding by the stream shushed her children and gathered them to her at the sound of hooves whispering through the long grass.

Dempsey read it over. It worked. He looked out the window. It was time for the little fellow to come home from the school. He had not been very happy about moving to a strange school but he had settled well. At first he had brought him to school by the hand but John had rebelled after the first day. Now he walked home along the sandy road by himself, proud of his independence. Dempsey watched for him every day pretending to be busy at some task. just happening to lift his head as it were, at the last minute to see the boy running to him. At other times he buried his head in his manuscript and waited for the grating of the latchkey, a dry, scraping noise and then a click. It was the sound he waited for all day in his self-chosen hermetical existence. It was human contact, like a phone ringing, a letter dropping through the letter box, the spark again that passed from God to Adam. He was blessed in this child.

There was the key to his story that he had searched for. Why had the younger brother left home? What was the dispute about? It was of course the servant girl Hannah, daughter of a landless labourer. The young man had lain with her. No, that was too Biblical. 'We are in love with thee and would know thee,' the elders of Babylon, dropping over the garden wall like a crowd of schoolboys. He had known the servant girl and she was with child. Nah. He had it away with her and she was up the stick. Nah again.

Whatever way the cat jumped there was a row. No daughter of a landless labourer was good enough for the Synnotts of Tomgarrif. The young man, as yet without a name, left home and found work on the building of the great bridge. Dempsey noted that the bridge, that *via dolorosa*, subsequently fell down. There was no explanation but he knew instinctively that it was not from the wind that moaned through its oaken piles. It was the bridge itself, groaning under the weight of sadness and horror that it had borne. From the date that Lemuel Cox signed his contract to the day of its collapse was thirty-three years, the age of Christ. And it gave up the ghost.

The idea stopped him abruptly. It was as if the story was writing itself. The young man had come home at the outbreak of the Rising to leave his wife and child in the care of his elder brother, but Clem had already gone with the insurgent army under Mr Harvey to batter at the walls of Ross. Clem's wife took her in and together they hid with their children by the stream while the yeomen harried the land. A baby was born there under the hawthorn bushes. They always pick their time. Indians gallop around the wagon train and babies decide to be born. Get hot water. The first time we smell the air we waul and cry that we are come to this great stage of fools. It would be no joke trying to pacify a new-born baby with Hessians beating the bushes.

The goat, as always, took the blame. The Hessians leaned down to peer through the brambles and the goat emerged bleating. They joked in guttural tones and shot the poor creature. Maybe they were hungry. Maybe it was a reflex action but the fugitives ate oatmeal

and water after that. Now two women waited for their men to return.
They heard gunfire and smelled smoke and the heavy sickening
stench of burning flesh. They came forth warily to begin to put the
pieces of their lives together and it was in the ruins of Tomgarrif that
General Moore found them. Almost unaccompanied he rode from
one shattered homestead to another pleading with the people and
signing protections. He knew as well as they did the implacable
ferocity of the yeomen. Clem's wife drew herself to her full height
and took her sister-in-law by the hand.

'We are the Synnotts of Tomgarrif, Sir,' she said 'and this is our
place.' The general raised his hat. Soon enough he would know what
it was to be hunted like vermin.

The key scraped in the lock and the child came with sunlight into
the kitchen.

'Well young fella, how did you get on today?'

'Okay,' said the boy noncommittally, throwing his bag on the
table. 'I got a *go maith*[1].' He grinned suddenly and opened the bag.
There it was, a gold star with *go maith* written under it. What more
could a proud parent ask for?

'I think I might have got one too,' said Dempsey, proud of his own
effort.

'Ah, so you fixed the drawer.' John misunderstood, but he was
not far off the mark.

'I did indeed,' said Dempsey and demonstrated yet another suc-
cess. The drawer tilted slightly to starboard but it retained its contents. It was a bit stiff but it would loosen up in time. A bit of
two-by-one and a few nails gave it the necessary support. Never
mind all that tongued and grooved stuff in the handyman book. A
practical man has no need of books.

'We'd better find you something to eat,' he said ruffling the boy's
hair, 'before you do your *obair bhaile*[2].' When John first went to school
he had been given a lollipop and a leaflet about head lice. He had
come home proudly with Elaine and told Dempsey about his lollipop and shown him his head licence. Everyone should have one.

1. good
2. homework

'There's a boy in my class called Seán Ó Dhiumpsa,' he said 'but I haven't met him yet.'

'What do you say when they call out his name?' Dempsey asked.

'I say *anseo*[3].'

He had cracked the system without even knowing why. He had made the necessary language shift and it worked. He was licensed to have a new name, a name for 'good wear'. But at least he would never be Jack Dempsey. That would be too much to inflict on any child.

'Would you fancy a bit of shepherd's pie?' he asked. He had begun to take pride in his cooking. Plenty of thyme, that's the secret. He watched the boy eating and he put the kettle on the gas. It was time for a cup of tea and a chat. The gas hissed and spluttered and Dempsey stacked his papers away. Sufficient unto the day and all that.

~

The end, it is generally agreed, justifies the means — after a period of adjustment and rationalisation. The Mad Gunner wrote saying that he had shifted the squatters out of the house. This was the first Dempsey had heard of squatters. The other tenants had obligingly done a flit. Forcible ejection was the least of the problems. Dempsey appreciated in microcosm the dilemma of the absentee landlord. His was not a life of gambling and debauchery in London but nevertheless the loss of the rent threw his financial calculations seriously off balance. It was the least, Mr McEnaspie wrote, that he could do for the son of an old friend. Went around with a length of lead pipe and asked them to leave. Dempsey pictured him, tall and gaunt like an old western gunfighter heading for his last showdown. It was shocking to think that his father's old friend could have met the same fate at the hands of a crowd of Balubas. He did not specify the nature of the people involved. The house was secure and boarded up but it was not earning any money. Dempsey felt a guilty relief that the

3. present

situation had been resolved without his having to take any action.

It reminded him in a way of the Quakers. They were like drops of oil in the great flood of insurrection, borne hither and yon but always keeping their identity separate, remaining true to their principles. He wondered at their individual feats of courage, staying aloof from the fighting, impartially ministering to the injured and homeless, hiding fugitives from both sides 'under the skirts of their garments' and carrying bodies from the streets when others feared to peep outside locked doors.

Yet their predecessors talked of Cromwell restoring order, which he did in a sense. Cromwell admitted to losing his temper at Drogheda which led to the infamous massacre. Dempsey thought of it as the Ah-sure-fuck-it syndrome that seems to take over in intractable situations. In for a penny — sheep as a lamb. What difference can it make now?

So Cromwell restored order. So did Wyatt Earp and so did the Mad Gunner McEnaspie, all variations on the same theme. Put manners on them; taught them respect.

Dempsey, like the Quakers, abhorred violence, not counting the noble art of self-defence, but he was relieved that his house was free of squatters. The ladies of Horetown who had been plundered and insulted throughout the early weeks of that fateful June, were glad to have some stalwart young men with sabres guard their doors from the mob that camped on their lawn and they were equally glad to see the red coats of General Moore's men as they came gingerly up the avenue. On one subject the Quaker prophecy was incontrovertibly right. The Lord had indeed spread the bodies of men on the earth as dung.

Looking across the bay one afternoon he could make out the distant bulk of Tintern. The king's champion William had granted that land. He fought the King's battles for him even into his sixties and each time had slain his man. The Mad Gunner would have approved. Every time Dempsey thought of Tintern he thought of Wordsworth and his assertion that everything he beheld was full of blessings.

'Stupid old fart,' he muttered aloud.

'What was that you said?' asked Elaine. 'Who's a stupid old fart?'

'Nothing,' he said sheepishly. 'I was woolgathering, as they say.'

They sat on top of a dune among the marram grass. She tickled his nose with a long seed stem.

'You're not much of a conversationalist,' she accused lightly.

'Ah no. I've a few things on my mind.'

He had not told her about the squatters. He pulled his jacket around him. The breeze had an autumnal nip in it. Elaine seemed happy enough with her pursuits but he wondered how they would face the winter. It could be very bleak and lonely for her and John.

'Where's he got to anyway?' He sat up and looked around.

'Oh, he's just gone mooching up along the beach. Don't worry about him. It's right up his barrow.'

Dempsey felt a prickle of irritation. Right into his barrow; up his street. Why could she never get the right ending, even on a cliché? There should be a society for the preservation of clichés. A ministry of clichés.

'Into,' he said with a touch of asperity.

'Into what?'

'Into his barrow; right up his street; in his alley; nose to the grindstone; ear to the ground.'

'What does it matter?' She sniffed.

'It doesn't matter. It doesn't matter at all.'

Elaine said nothing. She pushed back the hair from her forehead.

'I was just wondering,' he began, pretending not to notice her withdrawal from him. 'I was wondering as a matter of fact, how the Quakers got their land.'

She offered no suggestion. He pressed on, eyeing her covertly. She sniffed again.

'I wonder if they snaffled it by force and then changed the rules. Like when you were a kid playing chasing and you got into den, tip-off-the-ground.'

'Maybe they bought it,' she said deliberately. 'Maybe they paid through the nose for it.' She looked straight at him. 'Paid through the nose,' she repeated. 'Did I get it right that time? Over the odds. Through the nose.'

Well, fuck it, he thought, if she wants a row, I'm her bloody man. Why should he apologise? He spent his days trying to put words on paper to make sense and she could deconstruct the language as quickly as he put it together. He felt a quick spasm of justification and teetered on the brink. It was only a preposition. Still, a preposition can make all the difference.

'I'm sorry,' he said gently. 'I can be a bit narky at times.' He reached out and touched her hand. She did not move away.

'Do you still think it's a good idea?' she asked and looked at him again. He wondered what exactly she meant. The book; the cottage; giving up the job?

'Oh yeah, yeah. It's going great. I'd welcome an opinion at this stage.'

She smiled. 'Any of that manroot mallarkey yet?'

He had been giving her a daily tally of pages but still felt that she would regard it as a 'homemade' book. Americans use 'imported' to mean high quality. A prophet fetches a very low price in his own country.

'I have to get back to that. I have it all figured out now. The younger brother and the serving girl.'

'At least you didn't call her a wench.'

He felt offended. 'I'm not writing that sort of a book — the master be a pleasurin' of the young wenches.'

It was her turn to apologise. She leaned against him and put her head on his shoulder.

'I was only kidding. You mean I won't have a dashing highwayman or a swarthy villain to get me all worked up.'

'Oh I suppose I could lob in a few doxies with breasts throbbing like young doves and a masked avenger, if you like.'

'That's more like it,' she said laughing and nudging him off balance, 'and a manroot of course.'

'And a square root, and a beetroot and ...' He was stuck.

The line of thought fizzled out in laughter.

They heard the high excited tones of the child from far down the beach.

'Come quick. Come quick. Mammy, Daddy.'

They leaped up in alarm and ran. They could see him running towards them shouting and gesticulating. He was almost incoherent with excitement.

'A fish,' he said gasping for breath. 'A huge fish.'

'Oh,' said Elaine kneeling down to hold him. 'You gave us a fright. Where's this famous fish?'

John pointed. There was a dark shape moving through the choppy shallows of the long runnel. It rose to the surface with a sigh and sank again.

'It's a porpoise,' Dempsey declared in surprise. 'What's he doing in here? I thought they only came in hot weather.'

They watched as the creature reached the end of the runnel and turned, apparently seeking the open sea. The boy ran parallel to its course, straining to see it better. It rolled on the surface and sank again.

'Go on, go on,' urged Dempsey. He began to throw stones behind it nudging it towards open water.

'Don't frighten it,' warned Elaine. 'The poor thing is probably lost.'

'Must be the Gulf Stream,' suggested Dempsey, skimming the stones to discourage the animal from turning back into the cul-de-sac. 'It's not a fish,' he added to the child, 'it's a mammal.'

'A mammal,' said the boy. 'Would it eat you?'

They laughed. 'No,' said Elaine. 'They wouldn't eat you.'

The porpoise seemed to sense the pull of the sea. It rolled for an instant on the end of the sandbank, splashed its fluke in the shallow water and propelled itself into the deep.

'Good man,' called Dempsey, elated.

'Ah, he's gone,' said the little boy, crestfallen.

'He's gone home to his children,' said Elaine gently and gathered him to her. 'You wouldn't want him to leave his children. Would you?'

'No,' said the child doubtfully. 'I suppose not.'

'Good man. Good man,' said Dempsey and clenched his fist.

He blessed the creature silently. Go for it, he thought. Maybe Wordsworth had a point after all.

~

The east wind was always bad news. Even the slightest gust seemed to belly down over the dunes and blow smoke down the chimney. It was impossible to light a fire when the east wind blew and the cottage became dark and dank like a hovel. He found that he could never write during the time of the east wind. He would light the gas cooker but its spluttering and fizzing irritated and distracted him.

Eventually he found the solution at an auction, a portable gas heater. It came in a lot with an old weighing scales, some assorted crockery and a gadget for slicing hard boiled eggs with two of the wires broken and particles of petrified yoke clinging to those that remained. It went into the bin. He had no great need for a weighing scales and was half sorry the lot had not included a large turtle shell with *Midway* written on it in blue enamel paint. That went for four pounds, putting it totally out of reach. For thirty bob he got volume one of *Dr Johnson's Dictionary* with an introductory history of the English language, published by subscription, in Dublin in 1773. There was nothing there that would have interested Paddy Sedgwick.

The gas heater needed a little attention but it would solve the heating problem. He took it apart and found a little ball of cinder blocking the outlet valve. The feeder pipe was a bit loose so he tightened it up and taped it securely. It worked like a dream and he surveyed his work proudly. Instant heat and the thing almost had a personality. Like a benign Buddha it stood in the corner of the kitchen, muttering to itself and spreading goodwill.

When the wind brought rain it drove water up the roof of the lean-to kitchen and in under the flashing. A trickle would appear on the inside wall. Dempsey cursed it vehemently and pursued the leak with large tubes of bitumen glue. Theoretically, he reflected, he could have pursued his landlord but what was the point? For a few bob he could do the job himself. Anyway, it gave him time to think. There was a bit of a blockage in the story. It was all a bit ordinary. Like a good journalist he needed an angle. Dr Johnson had proved a major distraction. The old language of South Wexford was frequently referred to as Chaucer English but Robert of Gloucester was nearer the mark. Tomgarrif was no displaced Cockney. He was a solid West Country man who followed Strongbow to a new country and remained loyal through all the vicissitudes of history until the king's men came to burn the roof over his head.

Strongbow, down on his luck, also had a problem with smoke in his castle at Chepstow. He could never afford to install a chimney until a ragamuffin king, a wheeler and dealer from Wexford, made him an offer he could not turn down. This king too had the obligatory beautiful daughter. Now there was a story.

Dempsey sat on the roof, shielded from the wind by the ridge and looked about him. He could hear shufflings below.

'Is that you, John?' He looked at his watch. The child's head appeared at the edge of the roof. He was red in the face from the wind.

'I saw you when I was coming home,' he said, 'so I thought I'd come up and give you a hand.'

He clutched a bread roll in one hand. A sheet of ham lolled out like a pink tongue. He waved it excitedly. 'I made you some lunch,' he said. Dempsey lifted him from the ladder onto the roof.

'For me?' He was touched.

'I thought you might be hungry.'

He wondered momentarily about the method of preparation. They sat in the lee of the ridge and he put his anorak around them.

'I think we might dine out today,' he said tearing the roll in half.

'Do you like it?' asked the child eagerly.

'My good man,' said Dempsey, 'it's one of the finest meals I've ever eaten,' and he meant it. 'I might write about it in the newspaper.' He realised that he was hungry. He had been so engrossed in his task that he had forgotten to eat. The book showed how old felt should be renewed but the process looked very complicated. Plenty of bitumastic bunged into the holes and a few ridges of glue to break the momentum of the water, like a series of ramps. He thought of patenting the technique. Make a fortune.

In fact he could do with a fortune. He had dipped heavily into the few pounds that Dinny had left and still had no rent coming in. He had thought of selling the house but it gave him some sense of security to have it there for emergencies. The problem was how to explain the situation to Elaine.

'That porpoise came back again,' he said. 'I could see him from up here.'

'Did he?' said the child standing up quickly. 'Can we go and see if he's on the beach?'

'We can, just as soon as I finish here.' He pulled the boy down beside him again. 'Be careful you don't get blown away.' The porpoise was a stupid bloody creature. If it came inshore it could get stranded. 'Mind that glue there,' he warned but it was too late. The child had put his hand into a great splodge of the stuff and went to wipe it on his jersey.

'No,' yelled Dempsey, 'don't do that. God you're an awful man.'

They climbed down and Dempsey cleaned the glue off with some petrol from a can that he kept for emergencies. Carefully he wiped the little hand, examining each finger. 'Have to have you clean before your Mammy gets back.' Women have this irrational attitude towards cleaning things and people. Boys are naturally dirty up to the age of twelve or thirteen. Then they begin to comb their hair and conkers and marbles become vaguely apprehended memories. They begin to walk that perilous knife edge between joy and despair, that is called love and they wash, even behind their ears.

'Plenty of time for that.' He held the child's hand for a moment and then gently mimed a punch to the chin.

'Wash that smelly stuff off and we'll go down to the beach and see if our friend has come back.' A good walk would clear the head: then he would get something for dinner and warm the place for Elaine.

Occasionally Dempsey would break into a sudden sprint, darting up and down the dunes in a zig-zag pattern, with the little fellow panting behind him.

'Wait for me. Wait for me,' gasped the boy.

'Just testing. Keeping him on his toes,' laughed Dempsey.

'Why are you running though?'

Dempsey hunkered down and held the boy by his elbows.

'It's the guardian angels, do you see? I have to make them fit enough to keep up to the job.'

The child looked at him wide-eyed.

'Like when you were on the ladder. His job was to see that you didn't fall. I don't want him getting fat and lazy.'

The child frowned. 'Is that a bleezfnap?'

'A what?'

'A bleezfnap. I think that's what our teacher said.'

'I don't know. Can you tell me what it is?'

'He said if you say rude things about holy things it's something like that.'

'Aah! I see.' He drew the child towards him and held him. 'No it's not a bleezfnap. I just have to remind him now and again to keep up to scratch. He has a very important job to do.' If there are angels it is no harm to give them a reminder. He shivered. The wind had picked up.

The porpoise was nowhere to be seen. Sullen grey waves crumpled on the beach and the undertow hissed like a serpent. They stuffed their hands in their pockets and strode with heads down. The marram grass whistled its reedy song.

~

The first time they went to the chapel on Sunday he did not realise that in that remote place, men went to one side and women to the other; Epistle for the men and Gospel for the women. Dempsey was out of place and the subject of open curiosity. He sensed even a touch of hostility in some of the stares and felt like an infidel clumping into a mosque in a pair of hobnailers. They conformed.

It added a new dimension to the whole business of the Mass, a sense of forbidden fruit. He could look across the aisle to Elaine and give her a conspiratorial wink, sharers of a secret. He recalled a school friend who admitted that he first realised the need for underpants while watching the girls going up to Communion — manroot trouble again. There is a lot of it around.

The choir sang about waters streaming from His side and his
mind wandered again. It was Longinus with his spear who had
pierced Christ's side. No place could hide the man who had murdered his god. At Chepstow the river gate on the castle was called
the Longine Gate. Longinus had fled to the edge of the world to
atone for his terrible crime, or so the story went. The real reason for
the name was *long*, a Celtic ship, the Water Gate or Gate of the Ships.
It might have been from there that Strongbow set out on his great
adventure.

In times of spate the river rose over the mossy steps, threatening
to flood the castle. Water and smoke — he had a lot in common with
Strongbow. The roof was leaking again. The prosaic explanation is
most often the true one but he preferred the story of the Roman
soldier, haunted by guilt, wandering the world like the shades of the
unburied, seeking atonement for his terrible deed.

The writer takes base facts and transmutes them by subtle
alchemy into gold. The wind dashed the rain against the chapel
windows. There would be a puddle on the kitchen floor when they
got home but today it did not seem too bad.

'Let us now exchange the sign of peace,' intoned the priest and
Dempsey turned to Elaine across the aisle. She caught his eye and
smiled as he reached out to her. The spark leaped between them as
their hands met, contact that nothing could put asunder.

Late on a winter afternoon the porpoise appeared again, driven
by the gale and rolling in the troughs of the waves. He should not
have been there. He should have been basking by the shores of the
summer isles. They watched as the waves tumbled him over the
sand bar into the calm of the sheltered water. He seemed dejected
and sluggish. They huddled with collars turned up against wind and
rain and feared for him as he turned listlessly this way and that. A
trio of gulls dipped at him and rose again on the wind.

'He'll die if he's stranded there,' said Elaine.

'What can we do?' asked Dempsey.

She shrugged.

'We could feed him,' suggested the boy. 'Maybe he would stay
with us.'

'I don't think food is the problem,' said Elaine. 'I think he's just lost and tired.'

'Maybe when he's had a rest,' began Dempsey brightly, 'maybe he'll be strong enough to go home.'

They left it at that and went back to the cottage. The wind dropped with the tide and the pounding of the waves diminished. Just before dark he got up and reached for his coat. He paused. A drop of water fell from the ceiling and for an instant made a liquid chess pawn in the bucket on the floor.

'I think I'll take a turn along the beach,' he said casually.

'Sure, I might as well come along,' said Elaine.

She was wearing her high riding boots. The child read their thoughts and pushed his homework aside.

The sea was calmer by then but the water in the runnel had dropped to almost a foot. The porpoise rolled, exposing his white belly. The gulls circled, watching his struggle.

'We can't leave him here,' said Elaine, starting to wade into the water.

'Wait a minute. If we could get a sack under him we could haul him over the bar. He should be able to manage from there.'

Dempsey began to run back towards the cottage.

The water was icy cold, penetrating their clothes. Their hands pained from the cold and the strain. The creature gave them no help at all. It was a dead weight. The child patted its rough leathery skin and spoke to it. It lay on its side and regarded them sadly with one dark liquid eye, consenting to their struggle but seeming to say that it was to no avail. They heaved and slipped and splashed through the shallows. Their teeth chattered with the cold but eventually they rolled him down the steep seaward side of the bar and standing thigh deep in the breakers, they watched him slide into the deeper water with a feeble flip of his tail.

Dempsey felt a cold sense of foreboding that had little to do with the icy water.

'Come on,' said Elaine. 'We'd better get out of these wet clothes,' and, catching the child between them, they ran through the stinging rain back to the warmth of the cottage.

CHAPTER SIX

'I believe,' said Mr Synnott, 'you're writin' about Scullabogue.'

'Aye,' said Dempsey. 'I am.' He wondered if he was straying into some forbidden territory, breaking some ancient taboo. In the house of the hanged man do not mention rope.

'Aye,' repeated Mr Synnott, stretching his feet towards the kitchen range. He placed his right ankle deliberately over his left and sighed. He peered into his mug of tea.

'Of course it wasn't the fighting men that burned Scullabogue.'

'Does it make any difference?' queried Dempsey. 'I mean to the people who were in it?'

'Aye, I know what you mean. But it does in a way. To us that is.'

'You mean the mythology. Is that it?'

'That's right. After all you have to believe in something.'

'But what about the truth? Isn't that important?'

'That's a tricky one, as Pontius Pilate used to say.'

'Was your ancestor there at the time? Clem Synnott.'

'I wouldn't rightly know. Why do you ask?'

'Oh I sort of assumed you'd know.'

'Well it was nearly two centuries ago,' said Mr Synnott drily. 'The story gets a bit vague in that length of time.'

'I suppose it would,' conceded Dempsey, 'though I did use a bit of poetic licence. You see I put him there on Carrickbyrne Rock during the battle of Ross. I was going to write him into the battle but the times wouldn't fit.'

'Oh yes?' said Mr Synnott, sitting up straighter. 'I hope you're not going to bring disgrace on the family.' His smile took the harm out of the remark. 'Did you go up to see the place?'

'I did,' said Dempsey and was silent for a while. He had found little trace of the barn, just a few fragments of old stone wall. Dark fluid seeped from a silage pit on the site and fir trees rustled in the breeze. He had found the atmosphere oppressive in the lonely silence of a summer afternoon. Nettles and brambles prevented him from getting close to the gaunt and deserted Scullabogue House. He imagined that someone was watching him as he prowled about and the hairs prickled on the back of his neck.

'Not much sign of any barn there now.'

'No,' said Mr Synnott. 'It was demolished there at the end of the last century.'

'Who'd want to keep it?'

'Who indeed? But the fact remains. What way did you tackle it at all?'

'I can show you if you like.' It was taking a chance but there was no point in being coy. 'I have it outside in the car as a matter of fact. I tried to envisage how it might have seemed to a prisoner in the house who would have witnessed what happened.'

'A Protestant of course. He'd hardly be impartial though. Would he?'

'A Quaker, as a matter of fact, an elder who was taken into custody while visiting the Meetings of Friends in the area.'

'Ah!' It made a difference. 'Give us a look at it anyway.'

Dempsey went out and returned with a bundle of typescript in a large brown envelope. He leafed through the bundle and extracted some pages. He reflected that the left-hand margins were fine but the right hand ones were a bit ragged. The bell on the typewriter always seemed to come too soon, just when he was getting into his stride.

'It's a bit scrappy looking but legible,' he said, diffidently handing over the sheets.

'Sure, leave the lot. I'd like to have a gander at the whole thing if

you don't mind.' Mr Synnott reached into his top pocket and produced his glasses. Raising his eyebrows interrogatively he began to
read.

'Hmm,' he murmured thoughtfully, letting Dempsey know that
nobody could put one over on him.

'Elder Shackleton. Hmm.'

'I'll leave it with you,' said Dempsey. 'I think I'll take a bit of a
walk.'

He glanced back from the door. His father-in-law was frowning
as he read:

'I assure you, friends, you are in no danger here. I have spoken with
the officer in charge and he has given me his word and that of his
general, as he is called.' The man spoke carefully and distinctly and
his air of authority had a visibly calming influence on the people
crowded into the small room overlooking the yard.

'We must bear these privations with fortitude and place our trust in
God.'

The air was fetid with the smell of too many people in too small a
space. A bucket overflowed in a corner of the room where men and
women were obliged to relieve themselves. The window was secured
by several large nails.

'We could try to escape,' said a short, burly man clenching his fists.
'We could overpower the guards.'

'And what of the children?' said another. 'We could not carry them
to safety. There are too many people on the hill above.'

'Well there is one thing we can do, Elder,' said the short stocky man,
taking off one of his boots. 'We can let some air into this place.' As he
spoke he smashed several of the small panes of the window and a
welcome gust of air rushed in.

The guards outside, sturdy countrymen who had been lounging
about, leaning on pikes and staves, became alarmed. There was a
pounding of feet in the corridor outside and the bolts screeched as
they were drawn back. In a sudden silence the occupants of the room
became aware of the moaning of the people imprisoned in the barn
nearby.

'Who was responsible for that?' shouted a young man. His face was flushed and his hands trembled as he pointed his long barrelled sporting gun at the captives. Two men with pikes stood behind him in the doorway. 'I have orders to shoot anyone who tries to escape,' he shouted and there was hysteria in his voice. He was aware that most of these people knew him as a neighbour. He blushed. 'I'll shoot if I have to,' he reiterated.

'Friend,' said the first speaker, 'you may put away your weapon. We were not attempting to escape.'

The young man faltered and slowly lowered his gun. He backed away, exhaling in disgust at the stench. The Elder moved towards him.

'I would appreciate a word in private.'

'No,' said the young man again. 'You can't come out. Captain Canning would have you shot. There's been too many executed already.'

'Your captain, as you call him, knows me well and I have no doubt that he would trust me not to do anything rash.' There was almost a flicker of a smile on the man's lips as he spoke.

'Very well then. You may step outside into the passageway.' He grounded his gun on the flagstone floor and his companions closed and bolted the door. 'What is it you want?'

'These people are distressed,' began the Elder quietly. 'I would ask you, in God's name, to grant them even some food and fresh water. There are children, even infants in that room.'

'I am aware,' said the young man. 'You will soon be released, I promise you.'

'We have committed no offence, but even so I am prepared to pay for such food as you can provide.' He felt in his pocket and found a tenpenny piece. 'Will you refuse to accept King George's silver?' he asked with just a hint of irony.

'There is no need,' said his captor quietly. 'I will see that some food is provided for your people, Mr eh?'

'Shackleton,' replied the man. 'Elder Shackleton. These poor people are not *my* people, as you put it, but they are all God's people and never forget it.'

'They will be offered, each one of them, a chance to join us and to take baptism,' said the guard, drawing himself up to his full height.

The other man shook his head. 'They have already received the gift of baptism, my friend.'

'They can still take the oath and unite with us,' insisted the guard. 'They can unite with us in the common name of Irishman.'

'I should like to speak with some of the people whom you have imprisoned in the barn. I suspect that there are Friends there, you see. I should like to pray with them.'

'No, that will not be possible. I have already allowed you too much freedom. There are no Quaker prisoners.'

'I am not a dangerous man, my friend, but I am a prisoner.' He looked at his captor with a calm level gaze and the young man looked away.

'I cannot allow it,' he said. 'It would be against ...' He stopped. A noise like the roaring of the sea was rushing towards the house. It was as if a great wave broke about them and the yard and haggard beyond it were filled with a surging crowd of men and women shouting and brandishing weapons. The men guarding the barn were bundled aside and the doors were wrenched open. A man stumbled into the open, shielding his eyes against the sunlight. He was immediately confronted by a group which included a figure in clerical garb.

There was some exchange of words which the watchers in the house could not hear.

'What is happening?' asked the Elder of a man who had come in, hastily locking the outer door behind him.

'Trouble,' said the man addressing himself to the guards. 'Ross has been lost and the military are killing all before them. They say they've burned a hospital with a hundred sick and wounded inside it.'

'Well then, God help us all,' said the young man.

'Will we make a stand on Carrickbyrne?'

'Who knows?'

'You would do well to set us free,' said the Elder. 'We can speak for you and try to secure your protection.'

'It's not over yet,' said the newcomer. 'The priest is demanding that all prisoners join us.'

'But surely ...'

There was a roar from outside and they hurried to the door. Through the grimy pane of glass they could see a figure lying on the packed clay of the yard. Blood was seeping from his shirt-front and staining the earth. Two women emerged from the barn and helped him to his feet. Slowly they helped him back towards the dark interior. The crowd surged forward and the door was secured again with a heavy wooden bar.

'Christ,' said the guard. 'This looks bad. We should try to put a stop to this.'

As he spoke flames appeared at the base of the walls. People were running from the haggard with armfuls of straw. They were laughing and competing with each other to be the first to feed the eager flames. In seconds the whole building was engulfed in fire. Terrified screams could be heard above the uproar of the crowd.

'You must release those people,' said the Elder. 'I will do what I can to help.'

'Go back inside and make the people lie down. Stay away from the window.' The guard swung the door of the room open again and pushed him inside. 'Stay down,' he shouted again and slammed the door to.

Smoke had swirled into the room through the broken panes and with it came the heavy sickening smell of burning flesh.

'We must be quiet,' said the Elder, 'or these people will turn their fury on all of us.'

He moved among them talking quietly to one and to another, urging them to be still.

'We must wait and pray. There is nothing more to be done.'

'We could fight,' said the man who had broken the window, but one glance at the raging mob outside was enough to convince him of the futility of trying. He saw in one quick glance an infant wrapped in a shawl falling from a small window in the barn wall. It fell into the burning straw. A man picked up the already smouldering bundle and hurled it back into the blazing interior.

In a storm of sparks the roof fell and a cloud of dark smoke billowed upwards. The breeze caught it and sent it rolling like a stain over the fields. The noise of the crowd died away. United by what they had done, they stood silent, with blackened faces, staring at the charred shell of the building. Gradually those on the periphery began to drift away, distancing themselves from the obscenity. It had happened so quickly that many still found it difficult to believe the evidence of their eyes. The interior of the building glowed, a mass of smouldering timber and blackened, skeletal limbs.

'I fear,' said the Elder, 'that our situation as witnesses of this terrible thing is more perilous than before. I would entreat you yet again to remain as silent as possible.'

As he spoke a child began to whimper and a woman hugged it to her, soothing it and rocking back and forth.

'Our captor seems an honourable man but he would be powerless to protect us.'

Mr Synnott took off his glasses and rubbed his eyes. They should have fought back, he thought. Any red-blooded man would rather fight than see his family slaughtered. It was a bad business. No use harping on it now. He wondered how Dempsey was going to work his ancestor into the story. He was intrigued by the Quaker fellow. He read on.

It had rained heavily by the time the shattered army reached the camp at Carrickbyrne. It was as if a tide of defeat was driving the rebels onto the high ground. General Harvey sat on the ground with his back against a tree.

'There is a Quaker man here, General, under guard. He insists on seeing you.'

The young man carried a long gun cradled loosely in the crook of his left arm.

'What does he want?' asked the general listlessly although in his heart he knew.

'It concerns the barn, General. He wishes to make a search of the remains.'

'Remains? I understand there were no remains.'

'There are bones, sir, that must be disposed of. He says he must report the deaths and burial places of any Friends to their Meeting. He must write a report — in duplicate.'

'In duplicate.' The general almost laughed aloud at the thought. Atrocity reported in duplicate. He would see this man.

'Bring him forward,' he said, 'and what is your name, sir?'

'Synnott, sir,' replied the young man. 'I was one of the guards on the house.'

'And why did you not prevent this dreadful business?'

'Sir, we were very few. Who could have imagined that the people would have behaved as they did? There were deserters too sir, possibly more than took part in the battle.'

'I have been told that the fire was set by government spies seeking to discredit us.'

He glanced up just in time to catch the look of contempt in the young man's eyes.

'Bring the man forward,' he said again rising to his feet. This very day he resolved to issue a general order forbidding all plunder and murder under pain of immediate execution. In the meantime he would speak to witnesses and see if any honour could be salvaged from the smouldering debris of his noble dream. Disconsolately he kicked at a stone. A voice behind him said: 'General Harvey, you have not done well. Not well at all. I should be obliged to you for the loan of some paper and writing implements. I must make my report.'

With a sinking heart the general knew that the horror, once written down, would never go away. He turned to meet the level stare of the Quaker but he could not look him straight in the eye.

Mr Synnott brooded for a while after he had finished reading. Dempsey knew that he wanted to say something. He too was keen to know what his father-in-law's reaction had been. Would he take it seriously? Eventually Mr Synnott made his overture.

'I'll buy you a bottle o'stout, Jack,' he said by way of preamble. He liked to walk the half mile or so to the crossroads pub in the evening and have a contemplative drink.

'You're on,' agreed Dempsey. There would be time for the one before heading back to the cottage. He enjoyed the way Mr Synnott discoursed on one thing and another as he stepped it out, with the rolling gait of a man who had followed a plough. He might

point out an old ash tree and explain that the king had once
ordered all farmers to plant ash for arrows and tool handles and
yew for bows. It kept the kingdom ahead of France in the arms
race.

'The yew of course is in the churchyard to make sure the stock
don't eat the berries. Hard to imagine a churchyard without yew
trees nowadays.'

On this occasion he came more directly to the point.

'Harvey doesn't come out of it too well, does he?'

'Why should he? He hadn't much of a clue. He was a dreamer,
not a general.'

'But he meant well all the same.'

'Of course he did but he couldn't have known much about human
nature.'

'Ah still. That Scullabogue business was a kind of accident really.'

'No,' said Dempsey, 'it was no accident. It's the badness that's
there in everyone. We seem to need enemies to make us feel good
about ourselves.'

'Ah now Jack. That's a bit much. It was more about land than
anything else.'

'That's part of it I'll agree but not all of it.'

'What I can't understand though is why the people didn't fight ...
make a run for it even.'

Dempsey frowned. 'Did you ever see those pictures of the Jews
in the death camps?'

'Aye.'

Their footsteps rang on the stones of the road. Mr Synnott swung
at a dandelion, cutting the head off with a swipe of his stick.

'Why did they walk quietly into the gas chambers? I'll tell you
why. They were afraid they'd get into worse trouble if they didn't.
They were hoping against hope.'

'Ah, that was different. That was the Nazis.'

'Not a bit different. The Nazis were just ordinary blokes like you
and me. It was ordinary blokes that put people in the incinerators
and turned them into clinker.'

'Ah, now Jack, you're a gloomy huer at times. I think I need that drink. Tell us, was that me great-great-great whatever he was in your story?'

'Aye. That's Clem.'

'You say a young man. I always thought of him as old.'

'Well, he was eventually.'

'What way do you see him there at the fire?'

'I sort of imagined him arguing with the priest. They say a priest gave the order to burn the prisoners.'

'What would he have said?'

'Well, the bit about the baby. The priest said to burn the nits along with the lice.'

'That wouldn't go down too well, would it. And where does it go from here then?'

By this time they had reached the pub and Mr Synnott rapped on the counter. Dempsey felt furtively in his pocket trying to identify by touch the value of his loose change.

'That's just the problem. I don't know that I want to go on. I don't know the rights and the wrongs of it any more.'

Mr Synnott tilted his glass and peered into it thoughtfully.

'I still can't fathom why people would do such a thing,' he said.

'They did it because they were able to. Somebody told them it was the right thing to do. That was all they needed to hear.'

'Now Jack, you an' I wouldn't do a thing like that. I don't care what you say.'

'But would we stop it?'

'Begod but this is serious stuff. I think we need another.' He went to put his hand in his pocket but Dempsey forestalled him.

'My round,' he said beckoning to the barman.

'But what about Clem? You can't leave him where he is now.'

'I had that all planned out before. I've even written the battle of Horetown that happened later. That was easy.'

'Aye, I read that. Very good, very good.'

'I just don't know why Clem would have gone on.'

'Well, he tried, didn't he? There were good people. Even General Harvey was a good man.'

'And Sir John Moore on the other side.'

'Now,' said Mr Synnott, 'that's a quare one, even if he was a redcoat.'

He raised a finger to the barman and indicated the two empty glasses.

'None of them though,' continued Dempsey, 'could control the deep down ...' he thumped the bar, searching for the right word, 'the rancour, the malice that lies just below the surface all the time. It's always us and them, no matter where you look. We're always the good guys.'

~

Elaine could hear them arguing as they came up the drive. It was obvious that they had had plenty to drink.

'And who was it showed me how to dismount a horseman with a pike? What do you do with him then? It's not a bloody game, y'know.'

'All I'm sayin' is,' her father insisted, 'it wasn't the fightin' men that burned Scullabogue.'

'Well, you're a right pair,' she challenged, throwing open the door. 'We thought you had both fallen in the ditch somewhere.'

'Your father,' said Dempsey loftily, 'is a difficult man to reason with.'

'That's no news,' she replied. 'Give me the keys. We have to go home.'

'Anyway,' said Mr Synnott jabbing his finger at Dempsey's chest, 'you have to finish it now. Just like Clem, you have to try. Have to believe in something.' He swayed slightly and tapped Dempsey again. 'Have to believe in people. You gave your word.'

'You go in now, Dad,' said Elaine. 'We have to go.'

John had fallen asleep on the back seat of the car. She had covered him with her coat.

'I read your stuff,' she said as she eased the car out of the driveway. 'It's interesting. I want to see how it turns out. It's a bit like seeing the family album coming to life, if you know what I mean.'

'That's good,' said Dempsey but he could not rise to her enthusiasm. 'Your father thinks I'm too gloomy. He's not sure whose side I'm on.'

She laughed. 'I think you'd like to be a Quaker but deep down you'll never be anything but a 1950s Catholic with your notions of right and wrong and the necessity for punishment, even if you have to inflict it on yourself.'

He responded to her mockery. 'Is it that bad? Of course there is right and wrong. We just have to train ourselves, learn to stretch the old conscience. Your father tells me that the tradition in the family was that Old Clem refused to talk about the Rising for nearly half a century. By then he was some sort of a hero and had learned to play the game.'

'A cynic too! What else did you find out tonight?'

He could have told her that his story had foundered on the grim hunchback rock of Carrickbyrne; that like General Harvey, he had come to the end of the road; that he saw defeat staring him in the face — but he prevaricated.

'I've learned that the more I drink, the better your driving gets.'

'Get away,' she said, slapping him on the arm.

'He said too that sometimes when the wind blows from that direction he used to notice how the horses got jittery. He said he was nearly thrown a few times, going the road.'

'Well now,' said Elaine pensively, 'I never heard that one before but it figures in a way. Remember that time?'

'Will I ever forget it?'

The motion of the car was making him feel ill. He was glad to get to his bed.

CHAPTER SEVEN

He knew that his scheme was coming apart. He had aimed for a story of adventure and heroism, a saga, but it was unravelling, splaying like a cane without a ferrule. He tried to think of some way of telling Elaine that the game was up, that he had failed, had let them all down. He would have to go back to Dublin with his tail between his legs, cap in hand looking for his job back or something to tide them over. In moments of fleeting optimism he thought that maybe she would be glad.

He had become gloomy. The atrocities of the last days of the Rising oppressed him. He could see no glimmer of light, no hint of compassion. He could put no shape on this dismal chronicle of tribalism and revenge.

He came more often to Tomgarrif, listening to Mr Synnott's yarns, sometimes becoming impatient with his rambling monologue. It was winter and he was glad of the warmth and the company. He owed rent but had said nothing about it yet to Elaine. The cottage was lonely during the day and the blank pages had become a reproach. The child was happier with his grandparents and there was plenty for him to do around the farm. Nonetheless he felt, if he could not break through, things would very soon come to a head.

That east wind, though, at Bannow was a bitch. The way it tore at the cottage; the way the waves hurled the coarse shingle on the strand, piling it up in one place and gouging out great troughs elsewhere. The flying sand stung the face off him and blinded his eyes. He was not too sure where he was going.

It would be great if the ideas could leap by some intuitive process, from the mind to the printed page without the cumbersome process of rooting around for the right words. Perhaps, he thought as he trudged along the beach, he should have gone in for photography — writing with sunlight, as the seraphs do, filtering the image through silver oxide and imprinting it so that people see with new eyes.

This mood is self-induced, he thought. It's cold and I'm skint and I don't know what the hell I'm doing here at the arse-end of nowhere on a bitter January day.

He thought about Elaine. She was good at what she did. It would be childish to resent the fact. That riding centre was always full — horsey types talking in loud voices, glum-looking Germans in sleek cars with expensive looking women, just off the ferry. Did they know that they were on the Cork to Moscow road, that some Eurocrat had decreed that at some stage in the future a great *autobahn* would carry thundering juggernauts laden with cheese and butter for the starving kulaks all the way from the Golden Vale to the frozen steppes of Russia?

His feet crunched on the coarse gravel and the wind flattened his anorak against his chest. His face was numb with the cold. The Cossacks would be at home in a place like this. Show them how to ride horses too. It would be nice to go into that riding centre with the Cossack horde, have a quick pillage and drag Elaine home to hell out of it, where she belonged.

The Cossacks would put the wind up old Wordsworth too as they swept through Wales and the West Country — soften his cough, curb his enthusiasm for revolution. Your Cossack doesn't mess about. He smiled at the idea. Those Eurocrats had no idea what they were starting. And yet he knew that his resentment was irrational. He was jealous, not of any individual, but of the fact that Elaine was doing something that she was good at, while he was falling further behind. He would cut a sorry figure if he tried to throw his weight around. In fact, he felt, he already did. He had accepted some money from her father, a loan of course. Mr Synnott was an astute old character. Maybe he saw himself as a patron, *Il Magnifico* of Tomgarriff. That wouldn't be a bad old set up — live on a pension at Tomgarrif and write imperishable prose. If only the words would come. He left the envelope in Tomgarrif in the hope of distancing himself from what he had written and maybe gaining a new perspective.

The waves sliced diagonally at the beach, tumbling and sorting the coarse gravel. He heard from afar a dull detonation and looked up into the overcast sky, searching for a flare. It must be the lifeboat maroon. He could see them in his mind's eye, men who should have parrots on their shoulders, pushing their drinks aside in the low ceilinged pub and running to the quay; Blind Pugh clutched his stick in his aged hand and shuffled after them, probing the eternal darkness ahead.

The trouble was that story was already written. He could hardly improve upon it. And then he came upon the porpoise. It lay on its side and its eyes were gone. The black flesh had shrunk away from its teeth — small shovel-shaped teeth. The gulls had punctured the hard rubbery skin with a thousand triangular indentations. The softer white skin of the belly was striated and torn. Sea-lice lumbered in and out of the gaping, sand-filled mouth.

'Ah you poor bastard,' said Dempsey and stirred the carcase with his boot. Sand-hoppers sprinkled upwards from the damp sand and the scattered bladder-wrack.

'Ah shag it,' he said and stepped back in disgust.

'An old hulk on a lee shore.' That was how Cap'n Billy Bones described himself. Aye, Jim lad. That was the little fellow's favourite story. Dempsey had told it a hundred times, hopping on one leg as required and cringing like Ben Gunn for a piece o' cheese.

He turned his back to the wind and plucked the hood tighter. It would be good to get home. Elaine was coming home early. She would collect the child from school on the way and together they would go to Tomgarrif. He looked forward to the warmth and the company. This evening he would tell her that the game was up, that he had run aground, on the rocks, that he were becaalmed, Cap'n, in the Doldrums, ahar. Long John would carry it off, no problem. Somehow or other he would have to go back to work, to honest toil, to earning a crust. Jesus, but there would be a row.

He looked back at the porpoise. It seemed to be asleep. A gull, a great black back, landed beside it and stared at it speculatively. Dempsey thought again of the lifeboat and wondered what vessel was in distress. This was indeed the Skeleton Coast.

He skimmed a pebble at the gull and saw it flap into the air, circle and land again further down the strand. It eyed him malevolently. Far off on the beach a small black figure was labouring along, a speck, a manshape. He wondered why anyone would choose to be out there on such a day. There was something ominous about the figure and incongruously Dempsey wished that he was carrying a stick or some weapon. It was that way from the beginning. We howl at our loneliness and reach for a stone when we see a human shape.

The figure was waving and trying to run, but the yielding surface caused him to stagger. Dempsey felt a coldness setting about his heart. He knew who it was and he knew that something terrible had happened. And then he saw the smoke, a low, scudding plume, wisping out to sea. He began to run, conscious that his mouth was dry with dread.

'Jesus Christ, man,' croaked the policeman. 'Oh, Jesus Christ.' He staggered and pulled at his collar. His breath sawed in his chest.

'What is it? What is it?' gasped Dempsey, knowing already what he was about to hear.

'The child. The house. Oh my Christ.'

'What happened? What happened?' He grudged the time it took to hear. He seized the man by the shoulders. 'What happened?' He tried to shake the words from him by main force.

'The gas,' wheezed the policeman. 'The gas blew up. Oh Good Christ.' He put his hands on his knees. 'House went up like as if there was petrol in it. They've taken him to hospital. The doctor has.'

'Elaine. Is she all right? Is he ..?'

'There was nobody else there but the child. He's badly ...'

But Dempsey was gone, running blindly. All he could see was the image of his child, petrol blazing on his hands and clothes where he had tried to light the fire. Matches spraying in the air. Anyone coming in out of the cold is entitled to a fire and something to eat. That was what he had always said. Took a pride in it. One thing he could do right. The flames leaped up and hid the terrified face of the child. He felt his heart bursting with the strain. The gravel clawed at his feet, dragging him back.

Neighbours, shamefaced, guilty, reproachful, helpful. The cottage a smouldering wreck. A Garda car — low slung, menacing, dark blue, well sprung; cornering at speed. Black wintry hedges; naked trees, a touch of ice on the road. They learn to drive on a skid pan.

'Rang your wife's people. She's already gone to the hospital.'

Word travels fast. Some static on the radio. One-sided conversation. 'Don't know exactly what happened.' Consciously avoiding blame or accusation. Plenty of time for that.

Glass doors; trolleys; smell of disinfectant, ether. White coats and white faces turned towards him and Elaine shaking her head. Tears ran down her cheeks. Voices murmured but he could not make them out. He reached out for her and the room spun around them and he knew that it was too late.

'I was late,' she said. 'Oh Jack, I was late.'

He held her, unable to speak. Her parents lumbered towards them, helpless. Her sisters stared with enormous eyes. Her father turned his cap in his hands and hung his head. There were no words that could carry what they felt.

He was very gentle, the coroner, in his dark pin-striped suit. He spoke of the tragic accident and could not emphasise too strongly the necessity for reminding people ... extreme caution ... inflammable substances ... number of serious accidents that happen in the home. He looked at the bereaved parents. They were only children themselves. They would have preferred it if he had blamed them, punished them, made it official, but he knew that they would punish themselves all the days of their life.

~

Elaine lost weight. She was pale, like a wraith, a ghost of her former self. The house at Tomgarrif was quiet. There was no chatter at mealtimes, no conversation in front of the kitchen range. Dempsey saw his manuscript on top of the dresser but he could not bring himself to touch it.

There should have been a progression through shock and dis-belief, to guilt and grieving and maybe some day to absolution, but they were stuck, lodged in a crevice of guilt. She could forgive him for his carelessness and for not being there. She pitied his pain and his attempts to reach her but she could not forgive herself. The one time they had relied on her and she had been late.

He knew that it was his fault. The child had seen him light the fire with turpentine. Black smuts had settled everywhere but the fire had lit immediately. The gas heater had snorted and spluttered but he always said it was fine. Now Elaine flinched when he touched her and turned away, avoiding his eyes.

'Give it time,' said Mr Synnott, 'that's all we can hope for. You'll be needing something to tide you over.' He always coughed at awkward moments. 'Was there any news from up there, of the job like?'

'Oh, they can fix me up no problem. I dare say we'll move back shortly. Get out from under your feet.' He tried to smile.

'Now, now, now,' said the old man, 'there's no need for any hurry. There's always a place here for the pair of you.'

But Dempsey felt that they had to get away. Distance might help. Even the cold shock of the bare little house in Dublin that she disliked might stimulate them to thinking about the future. They could sell it and move somewhere else. Maybe. He wondered how to broach the subject. They could not go on like this anyway.

She shrugged when he suggested the idea and turned away. So it was all right then? Why can't you answer me? I didn't do it on purpose. It was an accident. Misadventure the man in the suit said. Speak to me.

'If you want,' she murmured. 'I don't mind.' Her hair was lank and hung around her face. He wanted to brush it aside but feared that she would draw back as if in disgust. He felt hollow inside.

He closed his eyes. He could see his blind spot swirling like a jellyfish or a nebula in deepest space. Anger spurted inside him and for the first time he thought that he was not entirely to blame. The thought had inserted itself into his mind like water trickling through a crack. No, she had no right to lay all the blame on him. Oh Christ he thought, that's not the way forward.

'Whatever you want,' she said, 'I'll go along with it.'

'It's just, ah, I thought maybe if we got away it would give us a chance.' Think positive.

'Yes, yes, that's true.' She nodded several times and turned towards him but her eyes were blank.

Bleak afternoon sunlight filtered through the branches of the cedar tree and showed up the dust under the sideboard. It glazed the old leather chairs with a yellow sheen.

'Have to get away,' she said and held her cold hands towards the fireplace. Specks of ash had fallen onto the hearth and she reached for the brush to sweep them up.

~

He knew she hated the Dublin house.

'We'll get somewhere else,' he said.

'It doesn't matter,' she replied. 'I don't mind.'

One afternoon she left. 'Going down home for a while,' she said as she dusted around. Dusted the television set and the hemispherical base of the aerial. He could see her face reflected in it, her nose comically enlarged. She dusted the mantlepiece and the clock, a green glass cube with all the works visible inside. She gave it a couple of winds.

'There,' she said and a cold fear settled on him. She replaced the clock but kept her hand on it for a moment. He heard it ticking in the silence that lay between them.

'It'll do you good,' he said brightly, subscribing to a fiction. He drove her to the station and carried her case. When he held her she was stiff and wooden and in a way it was a relief when she went.

~

In the couple of years after Elaine left, his life settled into a mould. He felt it gel about him and harden into something like ice. Objectively he knew that it was some kind of mania. His misery hung round him like a cloud, a miasma that swept along the streets, filtering into laneways, rising to the level of the eaves. He walked the street, pushing it ahead of him, with his hands dug into his pockets and his shoulders hunched. Dr Johnson used to tap his stick on the railings, deriving some sense of completeness, unity from the staccato rattle on the uprights. If he thought for a moment that he had missed one, he would go back and start again at the beginning. Eccentric, mad even. Dempsey would make for high ground, up by Phibsboro Church. The cloud flowed down the groin of Cabra road, rolling, trundling towards Navan. He tried to see if it would drain away down Infirmary Road, maybe swill into the river and be borne seawards, but no. It set as it moved, expanding around the barracks where sentries lurked at gates. It settled around the mental hospital and seeped into the park, picking up grass and leaves, enveloping the zoo animals. It froze on Oxmantown Road, trapping the ghosts of the Ostmen, Dublin's ancestors, like flies in Norwegian amber. He looked up to see if anyone might swim down from the rooftops and rescue him. His misery set in the mould of streets as metal sets in pigs.

He drank in the pub with the statue over the door — Hygeia, in a spit and sawdust pub. People talked. The pub had a door on either side of the corner. He always went out by the other door to avoid tangling the string of his life. Always the circuitous route. Never turn back.

He looked into the military barracks. A colonial freak, a barracks designed for India but dropped, maybe in an administrative slip of the pen, into Dublin. Don't Lucknow. That was a good one. But your slip is showing. Guns, menacing, cocky, almost strutting on disproportionately tall wheels. Captured in the Sikh Wars. Could come in handy. Very manoeuvrable in the hill country; the wily Pathan.

Never underestimate the Pathan. He chuckled at the incongruity of
it all.

'Drunk again, eh Jack?' said a familiar voice.

The Mad Gunner swam down from a chimney top, his arms
flailing and legs kicking at the mist. A winter sun probed its last few
ochre beams through the layers that swirled and seeped around the
houses.

The face came into view. Prognathous jaw, forehead villainously
low, a shambling man-like creature. Dempsey looked him up and
down and the humour of the situation struck him. So this was his
guardian angel, the one who would pluck him up by the locks and
drag him from the depths to the pure air above. He rocked back on
his heels.

'So am I, Gunner,' he replied tolerantly. 'So am I.'

A hand seized the front of his coat and he felt a button give.

'Don't get fuckin' smart with me, you little gobshite.'

The button fell with a dry click and rolled along the pavement. It
wobbled and fell, oscillating like a coin, describing a Moebius band.
'Wa, wa wa,' it said and died. Impossible.

'Don't get fuckin' smart with me,' said the old man again. 'If it
wasn't for ....' The rest of his speech was unintelligible, something
about a decent man, bloody disgrace. Pull yourself together.

But the threads were broken. They stuck out painfully like four
tufts of grey grass. Have to leave them for the moment to mark the
spot. Retrieve the button. Very hard to find a matching button,
certainly not a talking button.

'Bummin' your chat,' said the Gunner. 'Answer to me.'

There was some element of threat in his voice. Dempsey bent for
the button, trapped it, dropped it, flipped it and lifted it expertly. No
one could accuse him of being drunk. Sober as a lord. No, that was
what she would have said. Pull your coat together, that was it. It was
cold too. What was the point of it all.

There was a hand at his elbow.

'Take your bloody hands off me.' A man has his pride.

'Attitude,' said the Gunner, ' — block off.'

There were faces watching them, pale oval masks in the street light. Somebody laughed.

'Home outa' that.'

'Look after myself.'

The lights of the cars drew lines in the mist, red on one side of the road and yellow on the other. A time exposure photograph, they formed railings that kept him on the pavement. Footwork, that's the trick. When the legs start to go you're finished.

'Take your bloody hands off me,' he snarled and swung a great roundhouse at the face that swayed in front of him. The momentum of the blow almost toppled him but he felt his fist connect with bone. A stinging pain shot through his hand and a voice said derisively: 'Pick on someone your own age, ya bowzie.' The speaker need not have worried. The Mad Gunner had been in tougher situations. With the precision of a matador he felled Dempsey with a quick succession of punches, much to the delight of the gathering crowd. Dempsey was aware that he was sitting ignominiously with his back against a wall and that people were laughing.

'Good enough for him, the gouger,' someone remarked to general agreement but Dempsey had no breath to reply. He felt a hand on his shoulder and a voice told him to get up and to accompany the speaker to the barrack. He was conscious of being in the back of a car which seemed to make a couple of rapid revolutions. Bright lights streaked past. He heard voices and knew that he was in a police station. He saw the Mad Gunner deep in conversation with an officer and then the cell door clanged shut. His head was beginning to clear and he was conscious of the pain around his ribs. He remembered that he had been in a sort of a fight and, worse still, that he had lost.

He sat down dejectedly on the stone ledge that was the only furniture in the room. There was a stench of urine from the hole in the floor, which reminded him with a shock of his childhood and the old red brick barracks. The seat of his trousers was damp from the pavement. He leaned over slowly and put his forehead down on the stone. He was grateful for its coldness as his head was pounding. His blind spot seemed to have grown and danced before his eyes. The light fitting in the ceiling began to rotate and the room slipped sideways. Dempsey clasped his hands around his knees and shivered. He heard voices raised in argument and the heavy banging of a door. He closed his eyes. A voice somewhere in the building sobbed: 'I want to go home. I want to go home.'

He awoke in confusion and looked about him. The wall was pitted and streaked with grime and faeces. Graffiti extended from the floor up to a height of about six and a half feet, many of them scratched into the plaster. He wondered where prisoners got sharp implements to record their thoughts. He found himself grappling with the problem as if it was of vital importance. Maybe murderers and patriots during their last hours on earth had scraped their testaments on that same wall, their shout to echo through all eternity that they had once lived, had once been part of the great procession.

There were some in crayon in a stilted italic style that seized and engrossed his attention: 'Lynch first, Jack last.' Was it some cryptic incitement to mob rule and civil disorder? 'Krushchev will drive a road through US.' America or what? And strangest of all the question 'Who burns wonderful man to death?'

He recognised the handwriting from walls and hoardings around the city. Was this demented scribe obsessed with some apocalyptic vision of nuclear holocaust? Wonderful man, the paragon of nature. He sat up carefully and put his head in his hands. He was still shivering and his ribs hurt when he moved. He was out of his fighting weight with the Mad Gunner he reflected ruefully. Archie Moore was still fighting in his fifties. Age has nothing to do with it.

A key rattled in the lock and a bolt slid back with a small metallic screech. The guard stood looking down at him with his hands clasped behind his back. For an instant Dempsey thought 'This is it. Death in a police cell. At the very least a hiding.' He stood up stiffly.

'You're a bloody lucky man, me bucko,' said the guard. 'That oul' fella declined to press charges. Said you had enough on your plate.'

Dempsey looked down, saying nothing. The guard's voice softened.

'Off home with you now and clean yourself up and don't you find yourself in the Bridewell again, boy, unless you're prepared for a longer stay.'

Dempsey nodded. 'Kind of lost the head,' he mumbled.

'Aye well, you'll know better next time, I dare say.'

'Aye,' Dempsey nodded again anxious to go and to be free of the smell of despair. He wanted to wash and shave and somehow be his own man again.

After that he laid off the drink.

CHAPTER EIGHT

The shout reverberated in his head as Dempsey awoke. He was sweating and he could feel his heart knocking against his rib cage. He listened for a moment and the shout came again, further down the street. It was nothing, just some night walking straggler taking advantage of the darkness, an anonymous homebound loudmouth issuing a challenge to the world.

His heartbeat subsided as he realised that it was not a quarrel. His parents were long gone and their antagonisms silenced forever. He was alone with his thoughts in the darkness. The night was oppressively warm and clammy with that electric tension that presages thunder. He threw the blanket aside and contemplated the pale yellow rectangle of window.

Everything about that house seemed to be yellow, pale brick on the outside and yellow distemper within. He never had any interest in changing it. In fact, he reflected, he had very little interest in anything, but yet his mind ranged about, seizing compulsively on anything and everything, except the great Sargasso of loneliness that lay just beyond the periphery of conscious thought.

Insomniacs, he mused, occupy their time with useful things like reviewing their finances, devising wild schemes to make money or diagnosing their own incurable ailments. He had no need, so far as he knew, to worry about money and since he had laid off the drink his health never cost him a thought. He could recall times when he had lain there in the half darkness trying to focus on the bulb as the only fixed point in a spinning world. That was no joke. When he shut his eyes the world pitched sideways and toppled him into the abyss. The drink was no help.

Lightning flickered outside and he started. He was always afraid of lightning. The Da was never afraid of anything in his life, but he was, Dempsey admitted, an ignorant and unimaginative man at the best of times. He never allowed of the possibility that fear was necessary, a good thing, the preliminary to flight and self-preservation. Ajax defied the lightning but Ajax was as thick as a ditch too.

Dempsey slid out of the bed and closed the window. It was only a million to one chance but why shorten the odds? He looked out at the street of small, two-up, one-down houses and at his old Volkswagen standing slightly askew under the street lamp. He really should get rid of it, he thought but knew that he could never come to a decision. It was a kind of talisman, a link with that other world where he had once been happy.

Experts have shown that a Volkswagen is the safest thing to be in during a thunder storm. The shape will conduct even a direct hit around the occupant. He could hardly though, go out and sleep in the car. The neighbours would look at him even more warily and anyway, the rim of the flat wheel was touching the pavement. He would probably fry. Frankenstein could have used it to inject life into his creation. Better to leave it to the attentions of passing hooligans until such time as the Corporation should force the issue or tow it away.

He felt the urge to go for a walk, to tire himself out and dissipate restless thoughts, but another flicker of lightning deterred him. It ran along the electric wires like loose tinsel and thunder grumbled somewhere over the mountains. Reluctantly he lay back on the bed and put his hands behind his head. It would be a long time to morning and the sleep had gone astray. This was the danger time where memory lay in ambush, the witching hour when the walking dead shuffle about the streets. He smiled wryly in the darkness.

'Igor, the lightning,' he said aloud. Galvanised, that was the word.

Mesmer, Bowdler, Galvan; men who became processes. Shirt collars were trubenised. Who was Truben? Drifting, wool-gathering, words leading into labyrinths of inconsequential thought.

Thunder rumbled overhead and he knew the sound at once. It was the sound of the Guinness barrels on the Custom House Quay on that day long ago when his mother brought him to Dublin on the bus. The men wore sections of motorcar tube on their hands as they rolled the barrels over the cobbles. There was a smell of frying bacon from the wooden hut and everyone seemed to be in a good mood.

'Your father wouldn't approve of sending all the porter away to England,' she said with a smile and he had looked up at her, sharing but not quite getting the joke. The men were master controllers of the wayward barrels, proud of their skill and sometimes showing off by directing one with a nonchalant boot, sending it waddling down the small incline towards the quayside.

It was nearly Christmas and they had important business to do. There were lights and decorations in all the shops and towards evening lights came on in the trees in O'Connell Street. The trees were full of small birds that hopped about and twittered as if enjoying the excitement of the day. In retrospect, he admitted that they were probably hopelessly confused and distraught from the unaccustomed brightness.

They had tea in the Adelphi and the waitress brought a tiered stand of cakes. He had never seen such luxury. His mother had let him choose two because it was a special day. On the way to the bus they saw the illuminated Santa Claus on the front of McBirneys' shop. The reindeer galloped and the bobble on Santa's hat flapped up and down in the breeze. The lights reflected in the blackness of the river. He clutched his parcels and was glad his father was not there to grumble and chivvy them along.

Years later he heard a story about these reindeer. The whole thing was made in Germany and delivered to McBirneys with comprehensive instructions for assembly and wiring. A succession of electricians glanced at the instructions and threw up their hands in despair. At last someone got the bright idea of writing to the manufacturer requesting an English translation. The translation duly arrived with a footnote to the effect that they always printed their instructions in the language of the country to which they sent their products, to wit, in this case, Irish. Another example of that Teutonic efficiency that causes nothing but trouble.

The thunder rumbled again, further away, the deep bass note of full barrels, not the rackety clatter of the empties. The yellowness gave way to a deeper darkness and it began to rain, a deafening downpour that pounded on the roof and cascaded from the gutters. The air was suddenly cooler and fresher. Dempsey drew the blanket around him and began to give in to sleep.

In the morning everything looked bright and clean and the sun shone from a cloudless sky. The mountains seemed so close that he could see the patchwork of fields and plantations. A few wisps of cumulus sat on their crests.

'That's a brave morning,' said a voice and Dempsey turned to see a familiar figure making his way carefully along the pavement with the aid of a stick.

In recent years his father's old comrade in arms had become very stiff in the joints, but not too stiff, as Dempsey well knew, to stand up for himself still.

'Not a bad day at all, Mr McEnaspie,' Dempsey replied slowing down to match his pace to that of the old man.

'It's well for yourself, the idle rich,' said the old man.

'You're off to Mass, I suppose.'

'Aye, that I am. I haven't missed a First Friday in many a long year.' The old man thrust his head forward, struggling with his disability. Dempsey noticed that he had developed a slightly crabwise movement.

'Though it's gettin' harder to get down on me benders, so it is. The rheumatics.'

'Ah well, you'll get your reward in heaven, as they say.'

'I tell ye what though. The monsignor was goin' to put hassocks on the kneelers down there in Aughrim Street an' in the heel o' the hunt he changed his mind.'

'Would make life easier, though. Wouldn't it? Might pull in the crowds again.'

'Had the money put aside an' all an' some bollox gave him a spiff about the Penal days and people kneelin' on the bare rocks in all weathers and fellas walkin', be Jasus, to Jerusalem on their knees, be Christ, an doesn't he say he's puttin' the money to some worthier cause.'

Spittle sprayed from his lips as he denounced the injustice of it all.

'An' sure there's nobody in the place but oul' crocks like meself.'

The monsignor it seemed had, in the best Irish tradition, alienated his most loyal supporters.

He continued: 'I went down to the men's retreat one night an' sure I felt like a chiseller. There was nobody there under seventy-five, I swear to God and what does he preach about? Lust. That's what he goes on about.' He cackled at the absurdity of it all. If you kicked th'oul sticks from under the lot of us we'd of all fell over sideways. Lust, how are ye?'

Dempsey smiled. Time was, he reflected, the Mad Gunner could have delivered an interesting enough talk on the subject, but he was not going to remind him of that. It would be nice to have time to repent of your sins long after you had lost interest in them. Somebody else said that. Some saint. Anyway the First Fridays carried a cast iron guarantee of salvation.

'Ye know what I'm goin' to say to ye?' began the old man earnestly.

Dempsey waited.

'Now, maybe it's none o' my business but I'll say it anyway, seein' as how I was great with your Da.'

Instinctively Dempsey divined what was coming and he felt a momentary panic and the urge to escape. A bony hand gripped his arm with surprising strength.

'There's a lot of your Da in ye, Jack, a quare stubborn streak. I've watched ye grow up, so I can see it. A right little get at times, I have to admit, but by an' large ye've some of the fibre of your oul' fella.'

A back-handed compliment they call it and Dempsey had experienced a back-hander from the same source before.

'I don't like to see a good man go down, that's all and I know what

I'm talkin' about.'

Dempsey muttered something neutral, neither encouraging nor dismissive. He wanted the hand that gripped his arm to let him go. This old fellow had cropped up at intervals in his life, sometimes to admonish and once or twice to rescue him both from others and from himself. He had, in a way, earned the right to speak his mind.

'You're an intelligent man, Jack, an' all that but what you need now is a good kick in the arse. No wait a minute.' He gripped Dempsey's arm even harder. 'Don't walk away, like that. I know what I'm talkin' about.'

The spray of spittle came again and he spoke vehemently. 'You'll arse around for the rest of your life lookin' like a tramp. Why don't you smarten yourself up?'

'I'm all right,' Dempsey retorted angrily, pulling his arm away.

'Why don't you smarten yourself up and go an' see that young wife of yours? Jasus, you can't punish yourself forever or you'll end up in Grangegorman.'

That was below the belt and the Mad Gunner knew it. There is always someone in life that you are just not able for, someone who can get in that telling blow or knock the wind out of your sails when you least expect it. The Mad Gunner was always a step ahead, even if he was on Dempsey's side. He knew everything there was to know about fighting dirty, using the elbows, pulling a man onto a punch or hitting him where it hurt most without leaving a mark. A good man to have on your side.

'Lookit,' said Dempsey raising both hands and stepping back. 'I'm all right, I tell you. I've plenty to do.'

'Well, whatever you say. I've said me piece. All I can do now is fuckin' pray for ye.'

He waved his stick in the direction of the church.

'I'm headin' down this way, so I won't hold ye from any urgent business.' He leaned sarcastically on the words. 'Just mind what I say.'

Dempsey had hardly heard him. The old man, like the Da, had been useful with his fists. He had caught him with a perfect combination. Of course he should smarten himself up and go to see Elaine.

That would be easy. What would he say to her then and how would he look into her eyes? Staying away made the pain bearable. It had become the norm. In a way, she was dead to him and it was better so.

The 'Gorman was another matter, a latent fear that, like his mother, he might just give way sometime and that he would be taken away for good. He had seen his mother weaken and lose her grip on reality and he had seen the uncomprehending look in his father's eyes and his shame at her frailty. There was a lot of his father in him, according to the Mad Gunner, but his mother had left him a legacy too. He wondered at times if their unhappy relationship lived on in his own inner turmoil.

She had been used to better before she married Dinny but her family turned away from her. The Comerfords were anti-Treaty republicans and he was a Free-State soldier, the lowest form of life according to her people. She, with her education, who should have known better, had thrown herself away on Dinny Dempsey. He must have had something going for him, but Dempsey felt that she had long regretted her choice.

She had never fitted into army life and incessant quarrelling had worn her down. When they finally settled in Dublin she said that she felt like a piece of flotsam in the big city. She explained the word to him but he was confused by the fact that there was a musician of the same name on the radio and another by the name of Jetsam. They played duets. Perfect harmony.

Nobody was mad. That was a ridiculous idea. The Mad Gunner was not mad. It was the frenzy of battle that got to him. His mother was never mad. She simply gave up and withdrew into her shell. Doctors always have to put a name on things, a syndrome or condition. No, he would never end up in Grangegorman. That was a mad idea. The thought went round and round in his head.

Sitting on the bus, pondering the nature of madness and sanity his attention was arrested by the conversation of a foreign couple, an elderly man and woman who were conversing volubly in French. He regretted that he was never a great linguist but he knew enough to read the notice over the window.

It stated, in Irish of course: 'Emergency exit. In the event of an emergency, ask for the hammer in the driver's compartment and break this window.' Not just any window. There was probably a fine for breaking and escaping through a non-designated window. The sublime lunacy of the idea comforted him and he smiled unexpectedly. The French people smiled back. These Irish, they are so friendly.

~

A bell tinkled as he pushed open the door of Sedgwick and Son, Antiques and Fine Art. The morning light glinted on brass and rich old mahogany furniture. A stuffed pheasant stared at him from under its glass dome. He had once suggested to Paddy that they put up a new sign, Antiques and Junque, at which Paddy, the son referred to in the peeling gilt lettering outside, had laughed through cigarette smoke and gasped for breath.

'I like it. I like it.'

'If you want anything done, ask a busy man,' was Paddy's motto, usually with the rider: 'Jack, you look after things here. I have a game of golf with a chap.'

Paddy, in fact, did very little that could be called work but he met a great many chaps and a constant stream of business flowed his way. On sale days he perched nonchalantly on a high stool and in a vaguely aristocratic manner allowed his clients to relieve him of a bewildering array of bargains. He often remarked to Dempsey that you could in fact get money for old rope.

'Ah, Jack. The very man.' Paddy always made it seem that by turning up for work, Dempsey had bestowed upon him a particular favour or that he was the product of some fortunate circumstance.

'The very man I wanted to see.'

Dempsey waited.

'I have to nip out for a while this morning. You'll be able to look after the show I dare say.'

'I dare say I could. I don't think I have anything else on this morning.'

'No,' said Paddy slowly, as if giving the matter deep consideration. He flicked his cigarette ash sideways towards a brass fender
and fire irons. Dempsey's eye followed the trajectory. The smoker
always makes a pretence of disposing of his waste in a responsible
manner.

'You'll burn this place down around us some day,' he remon-
strated.

'You could be right, Jack. Desperate things, the fags. You never
indulged.' He looked ruefully at his nicotine yellowed fingers.
'Desperate things.' Guiltily he rubbed the sole of his shoe over the
blue-grey sprinkle of ash.

'Would you mind organising a bit of a catalogue while I'm out?
A few nice pieces coming up next week. Give a bit of a spiff.'

'No problem,' said Dempsey. In fact he liked to have the place to
himself, to potter about and examine things at his leisure.

'You have the old way with words, Jack. Never my forte. Had a
nice piece in this morning actually, just before you arrived. A painting. Interesting.'

'I saw an old character going out just now,' said Dempsey.
'Looked like a bit of a wino in fact. Did he bring it in?'

'Yes, as a matter of fact. Wino would nearly describe him. That
was the late John Clifford. Ever hear of him?'

'Clifford. No. What do you mean, the late? Sure he just walked
out the door.'

Paddy laughed and gave a short rasping cough.

'Jesus, I'll have to give these up. Take up aerobics or something.'

'Come on. What do you mean by the late John Clifford?'

'Oh, nothing really. It'll add a few bob to the value, that's all. The
punters love a story.'

'So what's the story, then?' asked Dempsey. 'We can hardly kill
off our customers just to make them more interesting.'

'Why not? Aren't we a nation of necrophiliacs? Spend half our
free time going to funerals.'

Dempsey flinched and Paddy looked away in some confusion. He
drew on his cigarette.

'Anyway it's a nice piece of work, the picture. It's up in the office at the moment.'

'I'll have a look at it. But what was the story on your man?'

'Ah yes. Hold on a minute. I'll just give Frances a shout.'

He went up two steps of the stairs that led up into the rear of the building.

'Frances,' he called, 'do you think you could bring us down that picture?'

He stepped down again and sighed as if the exertion had exhausted him. He took another long drag on his cigarette.

'D'you remember one time talking about the Hellfire Club murders?'

'I do,' nodded Dempsey. It was a dinner party on a warm summer's evening with children squabbling in the garden. Elaine had looked at him and there was a lustre in her eyes. That was a long time ago.

'The Hellfire Club,' he said slowly and felt a pain in the pit of his stomach. 'Yes, I remember.'

'Well, that was your man. John Clifford.' Paddy was quite excited by his discovery. 'I remember now. He wasn't excommunicated. He's a Protestant. That's what probably got him in bad with the bishop in the first place.'

'Ah right. But why do you call him 'the late'?'

'Well he'll be late soon enough by the looks of him. It's only a technicality. It was manslaughter, not murder.'

There was a thump on the stairs and Dempsey looked up to see Frances struggling with the painting in its heavy gilt frame. Frances, frail and elderly, had been with Sedgwicks all her working life. She was devoted to the firm and to Paddy who took disgraceful advantage of the fact. It seemed to Dempsey that she was happy to define her whole existence in the phrase 'I'm with Sedgwicks'. Sedgwicks without Frances would be impossible to imagine.

'Hold on there,' called Dempsey, hurrying up the stairs. 'Let me take that.'

Gratefully she released her burden. Dempsey brought the picture down and stood it on an elaborately carved sideboard where the light fell slanting across it. He stood back and regarded it. It was a portrait of a young woman in a reflective pose. She wore a light check summer dress and held a bunch of bluebells in her lap. She was looking down at the flowers with a hint of sadness. Warm sunlight fell on a bare shoulder and on one side of her face.

'It's good,' said Dempsey peering at the signature — 'Clifford '48' in bold strokes of burnt sienna.

'The frame is worth a few bob,' added Paddy speculatively. 'I'd say five hundred to a grand. A bit of a story would maybe push it over the grand. Anyway I have to leave it with you. Knock up something about the tragic death of an artist hounded by church and state. That stuff goes down very well nowadays.'

Dempsey gave a short laugh. 'You're a cynical so and so. Still it's a nice piece of work.'

His eyes were drawn again to the picture. The girl was seated on a rough piece of stone. The light fell through leaves and made green patterns on her skin. The surface was grimed with dust and he felt the urge to clean it. He blew at the dust. Cleaning was better left to experts. He had once cleaned an old picture, a portrait, with a domestic cleaner. It took all the hair off the subject. They had to get a restorer to paint on a wig. That early *faux pas* had almost got him the sack but it had taught him patience. He blew away some more dust and cleaned an area with his sleeve. The flesh colour, particularly in shadow, was warm and a glint of light in her eye reminded him suddenly of Elaine. He envied the artist who could capture the essence of a person in a few smears of colour.

He turned away and gazed out of the window. Traffic rumbled along the quays, everybody going somewhere. Everyone except himself.

'Mr Dempsey.' It was Frances. 'Mr Dempsey, are you all right? You don't look very well.'

'No, no, I'm fine, fine. I was just woolgathering. Won't be long now till Christchurch is hidden from us altogether.'

She followed his gaze across the river to where the great bulk of the new civic offices had begun to obscure the outline of the stately old cathedral.

'Strongbow wouldn't approve,' he said lightly.

'Desperate altogether,' she agreed. 'I don't know where it will end.'

She spoke as if there had once been a golden age when everything was in its proper place. It was difficult to say when the rot had set in. During the fiftieth anniversary of the 1916 Rising she had come upon a reconstruction of the battle at Mount Street Bridge on her way to work. Unaware of the film crew she had looked at the apparently bullet shattered windows and the bodies littering the streets. 'They're at it again, I see,' she remarked to a woman beside her.

'But it's yourself, Mr Dempsey, I'm worried about. You should get out and get a bit of sun on you. You should take a holiday. We work you too hard altogether.'

He was touched and made some noncommittal reply.

'No, no, seriously. You need to look after yourself. I know you've had a bad time of things but you have to get back into the land of the livin'.'

Again the same message. He wondered if people had begun to think of him as the late Jack Dempsey. He smiled to himself and she caught his eye.

'Now don't go thinkin' I'm a nosey old busybody but it occurred to me that Mr Sedgwick is going down the country for the long weekend, in fact down to your mother's part of the country, to play golf. Maybe you should go along with him and get in touch with your mother's people.'

'That'd be a good one,' said Dempsey, 'sure I don't know them from a crow.'

'That's just it, isn't it. You cut yourself away from everyone. It's not healthy. That's all I'm sayin'.'

Dempsey grunted. 'Everyone seems to know what's best for me.'

'I remember when you first started here. I just don't like to see you let yourself go like this. Maybe I'm talkin' out of turn but I feel it's my duty. You look rotten and I'm not goin' to stand by.'

It must be great, thought Dempsey to achieve that eminence of age and wisdom where you can direct your shafts of advice and criticism with impunity.

'I'll speak to Mr Sedgwick myself about it.'

Dempsey shook his head. 'That would really make his weekend, wouldn't it. Sure I never hit a golf ball in anger in all my life.'

'You don't have to. Just take the lift down, say hello and get the bus back if you want to. It'd get you out of yourself.'

'I can just imagine it, the Comerford clan and the prodigal nephew. That'd be a good one.'

'Now, now. Blood is thicker than water.'

The absurdity of the suggestion made him smile.

'And how do you know so much about me anyway?'

'Oh,' she replied archly, 'I have my spies.' She tottered away muttering to herself and Dempsey turned his attention to the scene across the river. Old Georgian houses were crumbling and decaying. Buddleia in mauve and crimson sprouted from mouldering brick-work and at the same time machinery chuntered away, pouring concrete over the place where intrepid Norsemen had fortified their clay and wattle village, in wild and barbarous times. Dublin crumbling and renewing itself. Strongbow, he mused, in his tomb in Christchurch would approve, so long as the ventilation works.

'The catalogue,' he muttered to himself and reached into his pocket for a pen. Some of the stuff had come from a convent, an inlaid George III bow-fronted sideboard and matching display cabinet. Very nice. Great women, the nuns, to preserve a bit of furniture. Mahogany roll-top desk. A set of silver fish knives. Old Waterford crystal. The list went on. There is a buyer for everything.

'Oh, Mr Dempsey. This was upstairs in the office. That man brought it in with the picture.'

It was Frances again with a long narrow bundle wrapped in newspaper.

'It's a sword,' she remarked. 'I know you're interested in militaria.'

'Give us a look.' He unwrapped the parcel to reveal a cavalry sabre in a black brass-bound scabbard. The blade slid out with a metallic whisper. The steel was somewhat discoloured and pitted with age.

'My God, that's a dangerous yoke. Be careful with that.'

Frances stepped back in feigned alarm. Dempsey examined the

weapon turning it this way and that.

'A dangerous yoke, all right. What's this? There's an inscription here. J.C. 1798. Now, that's interesting. I wonder ... ah, it doesn't matter.'

'The man said it belonged to an ancestor,' Frances volunteered. 'He said his great-great-grandfather or somethin', carried it at the battle of New Ross.'

'Good God!' said Dempsey sitting down suddenly with the sabre across his knees. 'That's extraordinary.' He slid the blade back into the scabbard. There was a brutally functional quality about the thing. This was no decorative dress or presentation weapon. This was a tool to split a head open or to disembowel a man.

'I'll buy this myself,' he said on an impulse. 'I'll put a reserve on it.'

'What would you want with a thing like that?'

'It's a long story,' he said. 'I'll tell you about it sometime.'

'Now's as good a time as any,' she prompted. 'I was just goin' to make the tea.'

'You know, a fellow tried to sell my father a burglar alarm once. A real smoothie he was. "Elderly people like yourself," says he "should feel safe in their homes." He came on very strong 'til the Da says "I have a burglar alarm" and he pulls out this old bayonet that he used to poke the fire, "and if you don't get the hell outa here, you'll be alarmed too." I won't quote his exact words but that was the end of the sales pitch.'

Frances went upstairs and soon reappeared with a tray of tea and biscuits. She made herself comfortable.

'And what was your long story then?'

'Ah, it's not much really. I once tried to write a book about all that Wexford business.'

'The Rising of 'Ninety Eight? Father Murphy and the Boys of Wexford? I remember all that stuff in school.

What's the news, what's the news
Oh me bould Shelmalier,
With your long-barrelled gu-un of the sea?'

She sang in a cracked voice and laughed at her effort.

'Ah yes. We used to learn that in school, with Madam Gavan Duffy. And how did it turn out?'

Dempsey shrugged. 'Never finished it.'

'Oh!'

'No. Things all went wrong.' He lapsed into silence and fingered the sabre. 'This thing just reminded me of it all of a sudden.'

'I see.' Frances was sympathetic but the desultory nature of their morning's work had put her in the mood for a chat. 'You never talk about your wife and I remember when you were married first.'

Dempsey stopped her with a raised hand. 'Do you mind? I'm sorry. I didn't mean to bring up the past. Just this thing sort of gave me a jolt.'

'Maybe it's what you need. You can't run away from things.'

Dempsey tried a diversionary tactic. 'You sound just like my father. "You have to fight your corner." That was his motto. Loved boxing. That was his great interest in life; that and the army.'

Frances said nothing. Instinctively she felt that he wanted to talk.

'He was in the army most of his life you know. Left it the day after the Congo funerals. Do you remember that?'

'Indeed I do. I never saw so many people.'

'He moved up to Dublin after that. Got a job with the Corporation. A grand cushy job he used to say, if it wasn't for the Balubas. That was his worst term of abuse. Anyone that made noise at night, they were all Balubas to him. He would have declared war on the Congo, you know, after those soldiers were killed.'

'Oh, it was a terrible business. They never got to the bottom of it.'

'They stood their ground I suppose, for all the good it did them. It's very warm in here. I think I'll leave the doors open, let a bit of air in.'

He rose and opened the double doors. Heat shimmered from the roadway and the noise of traffic boomed. A stench rose from the river but bearable because of the flood tide.

'Let a few customers in maybe. I'd better get back to work.'

'But what about your book? You never finished telling me about it.'

'Ah, some other time maybe. It never came to anything anyway.'

'Not yet but there's plenty of time. You're only a young fella.'

Ambushed by memories, he thought, picking up the sabre. Paddy could deduct it from his wages.

'I'd better get on with it,' he said. 'I'll have to put a notice in the paper as well. Can't sit around here gossiping.'

He picked up his list. 'Now what am I to say about this fellow Clifford?' He paused. 'Still, that's a hell of a picture. I wish I had a few bob to buy it myself.'

Frances sniffed. 'If you ask me I'd say she was a bit of a rossie. She has that look about her.'

'That'd look well now: Portrait of a Rossie, by the late John Clifford. I like it.'

Frances rose and gathered the cups. She brushed some biscuit crumbs from the chair. 'I'll have to get one of the lads from the workshop to give this place a good hoover. It's like a pig sty. Now, you mind what I said about the weekend. You can't mope around by yourself all the time.'

She looked again at the painting and patted her carefully permed hair.

'Huh!' she muttered dismissively and departed, rattling the crockery as she climbed the stairs.

The weekend. Sure, why not? The weather was fine. It might be mildly interesting to wander around the town his mother had sometimes wistfully spoken of. There might even be some insight there. He pictured her as a girl, strolling along the river-walk with her friends. He could look at his grandfather's shop and wonder about what might have been. He might even — forlorn hope — be received like the prodigal son, Ginnie's lad come home at last. Fat chance!

'Okay then,' he agreed. 'Tomorrow it is.'

~

The rain began at Maryborough as they came out of the hotel, a light drizzle that drifted in swirling veils out of the west. Soon they could see great herds of grey rain clouds snagged on the ridges of the southern mountains.

'Not much dust risin' today,' remarked Paddy, wiping the condensation from the windscreen. He flicked the wipers and for a moment the road stretched ahead. The windscreen became office glass and shapes distorted again. He drove on regardless, maintaining his course. The windscreen misted up and he wiped it again and flicked the wipers. Steady as she goes.

'Don't like to wear out the wiper motor.'

'What are you saving it for?' asked Dempsey, with a note of rising apprehension in his voice.

'Very hard on the battery, this weather.' It was obviously some deep-seated conviction and resignedly Dempsey let it pass, contenting himself with keeping his half of the windscreen clear. If he was going to die he wanted to see what it was that killed him.

A provincial town can be a dismal sight in the rain and this was no exception. The ruined military barracks loomed over it with daylight showing through blank windows and roofless timbers. For a century the licentious soldiery had left their money in the town and then in an excess of patriotic zeal after the evacuation, someone had burned the place almost to the ground. No doubt the Comerfords, ardent republicans though they might have been, had laid the foundation of their fortunes in victualling the hated oppressor.

'It's a pity they didn't leave the place intact,' said Paddy. 'I'm sure the nuns would have found a use for it.'

As they approached the bridge over the river Dempsey noticed the sign on a large garage and showroom: Comerford Motors, Main Dealers. In the Square were the premises J.W. Comerford, General Grocer, J.W. Comerford Vintner. They had done well for themselves.

'Well there you are,' said Paddy expansively, 'take your pick.' He pulled in beside the kerb where a donkey with water streaming from its back stood wretchedly between the shafts of a low cart. 'And to think I was hopin' for a game of golf this afternoon. Ah well!'

Dempsey took his leave, promising to ring if he should need a lift back on Monday. It was a relief to be on his own to reconnoitre the situation, to case the joint. The trip no longer seemed like a good idea. In fact it had all the attraction of stepping down to the O.K.

Corral to meet the Clanton boys. He turned the collar of his jacket up and decided to brace himself with a pint in the hotel across the way. The best advice is that you should never take a drink when you feel you need one and that you should never drink alone. The obverse of that coin is surely then, that you should always take a drink when you feel no need to and that you should spend as much time as possible in bibulous and gregarious company. The end result is probably much the same.

He surveyed the company in the hotel lounge, the usual cross section of Irish country society. He recalled O Henry's variation, 'the rude four-flushers of the hamlet,' and pleased with his acuity, decided to have another drink. A small bud of optimism began to open in his mind. A feeling of goodwill spread through him. Blood is thicker than water after all. It was not as if he was looking for anything from anyone. In fact it was he that was bringing *them* a gift. He was glad at last that he had come. He slipped from the stool and headed out into the rain, turning his collar up again as he crossed the street. The donkey flapped its ears and blinked the rain from its eyes. It shifted its weight on curved, untended hooves and gave a decidedly negative shake of the head.

~

'Is Mr Comerford about?'

'Mr Comerford?' The shop assistant raised her head from her notebook. She put a pencil to the tip of her tongue. A small purple stain appeared on her lower lip. 'Which Mr Comerford would that be?' She looked him up and down. Definitely not a rep. Definitely not a farmer in for groceries and a roll of barbed wire.

'Well, I don't know. The boss I suppose.'

Dempsey looked around. The back of the shop contained tea chests, baler twine in great stacks, implements of all kinds, buckets, gallon cans, all manner of hardware. An alleyway communicated with the premises next door, from which came the buzz of conversation almost drowning the sound of racing on the television. It might have been a shrewder tactic to have had a drink in there and sort of ease into the conversation.

She pondered the situation and tipped the pencil again to her tongue. 'Well old Mr Comerford doesn't come in any more so I suppose it must be young Mr Comerford.'

'Yes, I suppose so.' The king is dead.

'Is it about a car or somethin'?'

'Well, maybe. Definitely something.'

'You'll probably find him up at the garage. He's there most of the time.'

'Ah, right. I'll head over there then.'

'That'd be the best of your play.' Her eyes flicked down to the notebook and she jabbed a line of purple dots alongside a column of figures.

'Ten, twenty-three, twenty-seven, forty,' she intoned, dismissing him.

'Right then. Thanks a lot,' said Dempsey.

She inhaled sharply and began again at the bottom: 'ten, twenty-three, twenty-seven ...'

Blast it, he thought and stepped out into the rain. He felt the damp penetrating through the soles of his shoes. By the time he realised that the shop had stocked umbrellas he was soaked to the skin.

Young Mr Comerford, he figured, was not much older than himself. He exuded the bonhomie and confidence of a man on top of his game. His suit, impeccable in every respect stopped just short of being flashy. He shot a mean cuff with a discreet flash of gold cuff-link as he clapped a departing customer on the shoulder.

'That'll be all right. I'll look after it.'

He spoke with the assurance of hereditary power and influence, a natural for politics and *droit de seigneur*. He turned and regarded Dempsey with a flicker of puzzlement. Dempsey was aware that he cut a sorry sight. He brushed a wet lock of hair from his forehead.

'Desperate day,' he began almost by way of apology for his appearance.

'It is that.' An incipient double chin gave a slight wobble. 'Bill Comerford. What can I do for you?' He smiled, as Dempsey's mother used to say, from the teeth out and debated extending a hand, thought better of it and nonchalantly put it behind his back pending developments. Tumblers clicked in his brain. A trade in? A banger at the very most.

'You wouldn't know me, Mr Comerford, eh, Bill. Dempsey is my name — Jack Dempsey.'

No light of recognition went on. 'How can I help you, Jack? Jack Dempsey. It's a good name.' Again the smile.

'Well I was just passing and I thought I'd look in, y'know.'

Something flickered in the eyes. The suave manner faltered momentarily.

'Jack Dempsey, you say? Not from around here?'

'No, Dublin. As I say, I was just passing and I thought I'd say hello. You see, we're related and I just thought I'd look in ...'

'Well my God.' He reached forward at last and shook Jack by the hand.

'Dempsey, of course. Yes, I've heard of the Dempseys from my parents. My goodness your mother would have been my father's sister. Bit of a tiff there I gather in the old days. All before my time of course. Yours too, I imagine.'

'Aye, water under the bridge, I suppose,' nodded Dempsey. 'Well there you are.'

'All gone now of course, all that generation. My father is barely in it himself.' He looked suitably sombre. 'Ah well, ah well.'

Dempsey wondered what next. He was not a man for small talk.

'And what can I do for you, Jack?'

This was more direct, cutting through the formalities. If you want to borrow money get to the point and be done with it. Absurdly Dempsey wondered if he should mention the fatted calf. A smile tugged at the corners of his mouth. He began to see how he stood. Should he go for a fiver?

'No, nothing at all, Bill. As I say I just thought I'd look in.'

'Great, Jack, great. It's great to see you. I often wondered like, y'know.'

'Yeah, me too. You know how it is.'

'Yes, of course, old son. Look we really must get together sometime for a drink. Talk over old times. Catch up on the family history.'

Dempsey saw the flash of gold, felt the friendly hand on his shoulder.

'Next time you're passing. Give me a shout. Up to my tonsils here at the moment. You know how it is.'

'Yes, of course. That's the way it goes.'

The hand patted him on the shoulder and he found himself at the door. They shook hands amid mutual expressions of delight at having met and regret at having to part so soon and again he found himself in the rain. No mention of birthrights or litigation there. You have to admire skill even when getting the bum's rush. You could vote for a man like that. He felt he should have tried for a fiver. Even a tenner would not have been out of the question.

He looked at his watch. Sundown would be too late to get out of town. If he hurried he could catch the Dublin bus.

~

At least the bus was warm. He took his jacket off and spread it to dry on the luggage rack. Steam rose from his shirt and trousers. He slipped off his sodden shoes and spread his legs to allow as much warm air as possible to circulate. It was going to be a long evening and he had neglected to bring anything to read. He looked back at the town receding in the distance and wondered how his mother had felt when she looked back, like Lot's wife, at her childhood home for the last time. How she must have longed for a glimpse of that grey clutter of houses and the red sandstone spire of the church on the hill. She used to sit in the window of their upstairs sitting room watching the people going to and coming from devotions in the evening. She had seen Halley's Comet, she told him once, from the garden behind the house. Her father had shown it to her. It was tangled in the bare branches of the pear tree. She remembered when the Union Jack was hauled down outside the police station and a strange new flag went up in its place. How she had met his father he never knew but she had run away with him and that was it. A sudden dip in the road cut off his view of the town.

He looked at his reflection in the window. Dusk was gathering outside and as if by way of apology, the sky was breaking to reveal a spectacular sunset. He recognised that he must have presented a most unprepossessing appearance to his cousin. Smug, patronising bastard. He could have made a bit of an effort. Dempsey felt a sudden urge to drive his fist into that suave and smiling face. He clenched his fingers and imagined with grim satisfaction his cousin falling back with blood streaming down his immaculate shirt front. Let that be a lesson to you.

It was ridiculous. To be fair the fellow was only protecting his patch, like any cock robin. It was not his fault that the Comerfords had thought Dinny Dempsey an ignorant lout with the blood of patriots on his hands. Maybe they were right. It was a bad old time.

The sun was sinking in resplendent colours towards the North West and rising up in the distance, silhouetted against the light, was the great pile of the Rock of Cashel. He watched it as it seemed to grow out of the landscape, incongruously thinking of the theatre organ coming up from under the floor, a masterly and dramatic entry.

Who needs a book? he mused. The stories are all around us if we have eyes to see. There was a bishop of Cashel who put a king in his place. The king, Henry II, remarked that what struck him about the Irish church was the notable absence of martyrs. 'No doubt,' says the bishop, 'Your Majesty will soon remedy that deficiency.' Better than 'who's your fat friend?' anyway and grimly prophetic too.

It was a good story. Dempsey loved a yarn. It still nagged at him, the story of the Wexford men and their doomed uprising. He remembered reading *Treasure Island* and the sense of desolation that overcame him when he finished the last page, at the thought that he could never again read it for the first time. He could never again wonder how it would turn out. Never could he dread the sinister tapping of Blind Pugh's stick outside the door or watch young Jim climb to the futtock shrouds with Israel Hands in hot pursuit. There was that instant of release when Jim fired and Hands lurched backwards, staring in surprise and fell, turning in a slow somersault, dwindling and plunging into the coral blue waters below. Ahar, Comerford, ye swab.

A girl in Saturday night finery had boarded the bus out of the darkness. As she looked at him strangely before moving further along, he realised that he had spoken aloud. That was the trouble with a good yarn. It can take over from reality. That was the bit that Elaine could not understand. Little John had understood though. He had given Dempsey another crack at *Treasure Island* too. He shivered. He must be getting a chill. He turned his head towards the darkness outside. It was raining again and the raindrops driving against the glass streamed down the gaunt and sallow face that stared back at him. The girl, alighting at her destination, looked at him with momentary pity as she might at any maudlin drunk bewailing the cruel blows that life had dealt him. And each day dies with night.

CHAPTER NINE

Midsummer day, reflected Dempsey as he turned the corner onto Bachelor's Walk. Who would think it? He turned his collar up as a sharp wind sweeping down river plucked at his lapels. He shivered and suddenly short of breath he began to cough. Midsummer and it felt like October. The world teetering away from the sun and the nights starting to draw in.

He caught his breath again. It must be the unseasonable weather. Must have got a chill. Bachelor's Walk. Was this where young blades came to promenade and catch the eyes of passing damsels? Did Regency bucks have aerosols too? Scotty and Doyler had been there, extolling the merits of the skinhead way of life and assuring the world that Mary is a ride. Everything crumbles and decays, buildings, manners, society. He paused and coughed again, rasping for breath. Winter just around the corner.

A hand slapped him on the back.

'That's better, Jack.' It was his employer, looking decidedly chipper in blazer and flannels.

'That's what the guidebooks call a bracing day, eh, Jack. Bracing.'

'Is that the word?' wheezed Dempsey conscious of a pain in the side of his chest. 'I dunno.'

'Come on man, step it out.'

The phrase reminded him of his father. 'Walk in step, for Christ's sake.' That really irritated the Da. An occupational fetish no doubt.

'On the tiles last night, Jack?' Paddy gave a short guffaw. 'You look a bit hung over, I must say.'

'No, no. I guess I caught a bit of a chill last week. Feel a bit knackered.'

'Nice piece you did for the papers,' said Paddy. 'Looks well. I notice you didn't kill off the artist.'

'No. Trade descriptions and all that. I don't want anybody coming back to us complaining that they saw him walking down O'Connell Street.'

'No,' laughed Paddy, 'I suppose not. I looked him up, you know. Quite a story there. Seems the row with the bishop was about the stations of the cross in some chapel out the country. The bishop ordered them taken down and your man held out for his money. A brave man in those days.'

'When was that?' Dempsey was intrigued again.

'You'd have to ask Frances. She knows all about that sort of thing. Enjoys a good murder.' He laughed again. 'Y'know, we used to go out to Ireland's Eye, Maureen and I, in the old days. Take a picnic, that sort of thing. Have a dip in Kerwan's Cove. I'd always say to her that that was where oul' Kerwan murdered the wife. I can tell you it kept a civil tongue in her head for a while.' He chuckled again.

'What was the upshot with your man Clifford?'

'There was a hell of a row. The Yank who put up the money for the stations didn't want him paid. Neither did the bishop but I gather he got his money. Took an action against them.'

'Some trick.'

Paddy produced his keys and unlocked the security grids.

'There was a time when you could stroll in this town at night and look in the shop windows. Now it's like a bloody fortress. Give us a hand with this.'

The grid was a ton weight as they manoeuvred it indoors. The rooms were chilly so Dempsey left his overcoat on. An occasional viewer wandered in as the morning drifted by.

Paddy came pounding down the stairs.

'Jack, I'm going to have to leave things in your capable hands for a little while. Have to see a chap about a few bits and pieces.'

Left to his own devices Dempsey sat down and had a look at the paper. The notice of the sale looked quite impressive, especially the photograph of the portrait which featured prominently — 'a significant work by a colourful figure ... instinctive and sensuous portrait ... subtle and beguiling' and more of the same. Bric-a-brac, he reflected bleakly, the detritus of vanished lives. He felt the urge to lie down but knew it would appear incongruous to the viewers and strollers who prowled among the furniture, occasionally catching his eye and looking away quickly for fear of betraying their interest in some article or other.

It had become intensely cold. He began to button up his coat, but the effort was too much for him. There was something wrong. He had become feeble.

'Mr Dempsey.' It was Frances. 'I've brought you a cup of tea.'

'I don't feel too spry, Frances. I think I'll have to go home. Must have caught a bug of some kind.'

'Oh my God,' she said, alarmed. 'I'll call a doctor.'

'Not at all. Maybe you could get me a taxi. Just need to lie down for a while.'

The effort of speaking exhausted him. He wanted to escape, like a wild creature to his lair.

'I'll do that,' she nodded, and hurried away.

~

He woke to the clatter of the door knocker reverberating through the house. It was Paddy.

'Good God man you look terrible. When you didn't turn up yesterday or today Frances made me come and see how you are.'

Dempsey realised that half-dressed and unshaven, he was a sorry sight.

'I'm taking you to see a doctor,' insisted Paddy. 'I have the car outside.'

There was no point in arguing. The doctor diagnosed pneumonia, suggested hospital, which Dempsey refused in the obstinate way of invalids, and prescribed complete rest.

Paddy insisted. 'Go back and talk to him again, man. You're out on your feet. I'll drive you down straightaway.'

So it was decided with a phone call and Dempsey found himself in Emergency clutching his letter of introduction.

'Next of kin?' queried the secretary holding her pen over the form.

'Next of kin? Em.' He hesitated. The absurd thought occurred to him that he was officially an orphan. He gave Elaine's name and the address of Tomgarrif — 'but there's no need for her to be informed,' he added quickly.

'Just take a seat there Mr Dempsey and there'll be someone to see you in a few minutes.'

He looked about him. This place is a death trap, he thought. Nothing but sick people around, walking hatcheries of every conceivable germ and bug in the business. It's war all right and we are all the walking wounded. He was getting morbid.

There was a fellow in the ward who suffered from an ulcer.

'What do they know about an'thin?' he growled, dismissing the medical profession as a crowd of quacks and mountebanks. 'Any time I get a bit o'trouble I just tamp it down with a few fuckin' pints.'

Dempsey was too tired to argue. The fellow slipped out during the night and must have applied the remedy because he was back again the next day, the centre of a flurry of activity. The ulcer had perforated.

'You're a lucky man,' said the doctor to Dempsey. 'One lung was in danger of collapsing. We just got you in time. Let's have a listen.'

Dempsey pulled off his pyjama jacket and the doctor probed and percussed and applied a very cold stethoscope. 'Hmm,' he murmured but he kept his conclusions to himself.

What would he know about it anyway? thought Dempsey ruefully. He would have been glad of a pint.

The nurse handed him a bottle, a misshapen wrynecked receptacle.

'I need a sample,' she said in matter-of-fact tones.

'Right,' said Dempsey, anxious to co-operate, but he foresaw a problem. There must be some protocol about this business. He could hardly ask the nurse, an attractive young girl and anyway she had gone without saying how soon she wanted it.

The man across the aisle might be the one to consult. Some sort of a foreigner, he went on a lot about his bowels and the vind and the vater. Obviously an expert. Perhaps you just sit on the side of the bed and fill the bottle. 'Lovely weather and how's every little thing?' No, better to slink off to the lavatory with the bottle concealed about his person. A big bottle though. He was sure to meet someone on the way back. A dangerous lunatic with a concealed weapon. Is that a gun you have there or are you just glad to see me?

Cowardice prevailed. He lay sideways and slid the bottle under the bedclothes. He managed by careful manoeuvring to urinate what he reckoned to be a respectable amount into it. A furtive glance showed a sort of plimsoll line almost up to the now horizontal neck. This could be a delicate operation, a situation fraught with danger. Carefully he slid the bottle towards him but a minor miscalculation tipped it just sufficiently to send a small tsunami spurting all over the sheet.

'Oh shit,' he swore under his breath, faced now with embarrassing explanations. Conversely he could discharge himself like the man with the ulcer and drown his humiliation in a few pints. It was too late. The nurse had returned. Abjectly he mumbled about his accident. She was a very attractive young woman indeed. She drew in her breath without a word, whipped the bottle out of his hand and went to find some clean sheets.

With a bit of luck, thought Dempsey, I might be dead by the time she gets back. Paddy arrived with the traditional grapes and some magazines. Dempsey decided to exorcise his embarrassment by telling the story against himself.

'Ho, ho, ho,' chortled Paddy. He was the only person Dempsey had ever met, except for Santa Claus, who laughed like that. 'Ho, ho, ho,' he wiped a tear from his eye.

'You're a desperate bloody man.'

'Well,' said Dempsey, 'I'm glad I brought a little brightness into your life and me here on me bed of pain.' But he could see the funny side of it up to a point.

In the morning he watched the young nurses at work. Lithe and efficient they moved as if in a ballet. Elaine had been like that undoubtedly. He played the old soldier a bit and they forgave him for his mistake. He found that he was enjoying being looked after. The doctor came again with better news and told him that he could go home again in a day or two but that he was to take complete rest.

Word got around. A neighbour brought him some dinner. The Mad Gunner left the paper in every morning. It became a high point of his day, the rattle of the letterbox and the thud of the folded newspaper. Paddy called again and took him to the doctor. No exertion, insisted the doctor. He maintained that Dempsey had been neglecting himself, that he was completely run down.

Dempsey began to enjoy the luxury of idleness. He was definitely on the mend. The paper became his lifeline to the outside world. There was a report of a sale of fine art at Sedgwicks — some very interesting pieces — a portrait of a Mrs Francesca Curtis by the late John Clifford made £3,500. So he was dead again. There was a photograph of the painting and elsewhere in the magazine section, a feature article on a neglected genius.

So this was John Clifford. The photograph put Dempsey in mind of an old daguerreotype — the beard, the wild staring eyes. He was like some old Fenian or a gunfighter caught forever on the collodion plate.

There was an account of the Baltrasna Chapel controversy and a photograph of the bishop, the fastest crozier in the West. There was a lot of indignation at the power of the hierarchy in those far off days and at clerical interference in civil matters with a rider to the effect that things had not changed all that much. There had been a deal of controversy in the correspondence columns but the artist was on a loser. After all the bishop was bound to know more about sacred art than a man who got involved in a public brawl resulting in the deaths of two men. And furthermore he was a Protestant and wasn't there a suggestion of further scandal? Anyway the bishop said to get rid of the whole bloody lot and that was an end of it. The writer bewailed a lost masterpiece, another victim of clerical obscurantism and predicted an increased interest in any surviving work by Clifford. A bit of notoriety does no harm at all. All battles long ago.

He felt hungry and wondered what his neighbour would bring him for dinner. He decided to get up and have a shave. That always helped. He was still a bit wobbly on the legs but overall there was a definite improvement. People, he reflected, had been very decent to him. He was not used to that. It came as a bit of a surprise that anyone would notice let alone take the trouble to look out for him. He looked at the scruffy individual in the mirror and wondered. Maybe there was something there worth salvaging after all. He took a deep breath. The stabbing pain was gone.

Paddy was pleased to see him up and about.

'You know it was nip and tuck there for a while.'

'Well I'm grand now,' said Dempsey, 'grand.'

'Indeed you're not. You could be back on the flat of your back in a day if you don't watch it. I tell you what I'm goin' to do. I'm goin' to pay you a month in advance on condition you take a break.'

He unrolled a bundle that had been wrapped in brown paper. 'However, I've knocked a few bob off for this yoke. Mind you don't cut your head off.'

Dempsey took the sabre. 'Hey, I'd forgotten all about this. That's great.' He placed it on the table. 'I appreciate all your help. Are you sure you can manage without me?'

'No problem. Look I have to go.' Paddy made for the door in some haste and Dempsey realised that he had been without his customary cigarette. The consideration touched him as he watched his employer departing in a cloud of smoke. He became aware of the silence in the house and felt the urge to go out. The sun was shining. It would be good to be on the move.

He looked at the old Volkswagen. If it had been in working order he could have gone for a spin. Out of curiosity he got his keys and tried the engine. It wheezed, a bit like himself. Something snagged inside in the works and amazingly it spluttered into life. These Germans built to last. The engine protested. The car shuddered and backfired and suddenly the engine settled to a steady whine. He pressed the accelerator and the engine responded.

'Well I'll be damned!' he said aloud, pleased with his discovery.

There was still the matter of the flat tyre and tax and insurance but the knowledge that the thing still worked put a different complexion on the day. He let the engine idle and checked the shelf under the dash. The length of pipe was still there. He decided against trying to change the wheel for the moment. Maybe it would be better to get someone to come and have a look at it. He had forgotten how good it can feel when a machine actually works.

It was as if something had snagged inside himself too, the little acts of kindness done to him, even the laughter at his own discomfiture. It was a good feeling to be alive. He felt an indefinable seed of hope germinating inside himself. He would face up to things from now on and at least try to put his life back together. He was impatient to be on the move. The doctor had warned about not overdoing things but what would he know about it?

~

'They're a great oul' car,' said the mechanic. 'There you go now.'

He swilled some oily scum into the battery.

'Shouldn't that be distilled water?' queried Dempsey. It was a bit like the hospital where you hand your body over to total strangers.

The mechanic snorted. 'You'll get no distilled water around here.'

Distilled water must be for the quality, not for the likes of him. The mechanic slammed the boot shut and slapped the roof encouragingly.

'There she goes. You could invade Poland with a car like that.'

He drove out beyond the airport and turned off the main road into leafy country lanes. The hedges were white with hawthorn blossom and the sun was shining. He felt good. The engine hummed an even note. All the omens were good.

He glanced at a signpost, Naul five miles. He had never been in Naul. He drove on. Another sign and another pointed to Naul, two miles, four miles. He wondered if he had missed it. A fourth one said Naul nine, Baltrasna nine. All roads lead to Naul. He wondered if it existed at all or whether it was like the nexus of the Southern Cross, a theoretical point from which people take their bearings but never actually go there. Baltrasna nine. It was a toss-up. The name was familiar. Baltrasna, yes, that was the place with the famous chapel. It could be worth a look though the chapel was probably in ruins. On an impulse he turned the car in the direction of Baltrasna.

CHAPTER TEN

Dempsey saw the stooped figure of a man cutting grass on the verge outside Baltrasna chapel. The scene was one of rural peace, a Constable sketch. He pulled in to the verge, being careful not to trespass on the green sward, got out and engaged the man in conversation.

'Ah yis,' said the old fellow, 'I remember the Yank Finnucane, all right. Hehy, heh. A great man to buy a drink.'

He leaned on his scythe, glad of the opportunity for a chat. The triangle of grass in front of the chapel could wait for a while.

'Heh, heh.' He fanned himself with his cap. 'Used to come over every summer.' He chuckled again at the memory of some escapade and then assumed a solemn expression. 'Gone now this long time, God rest him.'

Dempsey waited for a suitable interval, out of respect.

'How the fucker didn't kill himself years ago I'll never know.' He laughed again. 'I remember one summer he bought one o' them whaddyacallems, one o' them Vespas, just to get around to the races an' that. Fell off an' broke his leg. A desperate man.'

The Yank, it seemed, was a character, given to the drink, but protected from serious harm by that special angel assigned to look after the wealthy. There is a *quid pro quo*, as the Medicis had earlier divined. In return for special consideration in this and the world to come, the rich make generous donations to the church and provide the wherewithal for the odd coat of paint.

'Had a couple o' pubs in the States, y'know. That's the on'y business to be in, I'm tellin' you.'

Dempsey nodded. It is received wisdom, the nearest thing to heaven — a couple of pubs in the States.

'Knew his business all right, the Yank. D'you know if anyone started a bit of a barney, the Yank'd hop over the bar with a bit of a lead pipe and put a stop to it.' Mine host, the tradition of hospitality.

'So what gave him the idea of restoring this place?'

The old chap shrugged expressively. The chapel was in itself, unremarkable. A barn-shaped, pebbledashed building, it was surrounded by a high wall and green, feathery ash trees. The gravel walk was in good trim, kept clear of moss and dandelions. The old chap followed his appraising look.

'I do a bit of tippin' around, like, just to keep things in order, like, y'know.'

'Did you know the fellow that did the window?'

'Ah, your man John Clifford? Jays, of course I knew him. Hell of a decent skin, he was. He lived around here for a while. A Protestant he was, but a very decent sort, all the same. Ah, well.' He shook his head. 'Ah well, there y'are now.'

'Is the place open?' asked Dempsey. 'I'd be interested in having a look inside.'

'Well now, I'm your man.' He rooted in his jacket pocket and produced a large, old-fashioned key. 'You have to keep things locked nowadays, even the chapel. There's that many gurriers around, they'd take the eye out of your head.'

The hinges creaked as he led Dempsey into the cool interior. It was a typical old wayside chapel with pale green walls and the occasional attempt at a gothic arch around the windows. The altar was an incongruous chunk of granite balanced on three stone legs, post-Vatican II decor crying out at the nineteenth-century plaster altarpiece that clung grimly to the end wall.

'Is that where the famous window was?' asked Dempsey pointing to the long office glass gothic-style opening.

'The very place,' agreed the guide. 'Jays, you should of seen the way he had it.'

He looked around. 'Jays, sure didn't I have to put three coats of emulsion over the whole bloody lot.' He lowered his voice and nodded apologetically towards the altar, 'Beggin' your pardon.'

'How do you mean? Were there pictures too?'

'Jays, pictures. He had all the bloody walls painted. You should of seen them.'

Dempsey looked around at the lime green emulsion. 'I'll hardly see them now, will I?'

'Indeed'n you won't. It took me a good three weeks to paint over them. Three coats, exterior quality too. The bishop wasn't havin' any of it. I still have to touch it up now and again.'

'What was it like?'

'Ah Jays, arson, rape, murder. You name it. He said it was a panorama of Ireland's sectarian history. That's what he said, Ireland's sectarian history.'

'That would keep him busy right enough,' observed Dempsey wryly. 'What put that into his head?'

'Wouldn't you know? The Wexford men. That's what he told me. The last of the Wexford men was buried on this site. I'll show you the stone outside.'

Dempsey felt a strange tingling on the back of his neck, as if the Wexford men were still there. Not the sturdy Boys of Wexford renowned in song and story, but the remnant of a scarecrow army, straggling down a country lane, hunted like vermin from the hedgerows, ridden down by mounted militia.

They stepped out into the sunshine. The ash trees threw lacy patterns on their faces.

'That's right. They came down that road,' he pointed with a bony finger, 'from Nobber in the County Meath, so my grandfather told me. He said his father seen them; seen the bodies thrun in a grave in that corner over there. That's why the chapel was built here.'

He showed Dempsey the stone, a slab of grey limestone. The inscription was eroded to a series of indentations. Medallions of white and orange lichen covered the exposed surfaces, reclaiming it, hiding the wound of the stone mason's chisel. By stooping down and looking at an oblique angle the shadow of a cross could be discerned.

So that was it, the end of the line. Within sight of their mountains, the blue frieze of Wicklow, with their faces turned towards home, they had met their fate.

He wondered what they had hoped to do; to slip through Dublin like foxes in the night and hide themselves in the mountains, filtering homewards week by week, month by month? When all else fails, turn towards home. It was his fate he felt always to start a story at the end and ravel it backwards. Turn towards home, he thought, even if it is impossibly distant. What else is there?

'And what happened to the window?'

'Hah. Don't talk to me about that window. Do y'know where it is now — this is a good one.'

He took Dempsey by the elbow. 'It's in one of them discotheques, in a pub down the town. A discotheque, do you mind. Isn't that a good one?'

'That's a good one all right,' agreed Dempsey absently. He was still visualising the ragged army, the fighting men, cautiously rounding the bend in the road. He pictured the troops drawn up to meet them, some stirring uneasily in their saddles, perturbed by the reputation of this peasant army, others fortified by stirrup cups, looking forward to a day's hunting.

'I said, it probably would still be here if he hadn't got involved with that oul' huer.'

'What was that?'

'The window an' that. It'd probably still be here if he hadn't got involved, like I was sayin', with that oul' huer.'

'Oh, I see.' In fact he did not see very well.

'That's why. The bishop told the parish priest to take the whole lot the fuck out of it.'

His Grace had a way with words. 'There was all that business of the court case and your two men up at the Hellfire Club.'

'What was that? It rings a bell.'

'Aye. All that carry on. I suppose your two men asked for it, but the fact of the matter was, your man Clifford was carryin' on with that oul' huer, and he a married man.'

'But he wasn't one of ours, was he? I mean it was none of the
bishop's business. No skin off his nose, if you see what I mean. What
happened about the court case?'

'Ah, manslaughter or somethin'. He done a year in the Joy. Went
to England after that.'

The old fellow retrieved his scythe from where it lay against the
wall. He rooted in his pocket and produced a long whetstone. Every
depiction of a peasant army shows them with scythes. More likely
to cut your leg off if you tried to attack someone with that, or
decapitate a comrade.

The blade whined.

'Right is right, no matter what. The Bishop had his job to do.'

He took an experimental swipe at the grass.

'A decent stick and all that. But you couldn't have that kind of
carry on in a chapel.' He laughed a short gargling laugh. 'All bloody
fine in a discotheque.'

He leaned on the word in a mixture of incomprehension and
contempt.

Dempsey hesitated, wondering if he should offer him some
money for his time but decided not to risk it.

'What's that discotheque place called? I might have a look in.'

'Mulciber's, they call it. It used to be a respectable house. The bar
is still reasonably okay.' He spoke as one who had given the matter
a deal of thought. 'Still, I dunno.' He paused, enlightenment setting
in. 'I tell you what. I could show you the place.' He put down the
scythe again. 'The grass will hould till I get back.'

He was right of course. The grass would last another day but a
story should be taken on the hop.

'And what do they call you anyway, around here?' asked
Dempsey as he held open the car door. 'I'm Jack, by the way.'

Diffidently, as is the usual way. A name is a powerful thing, not
to be treated lightly, a handle to get a grip on a person, even a
weapon to use against him.

'Oh Patrick is me given name but I'm known generally as The Pa.
Pa will do fine. It's followed me this many a long year.'

'What about the scythe?' They could hardly take it with them with the blade protruding out the window like a motorised Queen Boudicca, chopping the heads off passing countryfolk. There was a time once when he had carried some lengths of two-by-one in like manner only to have them swing wide on a bend, dislodging a very angry cyclist. That was in the days when he had enthusiasm for doing jobs.

'Sure, leave it inside the gate. I'll get back to it soon enough.'

There was a filling station, perpetually *en fete* with faded bunting and beside it an extensive licensed premises with an authentic Victorian reproduction shop front. An extractor fan wafted the smell of cooking into the street and Dempsey realised that he was hungry.

'Would you fancy a bite to eat?' he asked and his companion visibly brightened.

'Bedads, I wouldn't say no.'

Soft music enveloped them as they followed the neon pub-grub arrow into the dimly lit interior. It seemed to leak from hidden speakers and swirl like fog in the semi-darkness.

Fascinated, Dempsey watched his companion emptying a number of plastic sachets onto his shepherd's pie, turning it into a Jackson Pollock with a variety of multicoloured sauces. This was a man who appreciated good food. There had been no awkward wrangling at the cash desk. Pa had heaped his tray and Dempsey had paid. A good yarn is worth a meal any day.

'Anyway, you were saying.'

'What was I sayin'? Begod, I can't remember.' Pa scratched his temple and absently contemplated his almost empty glass.

'You'll have another,' said Dempsey rising and going to the bar.

Idly he contemplated the television screen. The picture, brightly coloured, was startlingly clear, unlike his own battered black and white. No wobbly line started at the bottom and worked its way upwards only to start again at the bottom as if the picture was mounted on a drum. The newscaster did not appear to be speaking from the depths of a blizzard.

He became aware of a woman observing him from the end of the bar. She appeared mildly amused. He caught her eye and looked back at the screen. In one glance he noted that she was a good age, wore far too much make-up for her years and let her hair grow too long. It curled in towards her chin like two hockey sticks, he thought incongruously. The eyebrows had been removed and a new pair pencilled in. Pencilled in. Right enough, that usually meant leaving room for adjustments later. She sat crosslegged on a high stool and looked like a woman who could damage a gin and tonic. She was somehow familiar.

Two pints appeared in front of him.

'Yiz'll have to be quick. It's nearly two o'clock.' The Holy Hour loomed like a great cantle lopped from the day. In an instant he resented the illogicalities of the licensing laws. It would have been pleasant to sit in the confessional half light and while away the afternoon in idle conversation. He turned with a pint in either hand and caught the woman's eye again. He felt a sudden dart of pity, almost contempt. If she got her hair cut she would not look so ridiculous. The eyebrows, permanently arched and the heavily painted face gave her the look of a geisha.

'Anyway you were telling me,' prompted Dempsey, seating himself once again.

Pa rolled his eyes in elaborate pantomime and jerked his head towards the other end of the bar. Dempsey smiled, misunderstanding.

'Do yourself a bit of good there maybe.'

'Tell ye later,' said the old fellow rolling his eyes again. He addressed himself to his plate, scooping up great forkfuls and munching with relish — and mustard and some brown sauce.

'I'll tell ye again.'

'This place must be going to the dogs.' Dempsey realised that she was standing behind him. Her voice was throaty as if raddled by years of cigarettes. 'Since when did you start frequenting the lounge?'

Pa drew himself up where he sat and wiped his mouth with the back of his hand.

'I've drank in better lounge bars than this one, me good woman.'

Dempsey turned to look up at her. On closer inspection he could see that she was an elegant figure of a woman, probably quite good looking in her time if it was not for the hair. Bangs, that was the name for that particular style. The word was almost off limits nowadays in polite company.

He thought he saw a white flicker of a scar on her chin.

'And who are you leading astray now, might I ask?' She looked appraisingly at Dempsey who began to get uncertainly to his feet.

'This gentleman is an associate of mine,' declaimed Pa. 'He's a very distinguished historian by the way. I'm assistin' him in his researches, if ye must know.'

'Indeed.' She looked at Dempsey again with a hint of mischief. 'If it wasn't obvious to me that he was a gentleman, I'd have you sent back to the public bar where you belong.'

Pa made a disparaging noise. 'This used to be a respectable house before all this.' He waved his hand to suggest the depravity of carpets and piped music.

Dempsey began to see the light. The woman pulled at her hair, twisting it between finger and thumb and brushing it forward across her cheek.

'Dermot,' she called to the bar, 'give this gentleman another drink and I suppose you'd better pull one for this old reprobate too.'

'Very kind of you,' murmured Dempsey.

'Yiz'll have to be quick,' urged the barman. 'It's well after two o'clock.'

There was no hurry on Pa. He still had a plate of apple tart and custard to attend to. The woman was turning away.

'Is there any chance ye'd show me associate that famous window of yours?' Pa kept his eyes down and Dempsey fancied he saw a flicker of a smile as the pint rose mechanically to his lips. She turned again. The eyebrows had arched even higher. The barman was pulling down the blinds and making the kind of noises that suggest that valued and esteemed customers have now become a bloody nuisance, to be discommoded and insulted at will.

'Yiz'll have to get a move on there.'

'By all means,' she replied, ignoring the flurry of activity. 'Come with me.' She led him into what he divined to be the long shed that jutted alongside the filling station. 'So here we are then.' The room was in almost total darkness.

'Wait there a minute.' She left him and he was vaguely aware of her fumbling around near a small podium at the far end of the room.

Suddenly there was a crash of percussion and Dempsey was blinded by lights flashing from all directions, even from the floor, which was now a pavement of luminous squares. Lights chased each other along what looked like garden hose draped along the walls. Rhythm pulsated from every quarter. The woman's image flickered like an automaton in flashing stroboscopic beams. Dempsey's shirt glowed under ultraviolet and he was aware of a speck of gravy, black like a mortal sin on the dazzling whiter than white.

'Jesus Christ,' he swore and suddenly it was dark and silent again. He heard her throaty laugh.

'Just thought I'd give you the full treatment. Diabolical, isn't it?'

'Well, it's not my scene, I have to admit.'

'Nor mine,' she agreed from somewhere in the intensified darkness, 'but it certainly packs in the youngsters.'

'Why Mulciber's?' asked Dempsey and waited.

'I'll show you now, in a minute.' She fumbled again and a glow appeared behind the podium, a tall gothic window that reached to the ceiling.

'Through the miracle of the rheostat I give you ...' she drummed her fingers on the microphone ... 'Mulciber himself and all his works and pomps.'

Mulciber fell, pin-balling off planets, plunging headlong into the inferno. Colours more vibrant than Van Gogh's glowed in dizzying whorls. Figures as terrified as those of Guernica looked up as if warding off a hail of fiery shot and Mulciber laughed as he fell, shorn of his celestial radiance.

'*From dawn to noon he fell,*

From noon to dewy eve, a summer's day ...'

The words came back to him from long ago and he murmured them in the tones of the old professor with the trembling hands. He murmured them almost like a prayer.

'*And with the setting sun,*' her voice beside him startled him,

'*Dropped from the zenith like a falling star,*

On Lemnos, the Aegean isle.'

There was a catch in her voice, the cigarettes again.

'You know the poem, then,' said Dempsey breaking the long silence.

'Oh yes. I'm familiar with Mulciber.' She paused. 'What's your interest in him, anyway?'

'Oh, not a lot really. I'm just naturally curious.'

'What do you imagine he's saying there?'

Dempsey looked at the face of the falling angel. Why the laugh, as if he had pulled a fast one?

'I really don't know. It's a bit of a puzzle.'

'Well, I'll tell you. He's saying, "Ah fuck it." That's what he's saying.'

Dempsey reacted with surprise. The language did not fit.

'He had everything going for him and he blew it, as they say.'

'Who? Clifford?'

'Mulciber. You know. Top of his profession; the golden boy but he always had to win. Everything else took second place.' She twisted the lock of hair nervously and it seemed as if there was a certain bitterness in her voice.

'It's a strange place for a work of art like that, if you don't mind me saying so,' ventured Dempsey.

She laughed, a short dry laugh. 'Oh, I got it for a song from the owner, an American. I think he was glad to be shut of it.'

'The Yank Finnucane?'

'That's right. Did you know him?'

'Not exactly. Heard about him though.'

He felt her withdraw from him both mentally and physically.

'Well anyway, now you've seen it.' There was a click and the lights died away.

'If you'd like another drink Mr ...'

'Dempsey. Jack Dempsey.'

There was a pause while Dempsey waited for the gag.

'If you'd like another drink, Mr Dempsey, you're welcome, but as they say, yiz'll have to be quick.'

Pa had dozed off in the comfort of the lounge and it seemed a pity to wake him. Dempsey took another pint and sipped it, illegally, without any great haste.

'Dermot will look after you when he gets back,' she said. 'I'll leave you to mind the sleeping beauty over there. Call again some time.'

Dempsey rooted in his pocket for his tablets. It is dangerous to state the exceeded dose. He blinked and looked again. Caution, keep away from children. Cynical so and sos these chemists. He had fallen behind with his dosage so he popped two into his mouth and washed them down with a swig from his pint.

There was a bottle outside in the car too — an expectorant but it was out of reach. Very strong stuff too. Great Expectorations. Dickens spent some time in Dublin. That would look well — *A Novel of Talbot Street* by Charles Dickens.

He had had enough to drink but he was trapped. This was the point in the movies where the coward panics and runs amok: 'We're trapped, trapped like rats I tell you.'

Dermot came and went, making great play of washing some glasses and scowling in Dempsey's direction. There was an agreeable lassitude creeping over him. Don't worry chaps we'll drink our way out of here. A good man in a tight spot.

CHAPTER ELEVEN

It was Pa's idea that he should spend the night in the sacristy of the chapel. The alternatives were spending it in some ditch or the arms of the law. There was a bench where he could doss down in reasonable comfort. He knew there was some vague ordnance against sleeping in cars when under the influence of drink. He took a rug and a cushion from the car and tried to make himself comfortable but every time he put his head down he heard his pulse banging frantically in his ear.

Perhaps it was an echo of the unfamiliar disco music, thumpa, thumpa, thumpa or perhaps he should not have taken the few extra swigs of his medicine in order to make up for lost time. It is dangerous to state the exalted seed. At least the heart was still pumping even if it sounded like a forlorn old lag banging on the pipes in the depths of some dark-pile of a prison.

He sat up and put his head in his hands. Vague whisperings sounded around the chapel, the ash trees grooming their lacy foliage. He listened. There was white noise in his head and a great silence all around save for the whispering of the leaves. The dead of night. He regretted thinking of the phrase but it was apt. He looked at the glow-worm dial of his watch. Two-thirty.

There had been a plan to build a nuclear power-station at Carnsore, Hieron Akron, Ptolemy's headland of priests. A distinguished senator had assured the public that there would be no more danger to the public health than would come from wearing a luminous watch or for that matter, from the Wicklow Mountains. The friendly giant of nuclear energy would see them all right.

He looked at the watch again. Two-thirty-two. Furthermore, if the power station were to blow up, the prevailing winds would dump the lot on England and Wales. Why else would God have decreed that the prevailing wind should come from the South-West, if it had not been to spare the good Catholic people of Ireland from leukaemia and genetic mutations? No the watch was the real danger. Mutants always come for their victims in the dead of night, like mummies or zombies, the walking dead, dragging tattered funereal bindings as they shuffle inexorably towards their prey.

He listened. There was definitely a shuffling sound on the other side of the partition. This place had been painted by a murderer. A skeleton army lay buried in the grounds. He lay down again, wrapping the rug about him and tried to sleep but the shuffling came again and he felt his skin crawl. Maybe the old fellow was a Hitchcock character who would burst in at any moment with his scythe. Maybe he was some rural mutant product of inbreeding, some Hill Billy retard who got his jollies from decapitating unwary wayfarers. 'Come into my parlour,' said the spider to the fly.

He said it again to make himself laugh, as he imagined Boris Karloff might have said it, deep and resonant and sinister.

A bleary light crept in through the glass over the door. A dark shape became visible, an old clerical mackintosh. The shuffling came again, more persistent this time. What would the Da have done? He would have waded in with a roar, ghouls or no ghouls.

Dempsey stood up and braced himself.

'Okay you bastard,' he shouted and threw open the door to the interior of the chapel. In the dim light he saw a sparrow whirring up at an angle into a crevice at the top of the wall. In sudden relief he laughed aloud and exhaled a great gasp of pent-up breath. He sat down weakly on the altar steps. His heart was thumping. The sparrow chirped in annoyance.

'Keep your shirt on,' said Dempsey. He pointed an admonitory finger. 'You're lucky I don't have a shotgun.'

He sat quietly and his heartbeat subsided. He remembered serving Mass with the lads and their version of church Latin: 'Adam cut the leg o' the cat. You can shoot him if you aim.'

'You can shoot him if you aim.' He looked up at the sparrow. A bright bead of an eye regarded him from the darkness of the crevice. A shaft of pale light slid along the wall from the high window and he watched it brighten as it searched the far end of the chapel, illuminating the green baize of the confessional.

Pure sunlight, he noticed, with no myriad of dancing specks as would be found elsewhere, no wandering spores of fungi, no pollen, no spirochetes, dust, caesium or strontium 90 to invade the air passages and lay the fragile victim low. This was a place of safety, a sanctuary. He might spend his life here like Quasimodo, secure in the sacred purlieus of Holy Mother Church. He could ring the bell to call the faithful and scamper, a benign hunchback, up and down the aisle with the collection plate. He closed one eye.

'The bells, the bells,' he groaned and laughed aloud. The laughter rebounded from the tiled floor and the empty pews. He felt decidedly better. The sunlight seemed to have taken the chill from the air.

He began to notice shapes appearing on the wall, shapes etched by shadows and light as in low relief. Perhaps he was a visionary. This could become a shrine, hordes of desperate people seeking cares, seeking guidance, kneeling at his feet, reaching out to touch his garments as he moved gently among them. Make a fortune. He looked more closely.

The images were palpable to his fingers. He was no visionary. This was more of a bad paint job. The painter had used a stone paint, an exterior quality without priming the surface. The paint had blistered in places and was covered in a maze of tiny cracks like the glaze on old china. He probed experimentally and with a click, a small shard of paint flicked off. The surface should have been sized and primed. Leonardo had the same problem — always in too much of a hurry to see the finished product.

Dempsey had tried to buy size when he had first started in Sedgwicks.

'And what size would you like sir?' said the shopkeeper and there seemed to be some essential ingredient missing from the transaction. It was like the communication gap between the zookeeper and the man with the load of antelopes. 'No, you don't understand. I have gnus for you.' He probed again, expertly with a thumbnail and several flakes detached themselves and fluttered like snow onto the toes of his shoes. It would be a simple matter to clear the whole wall, like a conjuror making images appear at the touch of his fingers.

He could see a hand clutching what must be a flag. By leaning sideways he could deduce that the flag was streaming in the wind like a plume of smoke. It was smoke. He picked some more. The hand held a twist of burning straw. He knew what it was. Ireland's sectarian history, the man had said. It was the barn. It was an infant hurled into the flames. It was like a blow to the solar plexus. Petrol blazing from his hands and flames hiding his face. Fluttering like a little bird and beating at his garments.

Dempsey felt his stomach heaving. Blindly he staggered outside, fumbling at the latch. He retched violently into the long grass. The scythe was there, leaning against the wall. There was a thin film of orange rust on the blade. He twisted as another paroxysm seized him and gasped for breath. Tears blinded him. There was no getting away from it. It could never be painted over. He leaned his forehead against the cold stone of the wall and shuddered. He must face up to things. He felt the resolve forming in his mind. He would go and talk to Elaine in the cold light of day and one way or another they could get on with life.

He pulled a handful of long dewy grass and held it to his face. It smelled fresh and clean. He wiped his hands and looked about him. His gaze fell on the stone that marked the resting place of the last of the Wexfordmen, the Croppy boys. They would never go back but he might, like old Clem, even if it meant an old age of bitterness and self-reproach.

He took his belongings from the sacristy and pulled the door shut behind him. He felt like someone embarking on a great voyage. If he drove straight away he could be there in a couple of hours. No, that would be too abrupt. It would be better to write, to prepare the ground, maybe even phone, but immediately he drew back from the idea. A phone call elicits an immediate answer. Better give her some time, time to reflect and maybe even forgive. He determined to write as soon as he got back to Dublin.

He sat into the car and took another swig of the cough mixture. It would be as well not to rush things. It might be better to wait until he had got his strength back, 'til he was in the whole of his health as they say. It would be wise to do it in easy stages, to pace himself as it were, to give it some time.

An idea began to knock at the back of his mind. He could retrace the footsteps of the rebel army. It would impose a pattern on his journey, give him a sense of purpose. There was a nice sense of completeness about the idea, an inevitability that would carry him along. He could pick up the thread of the story and wind it back until it led him home. The shortest way is sometimes the longest way or is it the other way around? The letter could wait a little while longer.

He felt hungry all of a sudden. He took another antibiotic. Maybe the doctor knew a thing or two after all. He could be in Dublin in half an hour as the roads would still be empty. A good breakfast and then who knows? He turned the ignition key and the engine sputtered into life.

~

Each day's journey would begin from his father's house. He could see them in his mind's eye like spokes on a great wheel. He would go north to Tara and Mountainstown, where the last battles had taken place, then west to Kildare and Hollywood House where Moore, invariably courteous, had insisted on paying the housekeeper for his dinner and drank water as the cellars had been looted. Then he would head south to Glendalough, to Seven Churches and to Glenmalure where the armies had almost drowned in the mire. Inevitably the spokes would turn and he would come to Bannow and then to Elaine. There was a poetic unity in the whole scheme convincing him that it could not fail. It looked good on paper as he pinpointed his objectives on the road map.

~

He could see why the High Kings of old had made Tara their eyrie
and why people worship their gods in high places. The place had its
own aura of menacing power and regal solemnity. Those who came
to Tara came either in triumph or as hostages. It was no wonder that
the rebels came there as if to draw on its ancient strength but hunger
and whiskey did them down.

He shivered. Pillars of rain marched across the plain from the
west. He coughed. He must renew the prescription as directed. He
was not out of the woods yet. Brightly clad tourists moved below
him and sheep nibbled the grass all about. The tombstones in the
graveyard spoke of foreign wars. He was impatient to be away again
on his journey.

His quest brought him from Tara, northwards to Mountainstown
where the last rebel priest of 'Ninety Eight was killed. Corbally had
shot him. Squire Corbally, the priest-killer, a Catholic too. 'Only one
of our own can kill me,' said the priest before the battle, the skirmish,
the scuffle. Corbally, the loyal Catholic, the renegade, the Uncle
Tom, depending on how you looked at him, did what Protestant
bullets could never do. The priest died by the little bridge and his
blood is wet on the stone to this day.

Dempsey hacked at the concealing nettles with the length of
gun-barrel piping that always rattled on the shelf under the dashboard. Some bloke up in Kilmainham made those shelves. Made a
fortune. It was a wonder the Germans never thought of making
them.

There was no blood on the stone. There was an inscription,
illegible of course, and a vague shape which was probably a cross.
Again the elements had cheated him. Lichen camouflaged everything.

He took a photograph, hoping that some trick of the light might
reveal the message. He even hoped that the dead priest might
appear on the film, violent energy imprinted on the light-sensitive
plate. It has been known.

He photographed an old gnarled ash tree, imagining how it might have looked on the day that Corbally and his detachment of the North Meath Militia trotted down that narrow road. The North Meath uniform — red coat with black facings, just like the North Cork. The Wexford men must have felt that Nemesis had found them, that the old enemy had sprung from nowhere to have another go. The power of colour. It was a pity that none of that could come out on the film. Anyway he had run out.

~

The pharmacist gave him another film.

'Free?'

'Yes, it's included in the price of processing.'

'That's very nice of you,' said Dempsey. It was a while since he had got anything for nothing.

'Just part of the deal,' said the pharmacist. 'Now if you're really going for high quality colour, that's a different matter.' He launched into a discussion of technicalities and Dempsey nodded without understanding, anxious not to be taken for an impostor.

'Call back in a couple of days,' said the man in conclusion and Dempsey left the shop, idly turning the box of film in his hand. That was how drug pushers operate. They give you a few free samples until you get hooked and then they have you for life. The problem would now be how to give up photography. He might become one of those people who lie in wait for the unwary and spring upon them like the funnel-web spider, with a bundle of snaps. Or he might develop an interest in filters and light meters and assorted gadgetry. This free film business was only the tip of the iceberg, thin end of the wedge, rock we perish on. That film had been in the camera for years. He hoped it had not perished too.

There was a chap once who lectured about shipwrecks along the south Wexford coast. 'The captain was drowned,' he said sadly, 'and despite the efforts of the Kilmore lifeboat, the crew were ... the crew were ...' he searched for a rhetorical flourish, 'perished too.' What else could have been expected?

At long last something clicked in his head. The story that he had begun needed another half, an antiphon to rebellion and battles. It needed the story of the retreat and of Clem making his way back through mountains held fast in the grip of winter; Clem lying low in smokey hovels, scavenging from starving country people and shivering under the pitiless stars.

Dempsey was cold. His cough was troubling him again. He really should have gone back for a check-up. But he had embarked on a plan and the pattern could not be broken, like Dr Johnson with the railings. He turned up the heat and set off in the direction of Bannow.

CHAPTER TWELVE

There was a bend on the familiar road where Dempsey had always imagined that the car could fly. It was simply a matter of going straight through the flimsy fence instead of taking the turn and the ground would fall away below. Centrifugal force would give the extra impetus. They used it to sling rockets around Saturn, so why not?

Why not? That would be the way to arrive home, spiralling down out of the clouds, an Immelmann turn, just for show and coming to rest, light as thistledown in the haggard. It is better to travel hopefully. In his euphoria he had given little thought to arrival. Presumably they would be glad to see him. She would understand and share his optimism and newfound sense of purpose. They could make a new start.

There was a story he had read somewhere about a fellow who stepped out one evening to buy himself a cigar and returned twenty-five years later. 'I waited for a streetcar,' he replied to his wife's understandable query. There was Rip Van Winkle. There was Ulysses. He was in good company. His rag-bag mind offered further examples. He wondered why he always cloaked serious matters in absurd and trivial comparisons. There was a gambler in *Showboat* who wandered off for a whole generation and was warmly received by his elderly wife and his middle-aged daughter. Anything but face reality. All might yet be well. Oh yet defend me, friends. I am but hurt.

At last he came to Bannow. He stopped the car at a distance and climbed a sand dune. The wind shrilled through the stiff marram grass like ... Chico. Or was it Gummo, Zeppo, Harpo?

Look at it, he told himself. Look at it. A deserted ruin, bare gable ends giving the impression of a great molar embedded in the sand; sightless windows, a black hole where the door used to be. The sand had sifted inside. He was afraid to approach.

He sat down heavily under a weight of weariness. His mind was like putty. He could not think. The wind whistled. One of them never spoke. Dumbo? Larry? Mo? Curley?

The waves made their familiar patterns, rhombus, trapezium, opening, closing, angles narrowing, coalescing into a single line, crumpling on the sand. He could never go back. He was a stranger there. Always the wind blowing, plucking at his shirt, tempting him. The pain. A void that could never be bridged. Sand sifting around him, frittering away.

He heard a voice saying 'No use,' and realised that it was his own. It was enough to rouse him. 'No use at all,' he mumbled and trudged back to the car. Get away from here. There was always a line of sand down the centre of the road. Here and there a yellow weed had taken root in it. Long stems of summer grass brushed the side of the car. A thistle lashed against the windscreen. Away, away the engine whined.

He saw the bend and pressed hard on the accelerator. That was it. A fence post shattered, barbed wire screeched on metal and suddenly he was flying.

~

As his vision cleared he found himself stumbling along a familiar road in the wake of a red-coated horseman. A noose constricted his breathing. He was obliged to hold the rope to prevent himself from suffocating. It seemed as if his head was bulging and must soon explode with the pain but he had to keep up the pace. The horseman never looked around but he knew him all the same. This was retribution at last. The man never spoke but occasionally he jerked the rope or kicked his mount into a trot. The May blossom was gone from the hedgerows. It had been an unusual year for May blossom, the best anyone ever remembered, a good omen. There were two brothers in the army, two little dark-skinned men, the Quick Men, as they were known. He had never known their names. They had commented on the May bush. It would be a good year for them, they said. A good year for haws. They scattered haws and sold the seedlings for quickset hedging. They laughed. The countryside seemed covered in snow that June, what with blossom everywhere. One of them was hanged in Edenderry. He knew nothing of the other. The haws were green and small.

There were men blocking the road, horsemen. He knew them at once, Hompeschers in their distinctive green and red. Extravagant plumes wagged on their turbaned shakoes. They were laughing as they looked at him, enjoying a joke with his captor. They drew back and let the strange pair, horseman and prisoner, pass. The rope tightened on his throat and pain seared through him. There was a ruined cottage by the roadside and the smell of woodsmoke in the air and the sharp, salty sea wind.

They left the region of low hedges and the countryside softened around them. Ash trees inclined to form an archway over the road. Sunlight slanted through lacework, blinding him. He closed his eyes and stumbled on. If he was to hang it made no difference now. Nothing made any difference, not since Ross. All the rest had been either blind fury or an animal instinct to survive. Grandiose plans and stirring rhetoric. What did it matter now? Had it not been for the rope around his neck he would have laughed.

And then he knew that he was dead. Hanged. He felt no pain. He heard bees and the sound of leaves rustling. He opened his eyes. The horseman was gone. Bees were working industriously at a clump of lupins, investigating snapdragons, creating a living orrery around a clump of marigolds by the roadside. He sat with his back to a tall gatepillar and watched them. They nodded their heads and carried on with their work, pleased to be noticed but intent on their task, like children hungry for praise. So this was what heaven was like after all. He was absolved and all his suffering was at an end.

~

'They called me at the hospital,' said Elaine. 'They said you were in an accident.'

'I don't think so,' said Dempsey hesitantly. 'It just took me a long time to get home.'

It must have been a long time indeed. She looked older and thinner and he was sure that there was an incipient greyness about her temples. 'I'm sorry it took me so long. You must have had a very difficult time of it here. I should have come sooner but there were many hazards along the way.'

She was silent, regarding him warily. He realised that he was in bed in a familiar room; twelve small panes in the window; a cedar tree making dark diagonals across the rectangle of light.

'You should sleep for a while,' she said gently. 'You've had a nasty bump on the head.'

Tentatively he touched his forehead. It was bandaged — not for the first time, he thought. There was a binding of some sort around his throat.

'You'll have to keep that on for a while,' she admonished, 'until you're back on your feet again.'

A great wave of tiredness overcame him and he closed his eyes. He saw a straggling band fighting a doomed rearguard action on muddy country lanes. Walk in step, for Christ's sake. He recalled the cold and starvation of winter in the mountains and the wind cutting through rags of clothing and he drifted into sleep.

'You're an awful bloody man,' said the voice. 'You gave us a terrible fright altogether.'

He opened his eyes again. The sun had moved around, away from the window.

'We thought you were done for.' The man's voice was familiar, an old man, part of the place by the sound of him.

'So did I for a time but he must have let me go. I thank God for my deliverance.'

The man frowned. 'Be that as it may, I'm glad to see you on the mend.'

Dempsey smiled. He knew this old fellow.

'You have been well then,' he asked, 'all this time.'

'Aye not too bad, considering. By the way, the guards told us about your car. We went along with the tractor and hauled it out. You must have been doing a fair old speed.'

Dempsey said nothing. He puzzled over this information. There was some question there, the answer to which eluded him.

'I'll leave you alone then, for a while,' said the old man. 'I dare say you could do with a rest.'

The room was darkening and he wanted to sleep. At intervals he awoke and saw the moon sliding along the branches of the tree. He heard the familiar creakings and rustlings as if the house were speaking to him.

He awoke again to the sound of voices and a bright light shining into one eye.

'Really should have taken him in,' said a man's voice, 'but I think he'll be okay.'

The light shifted and fingers prised open his other eye. This had happened before. No more boxing. In the midst of the light he saw the familiar jellyfish shape squirming and writhing.

'I'm okay,' he shouted. 'I'm okay,' but the light had left him blind.

'Just be still a moment,' said the voice again and he heard Elaine saying his name.

'Elaine?' he asked and blinked to clear his vision. 'How in the name of Christ did I get here?' he asked between fear and hope.

'You had an accident,' she said slowly. 'The car went off the road.'

There was an inflection in the way she said it, like getting the story straight. Suicide, he thought ironically, is still a hanging offence in Ireland. Careful, careful.

'I remember now. I thought she could fly. Worth a try anyway. Douglas Fairbanks.'

The doctor was closing his case. He placed a jar of tablets on the bedside table.

'If they're needed,' he said to Elaine.

She thanked him. At least, thought Dempsey, they're not putting them out of reach, for fear that he might lay violent hands upon himself. Where had he read that? Castlereagh.

'What about Douglas Fairbanks?' Elaine turned after seeing the doctor to the door.

'I dunno. I read somewhere that he used to jump off things just for the hell of it, especially in the dark. Like Thomas Aquinas.'

'What happened to him?'

He was losing the thread again.

'Broke his legs, as far as I remember.'

'Aquinas?'

'No, Fairbanks. What am I rambling on about?'

'It doesn't matter.' She turned towards the window. 'You had us worried. You were rambling all night and calling for someone by the name of Tom. Who's Tom?'

'Tom,' he repeated. 'I don't know any Tom.'

'Daddy sat with you for a while but you didn't know him at all. I suppose he's aged a lot in the last few years.'

A silence fell between them.

'And the others?' he asked awkwardly. 'How are they?'

'Fine. The girls have grown up. They're away in college now. Working in London for the summer.'

He noticed that she still wore her rings. She was twisting them on her finger.

'That's good,' he replied. 'Young women of the world.' It was an awkward attempt at joviality.

'I wrote,' she said after a while, 'a few times, but I never posted them.'

'I wish you had,' he mumbled. 'I'm sorry,' he said after a while. 'I'm so sorry about everything.'

'I'm sorry too, Jack,' she said fidgeting again with her rings. 'We didn't do too well, did we?'

He said nothing.

'Well,' she said brightly, turning towards him again and assuming the air of the professional nurse, 'we have to get you back on your feet again, Jack.'

First name terms, like nurses always do.

Now Jack, none of your nonsense. Time for your medicine, Jack. Tuck in the blankets so that you can't move your toes, Jack.

'You'll have to wear that neckbrace for a while anyway.'

'Christ,' he said, involuntarily fingering the brace, 'for a while there I thought ... It doesn't matter.'

'I have to go to work,' she said, 'but I'll be back this evening.' She touched his hand tentatively, brushing a finger over his knuckles. Becoming self-conscious, she patted his hand comfortingly and left the room, giving him an awkward little wave.

~

'They were a grand car,' volunteered Mr Synnott, coming up quietly behind him. Dempsey turned from where he had been regarding the battered Volkswagen. The bonnet was sprung and twisted and the front axle looked sadly out of line. The car, with its shattered headlights and twisted fender had assumed a quizzical grin.

'A grand car altogether, but you've made a bit of a Paddy's arse of it, I'm afraid.'

'I can't argue with you,' agreed Dempsey ruefully. 'I suppose I'm bloody lucky to be alive.'

'I dare say.' He tapped the mangled metalwork with his stick. 'Used to be able to get three ewes in the back of a Volks.'

He pronounced it 'yeos' and for an instant Dempsey's mind went off on another tack.

'Aye, I see what you mean.'

'I'm afraid she's had it,' said Mr Synnott finally, having prowled around the car and peered gloomily underneath.

'Chassis's gone. You're a bloody lucky man, all things considered.'

'I suppose so,' agreed Dempsey resisting the urge to nod. His head felt like an egg in a very small egg-cup.

'I'll have it taken out of your way as soon as I get organised.'

'Ah,' snorted the old man, 'don't be bothering yourself about that. That doesn't matter a damn. It's yourself and herself that matters.'

Dempsey said nothing. He had no reassuring platitudes.

'Y'know, I always felt you might come back. It'd be for the best if ye could make a go of it again. Herself has never been the same. Never been able to forgive herself for what happened.'

'Forgive herself? But sure it was all my fault. I don't want to go into all that again. I know she could never look at me without thinking ... you know ... without it all coming back again.'

He had not looked for this conversation. He knew now that coming back had been a mad idea, like most of his mad euphoric schemes — a blind leap in the dark. Now that he wanted to get away he had no means of transport. It stood before him spavined and reproachful.

'Well now, between you and me, she blames herself still. There was a sick horse and she was delayed. She could have left it to someone else to look after but she didn't. She assumed you'd be at home anyway.'

'I never knew that,' mumbled Dempsey. 'I never knew that. Oh, my God.'

The old man gripped his arm.

'Jack,' he said, 'Jack, there is no blame. Ye did your best. It just happened. I've said as much to her. There comes a time when ye must stop punishing yourselves.'

Dempsey was aware of the sound of pigeons in the trees. He heard the leaves rustling and small twigs clashing. He tried to put his thoughts in order.

'Funny thing,' said his father-in-law, 'when I saw the bees all around the gate I had a funny feeling. Isn't that a good one. And there you were right enough. Just like the story I used to tell you about Old Clem. The bees always know, y'know. A kind of an omen like.'

'Well I had the strangest dream then,' said Dempsey. 'I remember the bees. I saw yourself in it and I thought you were Tom Garrif.' He laughed self-deprecatingly. 'I always get the wrong end of the stick.'

'Tom Garrif. Well now. And we wondered about that. Y'know she sat up with you two nights on the trot. You were rambling on and talking very odd. Anyway that's all over and done with now.

You must look to the future.'

It was an unfamiliar notion. Dempsey shrugged and winced again.

'I dunno,' he said. 'I just don't know.'

'She's a very strong woman but the photographs nearly destroyed her. I never saw her so cut up. Did she say anything to you about them?'

'No, not a word. What photographs?'

'The ones in the car. She wouldn't show them to me.'

'Photographs?' he thought, frowning. They must have been the ones he had picked up from the chemist. He remembered now. He had not even bothered to look at them, just thrown them under the dashboard with all the other junk.

'No, she never mentioned them,' he said, suddenly fearful of what they might show. Ghosts, phantoms.

'I'm sure she'll talk to you about them in due course.'

Memory, thought Dempsey not for the first time, lies in ambush.

'I never knew you were a bit of a photography buffoon.'

Dempsey looked at him sharply, suspecting a jibe, then thought perhaps that he had traced the source of Elaine's uncanny gift for the telling phrase. The Nobel Prize for genetics; the isolation of the Malaprop gene.

'Not really,' he said. 'I usually get my thumb in the way or something like that.' There was a silence. 'So she went back to the nursing again. I hadn't realised.'

'Aye, this couple of years. Gave up the riding centre altogether.'

Dempsey felt unaccountably glad, as at the elimination of an old half-forgotten rival, a small vindication, guiltily enjoyed. He kicked at a tyre, pensively as he had seen experts do, a diagnostic technique that rarely bodes good.

'Your stuff is all inside in the house. We put it in a holdall, your camera, tools and such. It's a wonder it wasn't stolen.'

Dempsey took it that he alluded to the camera. He had assumed the guise of the photographer, the kind of man who put the safety of his equipment before his own; a man who would keep clicking away amid a storm of shot and shell; a man who filched moving and luminous images from the squalor and majesty of life. He should have cases of attachments and accoutrements, mysterious light meters and flash bulbs, like a real photography buffoon.

CHAPTER THIRTEEN

He was sitting at the table in the kitchen when she arrived home.

'The guard was here again,' he said, toying with a mug of coffee, 'about the accident. He seemed to be suggesting that I did it on purpose. Sort of dropping hints and looking at me sideways. You were proceeding in a northerly direction in your vehicle,' he said ponderously and gave a wan smile.

She busied herself at the stove. 'And what was the outcome?'

'Oh not much. Just to be more careful any more.' Any more implies a negative. It should be in future, but he was hiding in the quaint diction of the policeman. The man of a thousand voices.

She turned from the stove and said levelly, 'What really happened, Jack?'

It was the first time she had used his name familiarly, not like a nurse. He looked up at her from where he sat. 'Would you believe me if I told you I was trying to fly? I was just too tired to go the length of the road; all those bends and corners; all those gear changes. Everything gets tangled up. I wanted to fly, away out over the water and over the land. For a minute I thought she could do it.'

They were aware of the clock ticking on the shelf. The room was darkening. He thought of his thread of life, paying out behind him and tangling and twisting into inextricable knots.

'It's like an arrow,' he went on, explaining it to himself. 'You shoot it up and up, up in a straight line but gravity starts to work on it even

from the start, pulling its path into a curve —' he sketched it with
his finger on the table — 'a parabola, pulling it down. I wonder if
the first half of the curve is the same shape as the second half. I just
wondered.'

She watched him guardedly. 'And you didn't fly?'

'No, no,' he shrugged, 'bit of a disappointment really. I suppose
you think it was a bit mad.'

She lifted the kettle and shook it. Shards of lime rattled inside.
'Empty,' she remarked unnecessarily, going to the tap.

'I went back, you see. To the cottage. I was going to come and talk
to you but then I became afraid and wanted to get away.'

'Afraid? Of what? Of me?'

'Just not able to face you after all this time. Afraid you would still
hate me for what I did.'

His voice came dull and flat to her ears. There was no tinge of
self-pity or exculpation.

'Not you,' she said after a while. 'Not you. I have never forgiven
myself.' She snatched at her bag and put the package of photographs
on the table. Bright and shining they slid from the envelope and he
stared at them. Christ, he thought, these have been in the camera all
the time. Pictures from another world: one of Elaine and the little
boy on the beach; another of the two of them in the water. She was
shading her eyes against the light. There was one of the three of
them, a delayed action shot where he had set the timer and dashed
back to stand beside the car.

He regarded the scattered images without touching them. He
knew that she was weeping now.

'In that time I ...' he began, rising and going towards her. 'In all
that time I never blamed you for anything that happened.' He felt it
was the truth, insofar as anyone knows the truth.

'But, oh Jesus, I never thought ...' He touched her awkwardly on
the shoulder. She wore a navy uniform cardigan. 'I never realised
you blamed yourself.'

She turned towards him and leaned against him as if overcome
with a great weariness. He put his arms around her and felt tears,
wet against his shirt. 'Oh Christ, what a fool,' he said. 'What a fool.'

She was sobbing silently with little animal shudders. He could smell her perfume and felt the softness of her hair against his cheek. A tear slid down the side of his nose and tickled him. He wished he had a free hand to wipe it away. He sniffed and sniffed again and a third time, louder than before.

'Still sound like a boxer,' she said with an attempt at a smile. She pushed him gently away. 'I'm sorry,' she began again, wiping at her tears, ineffectually with the back of her hand.

'And so am I,' he interrupted. 'You have no idea how sorry.'

He checked himself. You could hardly come back like Lazarus from the dead and expect to sit down for a cup of tea and a chat about old times. Lazarus, they say, carried the smell of the tomb with him to his dying day, that is to his dying day, take two, to be exact — the absurd breaking in again, like a deranged chorus.

'When I saw those pictures that you had kept,' she began quietly, 'I knew that I had to say something.'

He realised her misapprehension and went along with it. A drowning man is hardly very choosey about the kind of rope that is thrown to him. Aircrash survivors in the high Andes eat their less fortunate fellow passengers. Say nothing. All may yet be well. Even the Pope has pronounced on it. The chorus urged him on, gibbering at him from the shadows. Some day he would tell her that he had never known about the photographs, but not yet. Not yet.

'I think I know what you mean about gravity,' she said sitting down at the table. She began to sort wearily through the photographs, devouring them with her eyes and biting her lower lip. Furtively he studied them over her shoulder, recognising the bridge where the rebel priest had died. Fortunately no spirit had decided to manifest itself. There were enough ghosts for one afternoon. He knew that he would always blame himself for what had happened, as Elaine would blame herself. There are dark corners in every human heart that no one can look into without flinching. But if she could share his pain he would gladly carry hers. It hurt to look at those images of the past but he realised that he was glad of the pain.

Her mother came shuffling into the kitchen driven by the instinct to cater for the menfolk. She was old and walked with a stick, but a fierce pride decreed that she should have a meal on the stove for the working men.

'You might like to see these pictures that Jack brought me,' said Elaine, spreading them again on the table. 'Sit down there now and I'll start the dinner.'

The years fell away as he watched her and he felt a surge of terrifying hope.

'I'll just step outside for a breath of air,' he murmured. 'I won't be long.'

The breeze was cool on his face. He leaned against the cornerstone of the house and looked up at the trees. Shadows gathered under the cedar and the sycamore and invaded the orchard and peace descended about him as Tomgarrif welcomed him home.

~

Without a conscious decision Dempsey began to help around the farm. At first he was regarded as something of a convalescent and any attempt at physical effort was advised against. He found that he was an instinctive holder of ends of timber as they were being sawed. He would pick up an unattended fork and tidy a pile of potato haulms for no good reason except the pleasure it gave him to look back on his work. He liked the rough and ready approach to building and repairs and the way fine tuning was as often as not accomplished with the belt of a spanner.

An iron bedstead complete with brass knobs made an excellent fence at a gap in a hedge. Rust was tolerated on machinery as long as it presented no threat to the workings of the engine. A hen took up residence in the Volkswagen which had been towed behind a shed. It seemed the logical thing to throw in a few handfuls of straw to make her comfortable.

'That'll stop her layin' out, the divil,' said Mr Synnott approvingly.

He was allowed to drive the lorry beside the harvester to catch the grain as it gushed from the chute. He took a pride in his skill and stuck his elbow nonchalantly out of the window. He walked the land by himself, woolgathering, letting the tranquillity of the place sink into his soul. He particularly relished the evening when the heat and dust of the day were laid to rest and long shadows stretched from trees and hedgerows. He felt a disinclination to look ahead or to contemplate the future. He felt better without the ridiculous neck-brace and enjoyed the feeling of being able for physical work. The summer was coming to an end and August was trying on its autumn apparel. It was time to consider the future.

'Did you ever think of finishin' that story of yours?' Mr Synnott asked one evening out of the blue. He was leaning on a gate with one foot on the lower bar, regarding with satisfaction a field of stubble. The combine had left long parallels of straw and chaff. 'We'll put a match to that,' he added, meaning the straw, Dempsey presumed.

'Oh, that,' he said, 'oh aye. I've been turning it over in my mind this good while. I have a few ideas all right.'

'Good,' said Mr Synnott. 'That's good. A pity to let it all go to waste. I mightn't always agree with you but it should be written down. That envelope is still below in the house with all your stuff in it.'

Dempsey felt a chill creep over him. He had not thought about actually facing the blank page again. Neither had he given consid-eration to reading what he had written in that other time, the feelings that had prompted a phrase, the fortuitous happenings that had crept into and lodged in his fictional world. Perhaps a line or a scene recalled might wrench at the wound which he had only just begun to believe might heal.

'Well, they're just ideas still,' he said cautiously. 'I still have a few things to straighten out. A few avenues I need to explore.'

'Aye, you do that, Jack, but don't let it go too long. There's none of us gettin' any younger.'

He left it at that and Dempsey noted the unmistakable stiffness in his gait.

~

He stood at the window and watched the flames in the stubble field. The field sloped upwards away from the house and fire rippled along the horizon, silhouetting the branches of the cedar in stark black.

Sometimes when the breeze caught the flames they flared like a solar corona, shooting upwards and curling back upon themselves in graceful arabesques. He imagined horses' manes and Olympic torches and watched small figures flitting back and forth. The smoke, lit from below, rolled like great thunder clouds. He thought of his story and the countryside in flames. He was not aware of the door opening and of Elaine coming to stand beside him at the window and he started when she put her hand on his shoulder.

'What are you doing?' she asked and he thought there was a tremor in her voice.

'Just thinking,' he said, 'just thinking and watching the fires. It's as if a great battle was going on only there isn't a sound. Ghosts battling it out again over the same ground.' He felt her shiver.

'Don't talk about those things,' she said and was silent for a long time.

'Aye, I know what you mean.'

'Jack,' she said and he tensed himself. 'What made you come back?'

So he told her of his life away from her and dark streets and solitary walks. He told her about his drinking and of an old man who had threatened to knock his block off and of the night in the Bridewell. 'In fact,' he said, 'I think I was getting an ulcer or something because the stuff just stopped agreeing with me. I laid off it completely for a long time. You remember the Mad Gunner? Well he said the Da would have been ashamed of me. And to think that I was sometimes ashamed of him. I suppose I was a bit of a shit really.'

She shook his arm in disagreement, bidding him to go on. He became aware of her perfume and it came to him like a shock. He felt her hair brushing against his arm.

'I dunno,' he said. 'I was sort of locked in, you know, going through the motions, as they used to say about the Liffey Swim.' It was an old joke, coming unbidden to mind, but none the worse for that.

'I know what you mean,' she murmured.

'Sort of thinking it was temporary but never able to break out of it.'

He paused again, watching the flames. Black skeletons of trees flickered and danced. Spectral cavalry charged and silent ordnance blazed. 'Next of kin they asked for in the hospital and there was only yourself. I suppose I knew then subconsciously that I would inevitably come back, for better or for worse.' He sniffed. 'I felt like something moved inside me. Ridiculous thing for a man to say. Like a load shifting on a trailer or a cargo, maybe in the hold of a ship. You're not too sure what it is but you know something is different.'

'I know. I know,' she said again. 'I thought I hated you at that time. I thought you were the most self-centred, self-absorbed person I had ever met. I felt you gathered all the suffering to yourself and didn't want to leave any for anyone else, least of all me. I really felt you were punishing me by taking it all on yourself.'

'You couldn't have been more mistaken. I just felt I had no right...that I had lost the right...let you both down so badly.'

'Lightning can strike anywhere,' she replied.

'Lightning, yes.'

'We should have done better, but we didn't. Hating each other and hating ourselves won't bring him back. We owe him that much. Otherwise his little life will not have meant anything.'

'You're right,' he said softly, 'but I feel I don't deserve this.'

'Nobody really deserves what they get,' she said. 'You have to make the best of what you get. It took me a long time to come to that conclusion. A lot of sleepless nights.' She was pensive for a while. 'What was this journey you were going on about?'

'Oh that. I don't want to bring that up again.'

'Go on. Tell me.'

'Well, I'm afraid it was that bloody story I always talked about, or maybe one of your old man's yarns. I thought I was coming home from the Rising.'

'Still on your mind, eh? Is that what brought you here?'

'Partly. Some idea too that I should face things.' He told her about the little chapel away north of Dublin and how the poor Wexford men, those last emaciated stragglers, had found a resting place under a piece of rough Fingal limestone.

'Maybe I was a bit off my rocker,' he suggested, 'but everything seemed to fit. Mulciber, the artist called himself, a peculiar genius. A fabulous piece of work that window, but he seemed to be laughing at everything and everyone. Mulciber you see,' he hesitated, 'is Vulcan the God of Fire. I thought it made some kind of sense. And then in the chapel there was this picture of Scullabogue.'

She leaned forward and put her forehead against the glass. He imagined the coolness against her skin. The light fell on her shoulder, harsh yellow light from the flames, like the crude *chiaroscuro* of comic books.

'Do you think in symbols all the time?' she asked.

'Yeah, symbols, analogies. Never too good on logic.'

'So why, in the long run, did you come back here?'

He pondered for a while.

'I guess it sort of happened. I sort of picked up the end of a thread there and followed it. Sometimes I wonder if the old car made the decision for me. It's funny that she just made it to here and packed up.'

She gave a low reverberating laugh, the first time he had heard her laugh in the time he had been in the house.

'I found an egg in it today,' she said. 'It isn't entirely useless.'

He smiled and she was serious again.

'It's been so long, Jack. It's time to forgive.'

He bowed his head and she came to him and held him.

'Will you stay?'

'I will.'

'Come to bed.' She said it as if they had never been apart.

'Christ,' he said and groaned. 'That was something else I had forgotten.'

'What?'

'The old manroot trouble.' The suddenness of his arousal startled him.

Again she laughed, this time clear and uninhibited. 'I haven't heard that one for a long time.' She began to pick open the buttons of his shirt. He felt the warmth and softness of her body as he undressed her gently and led her to the bed. The light flickered on their nakedness and incongruously he thought those old Biblical chaps had it right when they said that he knew his wife. She had reached him from across the void and he exulted in her.

'So you'll stay then?' she asked again and lay close to him. She used to sleep on the other side of the bed but this was better. He could breathe more easily turning towards her. The influence of the deviated septum on the sexual mores of ... another Nobel prize.

'I will.'

'We could go away for a little while.'

'Good idea.' He wondered if it was all a dream, an illusion induced by alcohol. He passed his free hand down her back feeling the vertebrae and the little hollow at the base of the spine. She was no illusion.

'My parents would like you to stay.'

'You mean for good?'

'Why not? They're getting old. You don't want to go back to Dublin. Anyway you can't.' She was being playful. 'You haven't got any transport.'

'Seriously, do you mean for good?'

'Why not?'

'Okay, your parents want me but what about you? Do you really want me to?'

By way of answer she rolled on top of him and propped herself on her elbows, looking down at him.

'Yes,' she said and traced the line of his nose with her forefinger. 'Yes, I do.'

'Will we be well again?' He could not quite find the words.

'I believe we will. You know the Arabs break eggs at weddings. I'll look in the car again in the morning.'

'You know that old Wordsworth walked across the Alps and all the time he was thinking about reaching the watershed so that he could say he was in Italy.'

'So?' He knew she was laughing at him and his haphazard thought processes.

'So anyway he meets this peasant and he asks him how far it was to the summit and the peasant says "you crossed it ten miles back".'

'So?'

'So nothing. That's just it. So here I am. So somewhere along the way I crossed the watershed and I didn't even know.'

'Very illuminating,' she said with light irony and rolled away. 'What will you do about the job? Not that they'd want a jailbird on their staff anyway.'

'I'll talk to Paddy. I know he'll understand. We can work it out. I know he and Maureen will be glad for us.'

A door was closing on that other life, but he would regret very little of it, only the elegant plunder of the showroom and the kindness of good friends.

~

'It's good to be able to talk about things,' said Mrs Synnott uncharacteristically. Normally she left the talking to her more garrulous husband. 'I can see the difference in Elaine. You've done her good, coming back. It was the best thing that could have happened.'

Dempsey looked at the floor as if ashamed to take credit under false pretences. He was prepared to accept that there was a preordained pattern to events, over which he had little control. He felt a bit like an undeserving prodigal but his happiness offset any feeling of shortcoming.

'The girls will be well provided for, but it has done himself a power of good to think the place will be in good hands after our day.'

She made him feel that he had taken on a sacred trust, that he would not only work the land but would safeguard the spirit of the place for the future. They would have a future. No forked roads would ever sunder them. Everything fitted together. He belonged to Tomgarrif.

CHAPTER FOURTEEN

As time passed Elaine occasionally wondered about her husband. As with herself, no matter how things were going, there was always that residual sorrow, a sediment in their cup of kindness. He sometimes referred to the years of their Hegira, their time in the wilderness and she feared that things were not settled, that they were on thin ice.

It might be a momentary withdrawal, a vacant or faraway look that struck a chord of apprehension in her. She surmised sometimes that there was latent in him a frustrated dealer, an urge to huckster. Was he, she wondered, like a dog that has been cured of chasing hens or sheep, a sober citizen by day but at night — the call of the wild, under the pitiless stars, the yearning for the smell of fear and the warm taste of blood? A bit hard on the antiques trade, she admitted to herself.

The stream diverged from its natural channel and followed a cutting to where an old mill had once stood, the Cut of the Leat they had always called it. The mill was no more than a few shattered walls and the water plunged through the gap where a wooden dam had once blocked it and thundered into the pit, where a wheel used to turn. Above the fall however the water was dark and smooth as glass. Green weeds, combed by the current, swayed beneath the surface. Sometimes he would sit there lost in thought. One day, when she was sure that she was pregnant, she went and sat beside him.

'What are you thinking?' she asked.

'Difficult to say,' he said.

'Be careful you don't fall in there. We were always warned about the Cut of the Leat.'

'Say that again,' he said with interest.

'What? The Cut of the Leat?' she said it distinctly, her accent fracturing the diphthong into two syllables.

'There it is you see,' he said with animation. 'Everywhere else its *late* or *leet* a dam, but here it's *layat*.'

'So what?' Sometimes he had teased her about her south Wexford accent.

'That's the West Saxon break. Your ancestors imported it over eight hundred years ago.' He was excited by his discovery. 'King Alfred probably had a touch of a Wexford accent.'

'Get away. And is that what you were thinking about so seriously?'

'Well no, but it is interesting though, like maybe finding an old boundary stone.'

'You're a funny kind of a farmer all the same. My father, Lord rest him, didn't sit around like the village idiot, chewing grass and staring into the water.'

'Not everybody can be the village idiot. You have to train for it.' He smiled wryly. 'No, seriously look down there. What do you see?'

'Water. Weeds and water.'

'And it's dark and black, isn't it?'

She nodded.

'Now look at those little lads running on the surface, spiders and what not. Precarious existence.'

'Is that it? You're drawing a moral from it all.'

'Not exactly. Sometimes I look in and see only the depths and the blackness and I think of all that has happened and of our poor little lad left to wander all by himself in the dark. I think of him a lot of the time. Then sometimes I see the sky reflected and the clouds flying and little creatures skating over the abyss and for some reason I think he is all right. I'm not a religious man in the accepted sense but I do pray in an odd-ball sort of a way.'

'I think I know what you mean.' She sat forward clasping her hand around her knees like a young girl. A fish rose and made a circle on the surface. Concentric ripples spread.

'If things had worked out different I would have liked to send him to school to the Quakers in Waterford.'

'Why the Quakers?' she said, surprised. 'I didn't think you were a fan.'

'Just a thought. They came here in bad times but I think maybe they got it right in the long run. It takes great courage not to strike back. That's what I admire about them, though I don't think I'd be much good at it myself.'

The fish rose again and flipped over with a slight plop. The light glinted silver on its belly.

'I'm pregnant.'

There was a silence. He threw a long stalk of grass into the water, aiming it like a spear.

'You're sure?'

'I'm a nurse, God dammit. Of course I'm sure.'

He rose and walked away a few paces and stood with his back to her, struggling with his emotions. When he spoke his voice was strained and rasping.

'I never thought.' He coughed. 'I never imagined. Well, like, we got a second chance but I never imagined. Oh God.'

'Quite normal, really,' she said, understanding his confusion, 'all things considered.' It had been a joke of his about Wexford women — 'sturdy breeding stock.'

He came to her and gently lifted her to her feet. 'You'll have to be very careful,' he said solicitously.

She was determined that this child should not be born to any guilt or morbidity.

'It's not a disease,' she said 'and anyway I'm as strong as a horse. Which reminds me, I want to start keeping a horse or two again and certainly a pony when the child is old enough.'

'Well this is a day for surprises. I've no objection to horses as long as I don't have to drive one. I admit my failure in that department.'

'Well obviously I won't be riding for some time to come,' she said 'but I would like to get back to it in due course.'

They were putting their life back together, replacing the fallen pieces, brick upon brick but there were still one or two gaps where the segments did not quite fit.

~

The baby was a girl and they were overjoyed. She was born at Tomgarrif at Elaine's insistence.

'We were all born here,' she said 'and I see no reason why we should change.'

'Do I go and inform the bees?' he teased.

She maintained that the bees had to be told of any birth or death in the family. He was not sure if she had told them when her parents died but she maintained, with a wistful smile, that she had.

'You owe them that much,' she said half seriously, 'after all it was the bees who found you first when you came home.'

So he went in great good humour and declaimed to the bees that Mr and Mrs Jack Dempsey of Tomgarrif in the county of Wexford were delighted to announce the birth of their daughter, to be named later — most probably Elaine, although her mother protested. He liked to think that the bees were pleased with the news.

'Now,' said Elaine, 'I've done my bit so I want to ask you a favour.'

'Say the word,' he replied expansively, studying his daughter's perfect little fingers. 'Ask away.'

'I want you to finish your story.'

He hesitated. He had seen the brown paper bundle in the bureau drawer but had refrained from lifting it out. There was horror in that story which, when he had written it, had been theoretical and imagined. He doubted if he could read of fear and charring flesh without being plunged again into the deepest despair.

'Sure, where would I get the time?' he parried. 'Sure you have me run off me feet, not to mention this young lady here.'

'I just want you to do it. I know it's still in there somewhere.'

'I will sometime,' he agreed. It was a technical evasion. He should have said shall. Even Oscar Wilde, arbiter of style, had problems with will and shall. 'I will sometime. Sometime when I have the time.'

'You owe it to yourself,' she persisted. 'Don't hide your light under a garret.'

'Bushel,' he said. 'You hide lights under bushels.'

'Whatever. And you owe it to others too, my father and me and little John. It was so much a part of his life.'

Below the belt, he thought, but it was a blow like that which had once spurred Dr Johnson into long delayed activity, even if the end result was no great shakes. The one below the belt is the one that does the job.

'You're right,' he agreed. 'You're absolutely right. Unfinished business.'

~

He slid the envelope out of the drawer and looked at it from several angles. The paper was scuffed and limp from handling. He would undoubtedly have to make changes. One of these word-processors would be the man for that. You can slide paragraphs around and make spelling changes at the touch of a button. He could make over a room for his writing and build a desk for the word processor. That was the solution. He would look into it as soon as possible. He slipped the envelope, unopened, back into the drawer — Regency, in burr walnut, a nice piece of furniture. He recalled in embarrassment how he had once suggested to Mr Synnott that he might consider selling it.

When their baby boy was born she raised the matter of the book again and he explained his plans.

'Right,' she said, 'no problem. As soon as I'm up and about we'll get that room organised.'

He agreed and went so far as to buy a desk, a unit designed for a computer, word processor and printer. It came in a simple, self-assembly kit.

He gave it his best. His Philips screwdriver did not fit. It chawed and mangled the screw heads. He looked in the holdall in the back pantry where the tools were kept and found another larger one which completed the mangling of the screws. He also found the invaluable length of gun-barrel which had hardly ever been used, a vulcanising kit, a torch with no batteries and the usual bits and pieces that people keep until the time is propitious for throwing them away.

He tried tapping gently with a hammer using generous quantities of glue and foul language and the structure stood up against the wall, slightly askew, with an aggrieved air. He knew that he could never entrust to it a delicate electronic device. On the profit side, he put the holdall into the boot of his car as a safeguard against any emergency and went to play with his children. Progress was reported and Elaine warned him that she would hold him to his promise.

'Some people,' he maintained, 'write when they are young, full of piss and vinegar, child prodigies, that sort of thing. I'm more of a late developer, a sort of elderly child prodigy. Maturing like good old wine.'

He could always deflect her with a bit of clowning and sometimes he even deflected the niggling voice inside himself. 'If it's in you,' her father used to say, 'it'll come out in its own good time.'

One day he found her with the pages spread out on the rickety desk. She had been reading it.

'You've never even opened the envelope,' she accused 'so I thought I'd better do it for you.'

He spread his hands. 'It's a fair cop, guv'nor.'

'I've been reading it as you can see. I never read it all in one piece. Now I find myself believing it and looking out for the people. Even going along the road I half expect to see soldiers. You caught something there. I want to find out the ending — no matter how grim it may be.'

'That's just you Wexford people,' he retorted. 'You always go on as if the whole Rising business happened the week before last.'

'Still, you'll have to finish it, even for my satisfaction.'

'If only to get a bit of peace, then,' he grumbled. 'I'll read what's there and see how it hangs together.' He would not admit to her his fear.

Writer's block, he claimed, prevaricating. Resting, dear boy, resting, as the down and out actor says, not admitting that he is a bum. 'I'll read it, anyway,' he repeated and shuffled a few pages.

A name caught his eye: Sir John Moore striking camp at first light in torrential rain; men soaked and shivering from sleeping in mire; guns sinking up to their axles and all the while the watchers on the hilltops dogging his footsteps and fleeing before his scouts. I wonder what happened then, he thought and picked up another page. She left him there with a supply of biros and slipped quietly from the room. She saw him picking up a pen and making a note in the margin of a page. Twenty pence worth of biro would have to supply the place of expensive hardware. The desk gave a welcoming creak as he leaned an elbow on it and picked up another page.

~

No matter how much a man may love his children, it is always a relief when at least one of them goes to bed. Irrespective of the number, it is a relief to get one down. Elaine sat by the fire knitting. She had become very adept at the art and was preparing, for another baby, impossibly small jackets with elaborate designs which the wearer was unlikely to appreciate. As far as Dempsey could see, small babies were engaged in a villainous conspiracy to soil as much clothing as possible. As soon as they were changed they looked around calculatingly, before blasting off at one end or the other and then relaxing with a smirk, knowing that someone would have to get up and undo the damage.

Elaine loved small babies. He loved the half and half stage when they began to talk, to put language together, to invent new words and to master concepts. It had always been so. His daughter was propped on the couch studying an indestructible cardboard book about animals, in which the hero was Mr Lowly Worm. Dempsey gazed into the caverns of the fire, watching colours come and go.

Dark shadows flickered over white-hot coals and vanished again.
Shelley had that thing about an idea being like a fading coal. By the
time you pick it up in a pincer of words it is dull and lifeless. But
what about skill? Dempsey mused. He had taken Elaine's mare to
the farrier and watched him beating the glowing iron into shape.
Certainly it dulled before your eyes but human ingenuity worked
on it nonetheless. Could it not be the same with ideas? He had
written his book so often in his head and had drawn back repeatedly
from writing it down to the end. Yet sometimes he had found that
in sitting down with only the germ of an idea, his mind had become
more supple as he worked and although he crossed out and rejected,
occasionally the end product was better than the original starting
point. It was an idea worth taking up with Shelley if ever he should
meet him.

Elaine interrupted his train of reverie.

'I thought you'd be interested.' She had been telling him something.

'In the paper. Remember that chapel you told me about and the
painter fellow.'

'John Clifford. What about him?'

'It's in *The Times*. It seems they've restored it or something.'

She forked over the paper with her knitting needles. He found the
report: 'Major masterpiece uncovered at last.' Baltrasna chapel, it
appeared, had been disposed of by the parish on the grounds
presumably that the faithful, one and a half centuries after Emanci-
pation, should bloody well have motor cars and could drive into
town to Mass. It had served as a potato store until a concerned group
had raised funds to make it into a heritage centre and venue for
uplifting activities.

It appeared that the extensive murals by the noted artist John
Clifford had been painstakingly uncovered and that the famous
window, once the centre of considerable controversy, in less enlight-
ened times, had been restored to its rightful place through the
generosity of an old friend and confidante of the artist himself and
with the aid of a bequest from America.

'I see she still wears the hair down,' he mused aloud.

'Who?'

'Your woman,' he said turning the paper around to show her the photograph. 'Mrs what's it? Bit of a scarlet woman in her day, if I remember rightly. Friend and confidante. Now I get it. That portrait.'

'Are you scoffing, by any chance?'

'No, just thinking it's a funny old world. Mrs Francesca Curtis. Married to some old bloke and had a bit of a fling with Clifford as I understand it. She must be well into her sixties by now. He painted a portrait of her among other things. We had the sale of it once.' He still spoke proprietorially about Sedgwicks. 'I think that was why the bishop had the whole thing painted over.'

'Well the bishop is long gone anyway.'

'That's about the tenor of the various speeches. Lot of stuff here about stagnation and clerical oppression; prisons of the mind and so on. Wonder why nobody said that when he was around. The old gunfighter.' He chuckled to himself.

'You seem very amused by it all. There's a story in there somewhere if you chose to find it.'

'I'm just amused by the way people apply their attitudes to the forties and fifties and pontificate on how people should have thought in those days. We're not so good at solving today's problems. Are we?'

'You have a point. But wouldn't you be interested to see it all the same?'

'Nah. Not from the sound of this. Old hat. Just an excuse for a booze up and for a few trendies to pat themselves on the back.'

'Very cynical,' she retorted. 'I thought you would be very interested. After all, you told me that you started the work of restoration yourself, picking off bits of paint like a vandal.'

'Why so I did,' he said surprised. 'I had forgotten about that. Maybe I should have gone along and made a speech myself.'

'You'll have your chance,' she said slyly. 'I see where there's going to be an annual John Clifford summer school, dealing with his work and so on. It's going to be some time around Easter though, a sort of early summer effort.'

'Summer schools,' he snorted. 'Heritage centres. Going around in ever decreasing circles and vanishing up their own agenda. He must be dead again.'

'Don't be such an old crank. You've always said you were intrigued by the fellow.'

He thought for a while. 'Yes, I was.'

'Well then, go and see it. And you could take the opportunity of talking to Paddy about that branch office or whatever.'

'Nah, no,' he said dismissively. 'There's no mystery about him now. Not now that he has been embalmed in a summer school. No I wouldn't be interested.' He flipped the paper aside. 'I'll see Paddy some other time.'

She left it at that but noticed that he took up the paper again and read the report with great attention. Her needles clicked.

The child had fallen asleep over her book.

'The baby will be born long before Easter,' she remarked casually.

'Ah, there's too much to be done around here at that time of year.'

'You're probably right,' she agreed. 'You probably wouldn't be interested.'

CHAPTER FIFTEEN

The manuscript awoke a kind of hunger in Dempsey again, an urge
to build, to make something coherent from the chaos of tradition,
that might possibly shed some light on the violence endemic in Irish
life. He evolved a theory, prompted by the story that O'Connell the
Liberator had always worn a black glove on the hand that took the
life of another. He concluded that John Clifford in his art had tried
to atone, to expiate the enormity of what he had done. Clifford was
no fallen angel. He was a conduit, a bearer of the divine spark, who
out of his own suffering and guilt had forged a metaphor for
violence. He liked the idea of 'forged'. It suggested Vulcan, the
smith, Mulciber's other guise, a consummate craftsman. He reflected
on the glowing coal idea. Yes, Clifford was something of a martyr,
hounded and silenced by a latter day Savonarola. Perhaps even a
saint, a flawed and tortured soul, striving always towards the sublime. That was good. That was worth writing down. It would in fact
be a very good idea to go along and have a look at his work, almost
to make a pilgrimage, to join the loose ends. He rationalised. Elaine
would have had the baby by then. She could spare him for a couple
of days. Her sisters were coming down at Easter for a week or so.
She would not be short of help. Easter was late, in the middle of
April. Fine weather would be on the cards. Everything suited.

'Then longen folk to goon on pilgrimage.' Old Chaucer had
caught it right, the stirring in the blood, the itchy feet, birdsong in

the wayside trees and a meeting of minds and kindred spirits.

It pelted rain over Easter and was colder than average but anyway, he went, regretting the whole idea. Tomgarrif was warm and
comfortable and it hurt to leave Elaine and her new infant, another
girl. What lunacy, he wondered, had persuaded him to desert their
warm bed at an ungodly hour and drive a hundred and fifty miles
in monsoon conditions in order to listen to some old bore waffling
on about Irish history. Whenever he decided to go anywhere he
immediately regretted his decision, but as he travelled along he
always found that he enjoyed a sense of purpose. Only when he
turned homewards would he become apprehensive about what
might have befallen in his absence.

He began to enjoy the journey; the sense of freedom; the company
of his own thoughts. His car was better than the old Volkswagen but
he thought, with the affection engendered by time, of how faithfully
it had borne him through many vicissitudes. It was no more now
than a rusty tenement for fowl. That had a ring of Chaucer about it
— *A Tenement of Foules*. He recalled another phrase more practical
than Shelley's: 'The life so short, the art so long to learn'. No use
sitting around on your arse waiting for inspiration. Get to work.
Time is short. He felt invigorated by his meditation and braced to
the task.

He enjoyed his new car enormously and had enjoyed even more
the pleasure of buying it from Comerford Motors, from young Mr.
Comerford in person — Councillor Bill Comerford in fact, friend of
the common man, going to run for the Dáil. 'Great to see you again,
Bill. Great, great. Discount? No, wouldn't hear of it. A man has to
make a living.'

'Great, Jack. Great. Sure you'll have a drink itself.'

He had paid over the odds and was never quite sure in his own
mind why he found the episode amusing. Just for pig-iron as they
say. Still, it was a grand car.

He found the familiar road again — Naul, nine miles, Baltrasna
nine. He followed the winding country road and came at last to the
chapel. He noted that his heart was pounding with an unexpected
excitement. The rain had eased. Water dripped from the black,

unopened buds of ash trees and the grey bark glistened like old pewter. The chapel was closed. A poster, partly dislodged by the rain, gave notice of the afternoon session. He had time to spare, time to mooch about and time for lunch. He wondered then in anticlimax what he was doing there. He found the stone that marked the grave of the last insurgents and stood looking at it in silence for a long time. There was nobody to whom he could express what he felt so he addressed himself silently to his long dead child. This stone had anchored one end of the thread along which he had found his way home. It had an almost religious significance.

'Well now,' he said aloud to himself, 'so here it is.' So what am I going to do about it? he added silently. It was a challenge and reproach. Some things should be written down. No use writing them on stone for the rain to beat upon and the moss to obscure.

'Ye won't get in yet,' said a voice startling him. 'It's not open 'til two o'clock.'

Dempsey remembered the voice but not the name. It was the man with the scythe, Old Father Time himself. He remembered a lost day and declined to introduce himself. The old fellow regarded him closely.

'So you're back,' he remarked, almost a challenge. The game was up. Dempsey grinned. 'I am,' he said, 'and how are you keeping?'

'Divil a bother,' said the old fellow. 'Still on the go. Aren't you the bucko that picked the paint off the wall and me lashin' on the emulsion for fear of the bishop?'

Dempsey felt like a schoolboy caught in the act.

'It sort of fell off, if I remember rightly,' he said lamely.

'Ah sure, don't I know it. Sure I made a fair few bob over the years puttin' on the paint and a few more bob, from this crowd, pickin' it all off again. Mind you I took me time.' He nudged Dempsey conspiratorially in the ribs. 'Made very heavy weather of it, doin' a couple of square foot a day. Restoration, says I. Not like an ordinary paint strippin' job.' He cackled, showing a yellow tooth. 'Always go for time and materials. None of your task work for me. Heh, heh.'

Time and motion, thought Dempsey, with not too much of the latter.

'Gettin' a few people in, all the same, I have to admit.'

He said it grudgingly as if countenancing some strange aberrant behaviour. 'Pays for the upkeep.' He shook his head. 'Comical oul' world.'

Dempsey asked if there was any chance of a look around. He made a move towards his pocket.

'Ah now,' demurred the old fellow, 'ah now. The last time I let yourself in didn't ye vandalise the place.' He cackled at the pleasantry and relented. 'I don't know but what it could be arranged.'

There was an inference in his tone and Dempsey offered the going rate and something for his trouble. He looked surprised and even a little offended but secreted the proffered note with practised ease.

'You're a gentleman,' he said with maybe a touch of mockery and produced the key. 'I dare say I can leave ye to it. I'll be back again two o'clock so take your time. Have to be back for this crowd.'

He made a wry face, dismissing all enthusiasts and opened the door.

He had more or less suspected the usual — wolfhounds and round towers and androgynous looking fellows in saffron kilts, with shields and spears. They would, he expected, be mugging grimly for the camera in some softly lit Celtic twilight. That was not what he found. Between the windows there were painted panels, where the Stations of the Cross would normally have been. The artist however had superimposed the story of Calvary on a recognisable Irish background, so that Christ dragged his burden across a blood-stained landscape, a landscape of burning buildings and gibbeted corpses. Onlookers turned away laughing and reached for their drinks like on some grotesque advertising hoarding.

Heavy handed symbolism, thought Dempsey, with a touch of condescension — laying it on with a trowel. He followed the familiar story. There indeed was the burning barn and the hand holding the blazing twist of straw. He remembered the morning so well and how it had hit him like a blow, but now the effect was dulled by time and by reflection. It was as if a membrane had grown over the wound. Maybe it was annoyance that someone else had stolen his idea, his thunder.

The skies were invariably dark. Smoke rolled and billowed. That was my idea, he thought with a stab of pique. The painter's style was harsh, almost brutal. The figures were crouched and simian. Colours were slashed across darkness — a suggestion of Goya. The window with the falling angel dominated the end wall.

There was no Calvary. He began again but could find no end to the story. He heard the sharp tap of a high heel on the tiled floor and looked around. The woman was watching him with an expression of amused interest. She moved from the doorway and her heels made a hard, echoing staccato on the tiles. A fellow student had told him once of his time in the seminary and how during study time or devotions the tap, tap of high heels caused every head to rise and every face to turn towards the sound. The lady dietician cum manageress was the only woman on the campus. He had often wondered how many vocations had been lost to the sound of stiletto heels. In later years he had noticed also the damage they do to floor coverings.

'So you've come back,' she remarked, 'the rather gloomy young man. I suppose you heard about the great unveiling.' She waved her hand at the walls in a vaguely mocking way. 'A monument to a genius.'

Dempsey shrugged, puzzled by her attitude.

'I'm not so sure about the gloomy but I'm grateful for the young.' He was surprised that he had made such a lasting impression. 'I see you put the window back.'

'Yes. It was a condition of the American bequest. Anyway I had got tired of it. I packed in all that disco stuff and converted the place back to serious drinking.'

'Your heart was in the right place then.' He meant it as a throw-away line but she looked at him oddly again.

'Well what do you think of it anyway?'

He hesitated, reluctant to explain the reason for his coming. An unpublished manuscript, even a completed one, has no more sub-stance than a feather or thistledown or even a half formulated thought. She brushed at the lock of hair in the manner that he remembered so vividly. The thin line of scar flickered for an instant.

'Well, to tell the truth, it strikes a chord. You see I've been trying for years to write a book. Never got it finished but couldn't get it out of my system. Your man's pictures sort of hit the same note, especially that one there. Scullabogue, the burning barn.'

'Oh no,' she said, 'that's not Scullabogue. That's an incident that happened on Lord Castlereagh's family estate in Ulster or so he told me. They say it affected his mind. Ultimately drove him to suicide.'

'Not Scullabogue? So I've been barking up the wrong tree.'

'What difference does it make?' she challenged. 'Isn't one barn the same as another? Didn't the people burn just as well?'

They looked again at the panel. The figures, oblivious to Christ's passing, went about their business with the frenetic efficiency of characters from Hieronymus Bosch.

'You seem to know a lot about it all,' he said, feeling somehow cheated.

'Yes, I suppose I do,' she replied and some of the tautness went out of her. 'I suppose I should. I saw him paint every one of them.'

'Ah,' said Dempsey putting the story together in his mind. 'I see.'

There was a long silence. A smile flickered across her features. He could see that she had been a striking young woman.

'Do you then?' she retorted. 'Do you indeed?'

'I'm sorry,' said Dempsey awkwardly. 'I wasn't jumping to conclusions. It's just that I remember his portrait of yourself. You see I was involved in handling the sale, although I wasn't actually at the auction as it turned out. I don't know what became of it.'

'I bought it,' she retorted. 'I bought it. I bought the damn thing for revenge.'

'Well you paid a fair price for it if I'm not mistaken. Expensive kind of revenge.'

'I'll tell you a story,' she said, 'though I don't know why I should.'

'I'm a good listener.'

'Our local postman was once bitten by a dog and he sued the owner. He got compensation too, three hundred pounds. Well he went on an almighty batter and had to go into the John of God's to dry out. When he came out he wanted to sue the man all over again for giving him all the money in one go — attempted murder, he maintained.'

Dempsey smiled. 'I get it. So you wanted to bump off the artist. I gather he had gone down in the world.'

'Not quite.' She shook her head. 'Just a loose end to be tied up. He once said that he would never part with the painting, that it meant too much to him. Like an eejit I believed him. After everything that happened I imagined that he meant it, even though I never heard from him again. It was a bit of a shock to see it in the paper after all this time. I bought it just to make a point.'

'I can understand that.' It was just like Comerford and the car. 'He also sold a sabre that belonged to one of his forebears. As a matter of fact I brought it with me. I was thinking of presenting it to this place if you think it would be of interest.'

'That's very thoughtful of you,' she said. 'It's going to be developed into a kind of a museum and so forth.'

'Do you seriously maintain that you were in some way responsible for his death, though?'

'I honestly wouldn't know and at this remove I couldn't care less.'

'Well I'd say it's a good investment at the very least. It must have meant a lot to you all the same.'

She was silent for a while gazing into vacuity, lost in thought. She shook her head and laughed suddenly and there was no bitterness in her laughter. The sound reverberated in the empty building.

'The Scarlet Woman. Is that what you're thinking?' She regarded his embarrassment. 'Well you might as well. Everybody else did.' She glanced at her watch. 'I presume you're here for this afternoon's talk.'

Dempsey nodded. There was over half an hour to go.

'I doubt if there'll be very many in this kind of weather.'

As she spoke a shaft of bleary sunshine illuminated the wall where the altar had once stood. Dempsey looked up at it. He wondered why it was the only space left blank. She read his mind.

'That wall is for the Crucifixion,' she said. 'That still has to be done.'

'How do you mean?' he asked frowning. 'He's dead now. Who's

going to do it?'

'That's just it,' she said. 'We are. That's what he said. "The Crucifixion hasn't happened yet," he used to say. "Wait for the final act and then I'll paint it." '

'I suppose the time has come, when you look at what's been happening in this country.' The sun had gone in again and rain spattered on the glass. Dempsey shivered.

'Not yet,' she said shaking her head. 'I'm afraid there's worse to come.'

Dempsey sat down in a pew and looked up at her. 'Now there's a gloomy thought.' He was beginning to feel sorry that he had made the journey. 'He must have been a morbid so and so.'

She sat in the pew in front of his and turned half way to talk to him.

'Far from it,' she said. 'He was one of the wittiest — always made me laugh. Said none of it mattered a damn in the long run. A mad world.'

Dempsey waited, knowing that she wanted to talk.

'Do you remember the summer of 'forty-eight?'

He nodded. 'A hot one, I've been told. I was only a kid at that time.'

'Yes it was. Mackerel skies. I remember the clouds clearing off. It was the second of July, the day John Clifford started working here. That was where I met him. I was fascinated by him from the start. The sun shone till the end of August that year. I had a pink check summer dress, just off the shoulder.' She plucked at the shoulder of her coat. 'I was twenty-five and married to a man twenty years older.'

'May and December,' he prompted lightly.

'Twenty-five. Getting on. No family and nothing to look forward to but standing behind a bar pulling pints for bumpkins.'

'Ah,' said Dempsey again and nodded, not wishing to deflect her. She stood up and walked a little way along the aisle.

'He had a kind of a bosun's chair,' she pointed at the crossbeams, 'rigged up there. You could haul yourself up and down in it. He used to move it from beam to beam as he worked.' She swayed slightly and hummed a little tune. 'People would come and watch him at work. The parish priest used to come in and sometimes he would give me a peculiar look. I spent a lot of time up here. I suppose at first he had his suspicions but my husband and the Yank Finnucane were friends and the Yank was putting up the money.'

'A tricky one,' agreed Dempsey. They were allies now. He knew that she wanted him to hear her side of things. 'You were in love with him then?'

She shrugged. 'I used to swing in the chair and talk to him. Just gently, back and forth.'

'Did that not distract him?'

'What do you think? Here he was with his vision of the Apocalypse and me watching him all the time — up and down his ladder, mixing paint, talking all the time about how religion was the curse of this Godforsaken country. A bit of a contradiction, don't you think?' She put her head to one side. ' "Proddy, Proddy on the wall," I used to sing, "Half a loaf would do yiz all." That used to make him laugh. "I'll give them the works," he'd say, "lay it on thick for you Papes, and I'll stick me bill in too." He never really gave a damn about anything except maybe being the best in his field.'

'That I can believe,' nodded Dempsey. 'Very jealous of their work, artists.'

He was picturing the scene, the heat of the summer, the coolness of the chapel, the creak of the rope over the beam and a young woman in a pink check dress, swinging backwards and forwards. She had slipped her feet from her sandals and tilted her head to one side. He could hear her song, taunting, teasing. A man of steel might have resisted.

'It must have caused a bit of comment in those days,' he prompted again.

She folded her arms and clasped her elbows as if protecting herself.

'Rows, you could say. Nothing but rows. Eventually I was read from the altar. Not him of course. I suppose he was considered beyond redemption. That altar there,' she added pointing to the place where it had stood. 'He was going to leave his wife and come away with me. We talked it all through.'

Noises off, thought Dempsey, the casualties who don't get to tell their side of the story.

'Went up to the Wicklow mountains to get away from all the wagging tongues.'

Dempsey waited.

'And that was where it happened — the two men being killed an' all.'

Silence again. He waited like an angler waits for the pull on the line, before striking.

'I've never told anyone about this,' she said after a while, 'and for the life of me I can't think why I'm telling you. I just had an instinct. There's something about you that makes me feel you might be able to make sense of it all.'

'Dunno about that,' Dempsey mumbled. 'I haven't had all that much luck at making sense of things.'

'Two men tried to rob us. One of them had a knife.' She spoke quickly, anxious to be done. 'John had the starting handle. He hit one of them and the one with the knife panicked. He held the knife to my face and said he would cut me.' She put a hand to her cheek. 'The other one got up and started to run. John went after him and hit him again. He left me there with the other man. I think the man was paralysed with fright. I could feel him trembling. When John turned round I saw his face. I was more frightened of him than of the other man. He came towards us and the man was shouting at him. I felt the blood on my face and then John had him by the throat. After that he went back and hit the first man again.'

'Didn't they say self-defence?' said Dempsey. 'I read about it in the paper.'

'Self-defence. That was what he said when he came back to me. He was all concern then but it wasn't self-defence. You should have seen the expression on his face. He enjoyed every minute of it, d'you see? Winning was what mattered. I can still hear him: "Had to stand me ground".'

Stand your ground. The old familiar advice. Keep your guard up.

'I see,' he said. There were noises outside and the sound of footsteps on gravel.

'Yes. He was a sort of hero after it all,' she said, 'and look what I got out of it.' She pulled back her hair and showed him the scar. It disfigured one side of her face from the hairline of the temple, raising a white weal across the cheek and narrowing to a thread on the curve of her chin.

'I'm sorry,' said Dempsey, with a kind of guilt. He looked away.

'It was murder, you know. I suppose I perjured myself. I think I was afraid of him after that. Do you ever really know anyone?'

'And then the bishop stepped in?' Light relief.

She gave a dry cynical laugh. 'I don't think the killing was the problem. I think it was the sex angle that bothered him. Anyway, how could anyone say a prayer with all this stuff looking down at them?' She laughed again. 'So that's it. That's the holy all of it. And look at him there, the bastard, laughing at the whole bloody lot of us.'

Dempsey followed her gaze to the window where Mulciber was falling. The light glinted on his face and he laughed — for the hell of it.

'I suppose,' she said, 'it makes damn all difference now.'

'Well Daedalus made it to land but doesn't Icarus still steal the show?

'I suppose,' she murmured with a wan smile. 'I suppose so.'

~

The speaker had put up his hours on many similar occasions, introducing the proceedings with the ritual obeisance to Guinness, a necessary preliminary in all such gatherings. The scattered audience of some dozen or so laughed obligingly at the witticism, establishing their credentials not only as thoughtful and concerned folk, but as people able to let their hair down and mix with the common man. Umbrellas dripped against the wall.

'A tribute to your hospitality,' he went on gracefully, bowing in the direction of Mrs Curtis who occupied, it appeared, the position of patroness of the event. Strange, mused Dempsey how notoriety acquires the patina of celebrity with the passing of the years. She had also pointed out to him that she had the advantage of money which enabled her to thumb her nose at the lot of them. He could see why Clifford had been attracted to her.

'Our distinguished speaker who will propound his fascinating theory of how the artist might have approached the painting of the twelfth station, the Crucifixion. Ably assisted as always by his equally distinguished son.' There was a spattering of applause and the distinguished speaker left off for a moment his frantic tussle with the slide projector. His son, a studious looking young man with a dangling forelock, continued to load the slide magazine which he forced into the machine with a resounding snap.

'Ready in one moment ladies and gentlemen,' said the speaker, emending it after a glance to 'lady and gentlemen.'

She leaned towards Dempsey and whispered conspiratorially 'Lumiere and son.'

The first slide was inevitably upside down. Dempsey smiled. In an age of instant communication we tolerate nothing less than slick perfection. If the pictures from the far side of the moon are blurred we grumble about incompetence and the price of the licence.

After some minor hitches the speaker began again, directing the images onto the blank gable wall and the audience became instantly absorbed. He had made a collection of mural paintings from the embattled towns of Northern Ireland, 'the efflorescence of mural painting,' as he called it, the artistic expression of sectarian and political hatred, that assaulted the viewer in an onslaught of vibrant images: union flags, tricolours, sunbursts of green and yellow republicanism and the hero king on his pacing white steed. Everywhere there were the hooded men, the rifles, the threats and promises. Some were crudely done as befitted the sentiments expressed, but some were powerful, beautifully executed and deeply persuasive, as emotive as Voortrekker monuments or memorials to executed Maquis, depending as always on your point of view.

'...with an armalite in one hand and a paintbrush in the other,' said the speaker, perhaps unnecessarily, and Dempsey remembered how Elaine had rendered it: 'an armalite in one hand and a bullet in the other.' Near enough. Every old phrase needs to be brushed off and tidied up now and again.

Drawing towards the climax of what had been an absorbing talk the speaker at last came to the core of his thesis. Dempsey's mind had been wandering, reflecting on the ease with which he had thrown his images on the wall. No patient labour with brush and paint, all summer long with motes swirling in diagonal sunbeams and a young woman with sunburned shoulders taunting and distracting him. A fly landed on the wall, merging with its shadow and flew away again unscathed, unlike some of its ancestors who undoubtedly had lost a leg or a wing to the work of John Clifford. They were not the only ones to have become limed and entangled in his vision.

'The Place of Skulls,' declaimed the speaker. 'When we consider the place of head-hunting in our past.' He tapped the bench with a cane and an image flashed upon the wall. 'Three black balls on spikes, as the writer described them as recently as the 1840s. Put there by the forces of law and order on the walls of police barracks. We have no need to go any further back — to King Dermot rolling a cloakful of heads on the floor and biting the noses off those of his particular enemies, or Cuchulainn, until recently held up as an example to schoolchildren, tying the heads of his enemies to the rail of his chariot.'

In a moment of awkward levity he referred to the origins of football in kicking about the heads of defeated enemies and adverted to the continued popularity of the game. The audience gave a small collective laugh, tolerating the light relief.

'I have contrived, if you like, a composite picture incorporating elements that Clifford, had he lived, would surely have used in his work.' He tapped again and on the wall appeared his Calvary: a collage of the foregoing images superimposed on a Clifford sky; low flickering flames on the horizon; the scattered entrails of an upturned vehicle in the foreground; the crosses on the hill and the *Ton Ton* figures of the paramilitary gunmen at the foot of the cross. A jumble of skulls rolled into a suburban Golgotha.

There was a gasp of appreciation from the audience and Dempsey, though slightly sceptical of the ersatz nature of the image, was impressed. He wondered about the process and thought irrelevantly that it was a bit like the computerised fight between Marciano and Muhammed Ali. Marciano won, but then, given the times that were in it, he would, wouldn't he? He wondered if they should in some way press their buttons to vote in the approved manner of television audiences. The speaker had a point undoubtedly but he felt that it was all a bit over the top. The instantaneous nature of the business made him suspicious. There should have been more labour in the process. He felt vaguely cheated.

There were questions and a discussion ensued and suddenly the sun broke through again, blearing the image on the wall and all but wiping it away. Perversely he was pleased by its impermanence. Growing inside him was a determination that he would at last finish his book. It would be achieved through toil and long hours. It would be achieved, he thought virtuously, by no flick of a switch, but by labour and by midnight oil. It would be written too with love and with compassion and it would take his poor survivor home through suffering and many perils, as he himself had come home.

Suddenly he longed for Elaine and for his children. He was impatient to be gone. People were shuffling, retrieving umbrellas, putting on their coats. He went outside and stood apart from the group, looking at the stone.

After a while he became conscious of the silence. The branches above his head rasped in a light breeze. A hand touched his elbow.

'Are you all right?' she asked.

'Yes,' he said, 'I was just saying goodbye.'

She nodded, as if she understood.

'Have you far to go?' she enquired.

'No, not far,' he murmured. 'Not far. I've come a long way.'

'You're a strange one,' she said, tucking her hand inside his arm. 'I'll walk you to your car. Perhaps some day you'll tell me your story.'

'That's what I'm going to do,' he smiled. 'Some work of noble note may yet be done.'

'Not unbecoming men that strove with gods.' She laughed. 'Or devils for that matter.'

'I'll give you that sabre. I left it in the car.'

The grass verge was muddied and rutted by the departed cars. Dempsey swore vehemently. His front tyre was flat. At least it had stopped raining. Cursing, he reversed onto the roadway to give the jack a firm footing and got out again to change the wheel.

The woman stood by solicitously, reluctant to leave him although he had no problem with the task. He fitted the pipe over the T bar and whipped off the nuts. He smiled at the memory.

'Give me somewhere to rest my lever and I will move the world.'

'What's so funny about that?' she asked.

'Just an old joke,' he said and his annoyance abated.

He heard a loud guffaw and cat calls. A group of youths had appeared at the corner of the chapel wall. They seemed to be amused by his predicament. Balubas, he thought, dismissing them. That was it, Balubas. He had not heard that expression for years. Funny how some people derive pleasure from someone else's misfortune. Probably like the banana skin joke. The Germans, naturally, have a word for it.

'Why don't ye get a proper car, y'oul bollox?'

He felt his anger rising. He looked up and glared at the group. A pebble skittered in his direction along the road. It clanked off the side of his car.

'Cut that out,' he called and heard laughter in reply. The woman looked at him apprehensively.

'Don't pay any attention. They're only young hooligans.'

For an instant he wondered why they should go out of their way to antagonise him and figured that they saw him as privileged, well off, old, their natural enemy. That they looked shabby and under-privileged altered nothing. They were coming closer, sounding him out, growing in courage when he showed no reaction. There was a crash and a tinkling of glass. A stone had gone through the window of the chapel. At a glance he could see, even in the opaque version visible from outside, that the face of the angel had been shattered.

'Oh my god,' said Mrs Curtis putting a hand to her face. 'They're going to destroy it.'

'Cut that out,' shouted Dempsey, straightening up and advancing towards the group. He found that he still held the length of pipe in his hand. A pebble struck him on the face and a voice told him to go and fuck himself. In surprise he recognised the sabre in the hand of one of the youths. He heard his father's voice shouting 'Fight your corner. Have to teach them respect' and something snapped inside him. These were the sort that had beaten an old man and thrown him into a hole in the road; creatures of darkness and ignorance; the enemy. He swung his fist at a shape in front of him and felt it connect with flesh and bone. Dark shapes flitted across his vision and a fierce joy took possession of him. The youth with the sabre was backing away, swinging the blade in a wide arc. Dempsey saw the terror in his eyes and he knew that he had him. He struck with the pipe and it rang on steel. He struck again and with a howl the youth dropped the sabre and clutched at his wrist. He leaped backwards and tripped.

Dempsey was conscious of two terrified eyes looking up at him.

'No, mister, no!' screamed the youth cringing, with hands clasped about his head.

He raised the pipe to strike again and felt his arm grabbed from behind. She was surprisingly strong.

'Don't!' she screamed. 'Don't do it.'

He wrenched his arm free but the moment had passed. He hesitated and blinked. The roaring in his head eased and he looked down into the terrified eyes of the youth. He felt the muscles in his legs shaking uncontrollably.

He blinked again and felt cold sweat beading his eyelashes.

His vision began to clear. The boy began to inch away from him crabwise, and slowly Dempsey lowered the weapon. Suddenly the boy dropped his guard and ran. When he had got to what he considered a safe distance he turned and in a voice that still shook with fear, shouted 'Fuckin' lunatic.' In his mind he had again become the aggrieved party. His companions were nowhere to be seen. Every man for himself. Dempsey recalled a bright day and his terrified flight across the Curragh. He looked at the length of pipe, swung it and hurled it with all his strength over the hedge. It whirled against the sky, turning on an axis like a rotor or a sycamore seed. He was suddenly very tired. His breath snuffled through his nostrils.

The woman was white in the face, so much so that the line of scar was almost invisible.

'For a minute there, I thought ...' she began, still shaking from the shock.

Dempsey looked down at his hand. It was streaked with rust.

'You don't get many chances like that,' he muttered. 'That was a close one.'

'I think ...' she began again.

'I think you'd better get a grid over that window before it's all gone,' he interrupted. He bent and picked up the sabre, turning it this way and that.

'We had intended to but never quite got around to it.'

'Well, that's it then.' He wiped his hand on the seat of his trousers, forgetting that he had put on a good suit for the occasion. 'We'd better go before our friends decide to retrieve their honour. You'd better take this.' He retrieved the scabbard from where the boy had discarded it.

She smiled wanly. 'I'll say goodbye then. I'd better see about putting poor John back together again.'

'Piece by piece,' he said but he was thinking of something else. He extended his hand. 'I am in your debt,' he said formally. 'I have a few debts to discharge to a few good people. You'll be hearing from me in due course — I hope.'

He shook her hand and walked back to attend to the car. He started the engine and raised a hand in farewell. In a short while he came to a rise in the road and saw the sun glinting on the distant mountains. He found when he took a hand from the steering wheel, that he was still trembling.

It was dusk when he arrived back at Tomgarrif and the house was empty. He presumed that they had all gone somewhere to show off the new baby. He felt a gloom descending on him. The place had the desolate atmosphere of a railway waiting room.

He helped himself to a large whiskey and stood looking out at the fields. The rain had stopped and the sun was just sinking below the hill. Jackdaws called from the ruined keep. Again and again he went over the incident. He was undoubtedly in the right but he could not figure out how it had come about or at what point he had let go.

That was not respect. That was fear. There is a difference. He swilled the last of the whiskey around the glass and swallowed it, relishing the way it burned a track inside him. Does it all boil down to fear in the final analysis?

Long shadows reached out from buildings and trees, losing their sharpness as the sun fell away but thickening and gathering into amorphous blackness. The bulk of the tower house cast a great diagonal of darkness cutting across lawn and orchard as far as the gate, like an heraldic blazon, a bend sinister.

Strongbow might well have looked out from Tomgarrif tower, possibly on a tour of inspection. Strongbow, who according to legend, killed his own son in a paroxysm of rage. What had he achieved in the heel of the hunt but an effigy in Christchurch, worn and polished by the centuries, beside the mutilated, truncated image of the child? The legend said he smote the boy for his failure in battle, somewhere in the high pass of the Blackstairs mountains with the wind whistling through the gap and kites and ravens circling over the corpses.

When Strongbow smote someone he stayed smote, not smitten, a word for greeting cards and crooners, but smote, like Samson with his jawbone.

He contemplated another whiskey but decided against it. The winning is everything in the final analysis. McGuigan took the title from Pedrosa and the crowd roared approval. The whole country roared approval. He had settled down with a couple of beers to watch the fight, two little men battering the bejasus out of each other. Maybe the beer had been too cold, maybe it had been Pedrosa's eyes, sad like those of a baby seal, a good man beaten. No, he knew it was the crowd that caused his revulsion, the crowd baying for blood, for our man to win.

I won that fight today, he thought and looked at his hands. I had him down and could have finished him off, could have thrown everything away in one spasm of exultant joy. I could have reduced my whole life, defined it forever, in one downward stroke. His hands shook. There should have been black hairs sprouting from them and gnarled twisted nails.

The house creaked about him and the dog barked outside. He took down the shotgun and checked it. A Purdy, worth a few bob nowadays. He admired the finely chased scrollwork and ran his hands over the smooth walnut stock.

He stepped out into the gathering dusk. The dog looked at him expectantly.

'Stay,' he ordered, not wanting any company and the animal sank down, disconsolate, with its head on its paws.

He made his way along the headlands through fields of young green barley, viridian in the half light. He paused at the sound of a car entering the driveway and looked back as the dimmed headlights vanished behind the house. There was more light on the higher ground and he could make out the white shapes of the gate-pillars.

Elaine saw the dark silhouette just going over the curve of the hill and for some unknown reason she felt a chill. The children were chattering and squabbling with tiredness and the baby was demanding a feed. She left them with her sisters and started after her husband. The dog fell in beside her with a look of understanding.

A breeze had sprung up and the new leaves were rustling with a sound like the sea. She hurried her steps, feeling the wetness soak through her light shoes. The sound of the leaves was getting louder. She called anxiously, 'Jack, Jack. Where are you?' and listened for a reply.

A murmur of voices came to her from afar, the muttering of a great crowd moving behind the trees, indistinguishable one from another as if a great host were passing in the darkness. The dog whimpered and pressed himself against her shins. She listened intently, feeling herself shiver, although the air was mild.

Then she heard the shot from not far ahead and the echoes replicating in the distance, weaving their web of sound. The murmur of the crowd was gone. She began to run, almost tripping over the dog and twigs invisible in the shadow of the ditch.

She thought she saw figures moving on the crest of the hill and then she recognised Dempsey standing motionless by the gate-pillar. A great flood of relief washed over her and she ran to him.

He came towards her and his eyes were staring.

'Did you see them?' he asked hoarsely. 'Did you see them?'

'I did,' she replied 'a man and a little boy.'

'It was him,' he said. 'I just know it was John — and the man your father told me about.' He gripped her arm with his free hand.

'I know,' she said softly. 'I know.'

'I came up here,' he said, 'I don't know why. I was confused. I wanted to talk to someone but there was no one around. So I came up here.' He was trembling.

She put her arms around him and gradually she felt the tension leaving him, ebbing away.

'It's all right now, Jack. It's all right now. We can go home now.' She rocked him gently as she would a child.

'Gathered to his ancestors. Isn't that the phrase?' he said softly and his voice was still hoarse.

He stood back from her and broke open the gun. He took out the unused cartridge and looked at her.

'Shall I?'

'No,' she said, 'some other time maybe.'

He slipped the cartridge into his pocket. The moon was up. It struck a silvery glint from the roof of Tomgarrif. He put his arm around her shoulder and felt the warmth of her body. He realised that he had not eaten since morning.

Lights had come on in the house throwing bright rectangles against the darkness.

'Let's go down,' she murmured. 'You must be tired after your journey.'

From below came the high-pitched voices of the children, shrill with excitement as they chased about the house.